A Sporting Chance

Mr. Pemberton was made speechless by Vanessa's ingenious idea. He smiled as he said, "I will do just as you say, Miss Lester. I will hold a hunt. I like to hunt. And my aunt will be happy, too."

"I also like to hunt. I hope that you will allow me to ride neck or nothing, sir," Vanessa said with a quick smile.

Mr. Pemberton reached out his hand and briefly clasped hers. "You may do just as you wish, my dearest of friends," he said quietly.

Vanessa was quite taken aback. Quick color surged into her face as she stared in astonishment at her companion. With any other gentleman she would have known precisely how to take such an intimate address. But Mr. Pemberton was very different from all the other gentlemen she had ever known.

Mr. Pemberton laughed again. "Neck or nothing it is, Miss Lester! We shall see some sport, shan't we?"

Yes, we shall indeed, Vanessa thought to herself.

Lady Cecily's Scheme

❦

Gayle Buck

A SIGNET BOOK

SIGNET
Published by the Penguin Group
Penguin Books USA Inc., 375 Hudson Street,
New York, New York 10014, U.S.A.
Penguin Books Ltd, 27 Wrights Lane,
London W8 5TZ, England
Penguin Books Australia Ltd,
Ringwood, Victoria, Australia
Penguin Books Canada Ltd, 10 Alcorn Avenue,
Toronto, Ontario, Canada M4V 3B2
Penguin Books (N.Z.) Ltd, 182–190 Wairau Road,
Auckland 10, New Zealand

Penguin Books Ltd, Registered Offices:
Harmondsworth, Middlesex, England

First published by Signet, an imprint of Dutton Signet,
a division of Penguin Books USA Inc.

First Printing, April, 1997
10 9 8 7 6 5 4 3 2 1

Chapter One

That fall of 1803 many in England were alarmed that the country was to be shortly invaded. The brilliant French general, Napoleon Bonaparte, was even then amassing a threatening flotilla in the French ports, most particularly in Boulogne, and a huge military camp was known to be on the French shore ready to embark across the Channel. Watchfires were built up and down the English coast, ready to be lit if invasion became a reality.

A trade embargo had been erected between France and England, resulting in brisk smuggling between the two countries. It was a profitable but dangerous business, steeped in tradition. Those along the English coastline, from the meanest of hovels to the gentlemen's country seats, had for generations tacitly supported and protected the freebooters with their silence. The excisemen, whose duty it was to capture and stop the freebooters, thus had a difficult time putting an end to the illegal trade.

The same tolerant light was not bestowed upon the spying that went on back and forth across the Channel. French and English spies traversed the smugglers' routes for profit and for patriotism. In one year alone, twenty-seven French spies had been discovered and deported.

Stirring times, indeed.

At Halverton Manor, however, Lady Cecily Lester had no interest in momentous events. Her interest was centered upon her daughter, Vanessa. Her ladyship was determined to see that the girl was credibly established. For Lady Cecily, it was a matter of paramount importance that her daughter was wed.

Lady Cecily was a widow of formidable character and mien.

Once handsome of face, discontent had marked lines from her nose to her mouth. There was a hard cast about her celestial blue eyes that did not lighten even when she smiled. Her figure was still good and her ladyship was never seen abroad except in the height of fashion. Her ladyship was the daughter of an earl and she had often and bitterly regretted that she had married so far beneath her station. She had been a younger daughter. Her father had been in precarious circumstances due to his excessive gaming and she had had no portion and very few prospects. The offer from a wealthy baronet had come at a most opportune time to save the earl from his embarrassments and his daughter from the humiliation of being left on the shelf.

Lady Cecily's gratitude toward the baronet had not endured. She had hated the country. The windy downs to the west and the wooded lowlands had not appealed to her aesthetic sense. Most particularly, she had detested the smaller society in which she had found herself. She could only view her neighbors with haughty contempt, for none of them could aspire to her own high birth. She had demanded of the baronet that they remove themselves to the metropolis, where one could be assured of being able to mingle with others of the same social stature.

When it was gradually borne in upon Lady Cecily that her husband would never forsake his ancestral estate in order to establish a prominent place in London society, she quickly came to loathe him. After the birth of their daughter, Lady Cecily had spurned her husband altogether. She had done her duty, she informed him. He had his heir.

Now Lady Cecily had cause to regret that long-ago rebellion toward her husband.

Sir Charles Lester had indeed made his daughter his legal heir. He had brought the girl up just as though she had been the male heir of the estate, training her in her responsibilities and duties toward the land and their tenants. In the end, at his death, it was brought to light that Sir Charles had bequeathed all that he had to his sole blood descendant.

Halverton itself and all its rents were settled upon Miss Vanessa Lester. Nothing was left to Lady Cecily except the right to remain at Halverton until Miss Lester was wed, at which time a generous settlement would devolve upon Lady Cecily. The baronet had known his spouse very well. Sir Charles had written dryly that he had wished to be certain that Miss Lester would have proper chaperonage at Halverton in the event that his death took place before Miss Lester was established in her own household.

"Ridiculous! Absurd," said Lady Cecily forcefully, drawing her Norwich shawl closer over her shoulders against the room's chill. She stared out the window at the long green that was bounded by the woods. The south lawn was awash with sunshine, but its pleasant contours left her unmoved.

She had made the same statement over and over since the baronet's will had been read nine months earlier. That future settlement represented to Lady Cecily the key to her freedom. Bitterly, she reflected that if there had been a male heir, Sir Charles would never have set up such an idiotic condition. Naturally a brother could have been expected to offer his protection to his sister. Lady Cecily would likely have had a reasonable pension settled upon her and she could have shaken the dust of Halverton from her heels as soon as her husband had been interred.

Lady Cecily would have returned to London at once. And perhaps, once she herself had reentered society, she might have sent for her daughter to join her. It was her obligation to see that the girl was creditably established in polite society, after all.

However, that was what might have been. Lady Cecily felt her present circumstances to be intolerable. She was obliged to kick her heels at Halverton while every fiber of her being yearned to be in London. But her daughter, Vanessa, had flatly refused to stir from Halverton. Lady Cecily could not go without her daughter, for she had no monies of her own to draw from and her daughter firmly held the purse strings.

Vanessa had quietly advanced the argument that it did not make sense to maintain two households, nor did she wish talk to arise that too early a departure from Halverton was certain to incur.

"It would be a disrespect to my father's memory to ignore the canons of proper mourning, ma'am," Vanessa had said.

"Pooh; nonsense. Sir Charles doted upon you. He would be the last to deny you any amusement that you desired," said Lady Cecily in her characteristically impatient way.

"But I do not desire it, Mother," said Vanessa quietly.

Nothing had moved her. Not all Lady Cecily's representations of the advantages of a London Season; of the delights of gathering an intimate circle of high-bred acquaintances and admirers; of shopping and entertaining and being entertained.

When these appeals had failed, Lady Cecily had resorted to cold, quelling lectures on a daughter's obligation to honor and obey her mother. But Vanessa proved equally impervious to these also, only remarking that she was perfectly willing to fall in with her mother's wishes once the period of mourning was at an end.

"I fully intend to have a London Season. Papa and I discussed it at length. But there is a time for all things, and it has not yet come. When I have put off black gloves, it will be soon enough to think of amusements," said Vanessa. The hint of a smile had touched her lips as she regarded her mother's set expression. "Pray exercise a little patience, Mother. I promise you that the time will pass quickly enough."

Lady Cecily had not agreed. She did not want to wait out a Season, which was precisely what would happen if she waited much longer. It would soon be impossible to lease an acceptable address in the fashionable quarter of London and naturally she could not consider residing in anything less than the most prominent area.

Another year at Halverton! It was insupportable. Lady Cecily recalled that she had last discussed the matter of taking leave of Halverton with Vanessa three months previously. They were in half-mourning now. Surely that must make a difference.

"It must make a difference!" said Lady Cecily, glaring about her at the pleasantly appointed drawing room. There was nothing for the undiscerning eye to object to in the graceful shield-back chairs, the velvet-covered sofas, the side table and crested mirror. But Lady Cecily had been often enough to

London to know that styles had changed. Vain and arrogant, that knowledge was enough to give her an impatient contempt for her surroundings.

With an angry swish of skirts she crossed the thick Oriental carpet to pull the heavy bell rope. The door opened and a servant appeared to inquire her ladyship's wishes. Without looking around, Lady Cecily said briefly, "Send Miss Lester to me."

"Very good, my lady." The door closed again.

Lady Cecily stared up at the painting that was hung to one side of the huge gilt pier glass over the mantel. The painting was of her late unlamented husband and was very well done. Lady Cecily fancied that the baronet's eyes gleamed at her, faintly mocking.

Lady Cecily turned sharply away from the portrait. She had never succeeded in besting the baronet. He had resisted all of her cajolings and manipulations. Only in the matter of begetting another heir had she been able to claim a victory; but that, too, had proven to be merely a hollow triumph. Even now, when Sir Charles had been in the ground for these last nine months, he continued to hold the reins of all their lives.

The door opened and Lady Cecily's daughter entered the drawing room. Miss Lester was a tall young woman, well-proportioned but slim. She wore a black riding habit with long sleeves and cuffs. The bodice was double-breasted and ornamented down the front with the same design that circled the cuffs. A black beaver hat accented by a single ostrich plume angled over her head, in striking contrast to the fiery lights in her dark hair. The long hem of the habit was caught up over one arm, allowing a glimpse of her black half-boots. She carried a whip and tan leather gloves. She had obviously obeyed her mother's summons just as she was leaving the house.

Gravely, Vanessa met her mother's eyes. Not for the first time Lady Cecily was struck by the thought that at nineteen years of age, her daughter was remarkably self-possessed.

"You wished to see me, Mother?"

"Indeed I did, my dear. It is high time that we had another little talk about the future. Pray sit down, Vanessa. I dislike looking up at you," said Lady Cecily, sinking into a silk-

covered shield-back chair. She did not offer a smile nor her
hand to her daughter. It would never have occurred to her to
do so. She had left the upbringing of her daughter to a nurse, a
nanny and, later, to a superior governess. Such small tokens of
esteem that might have been expected to pass between mother
and daughter over the years had never materialized. As for
Vanessa, she would have been greatly surprised if any such
shows of affection had been implemented at this late date.

Vanessa's dark brows rose slightly. She chose a comfortable
carved and gilt armchair near the fireplace. It had been her father's favorite seat. "The future, Mother? I thought we had dis-
pensed with that question some months ago."

Vanessa had sat down directly below the painting of Sir
Charles, thus affording Lady Cecily the opportunity to renew
her unwelcome observation of the striking resemblance between father and daughter. Vanessa had inherited the baronet's
well-formed long aquiline nose and large gray eyes, the dark
brows and heavy waving hair, as well as a firm resolute mouth
that could as easily display quivering amusement or obstinacy.
She was cast out of the same physical mold, as well, being tall
and graceful.

In fact, thought Lady Cecily with asperity, there did not
seem to be one characteristic that she could point to that was
of herself. The painted baronet's slight smile seemed to widen.
Lady Cecily irritably shook off the impression.

"I am not at all content nor satisfied with how we left it,
Vanessa. You will recall that I objected most strenuously at
the time," said Lady Cecily.

Vanessa smiled, in a manner disconcertingly reminiscent of
her father's expression. "I do recall something of the sort," she
agreed.

"Yes, and particularly to that ignoble condition of your father's will that virtually ties me to Halverton. I cannot support
it, nor shall I ever forgive Sir Charles for the insult he dealt to
me," said Lady Cecily.

Vanessa still smiled, but her eyes had hardened somewhat.
"I shall not sit by if you intend to vilify my father, ma'am. If
that is all that you wished to say to me, I shall take my leave of

you. There are matters to do with the estate which I must attend." She rose to her feet.

Lady Cecily was startled and exasperated. She quickly disclaimed. "No, no, of course not! How you do take one up, and over a completely innocuous statement. Do sit back down, Vanessa! I am getting a crick in my neck."

Her daughter did not avail herself of the imperious invitation, but merely stood looking down at her ladyship with a faintly quizzical look. Lady Cecily pressed her lips together. However, it was not in her plans to set up the girl's back and so she did not press the matter. Instead, she said, "No, what I wish to discuss with you was our going up to London for the Season. I was just thinking about it. We must be quick about our preparations, for it would not do to take up residence too late. Nothing is so detrimental as a bad address or as annoying as missing the first invitations."

"You go too fast for me, Mother," said Vanessa, drawing her whip through her slim fingers. "What London Season are you referring to?"

"Why, this Season, of course. We are out of full mourning and in scarce three months more we will be out of black gloves altogether. It cannot be thought odd in us to leave Halverton now," said Lady Cecily. At her most persuasive, she added, "You are nineteen, Vanessa. Another year lost without introduction into society and you will be twenty. On the shelf before you have ever been seen! My dear, you must think a little."

"While I appreciate your concern on my behalf, Mother, it does not alter the fact that we are still in mourning," said Vanessa.

Lady Cecily preserved her temper with difficulty. She managed a superior smile. "Attending a few quiet, select parties would be unexceptional, I believe. It cannot be thought shocking."

"No, I will agree to that much. However, you know as well as I that once we were in London it would not end at a few unexceptional functions," said Vanessa dryly. "And a whirl of social squeezes would hardly be considered proper, situated as we are."

Frustrated, Lady Cecily drummed her longer fingers on the arm of her chair. "Yes, yes! I do not forget the restrictions upon us. It slips your memory, Vanessa, but I was bred to uphold the sanctity of such conventions. However, it is not to be thought that we can wait another three months and expect to acquire a decent address in London. The Season will already have begun by then and there will not be a suitable residence to be had. No, we must make the necessary arrangements now or we shall be forced to wait until next spring."

"Then we shall wait, ma'am," said Vanessa.

"Pray do not be absurd!" said Lady Cecily sharply. "You cannot mean for me to spend another year here at Halverton. Why, it is not to be thought of. I shall go out of my mind."

"I am sorry that you are so repulsed at the prospect, Mother. However, my decision is the same as it was. I shall not show disrespect toward my father's memory by throwing off my black gloves too soon. You cannot expect it of me," said Vanessa.

"And what of me, pray? I have been buried in this forsaken place year after year after year. Is that nothing to you? I am your mother, Vanessa. Surely my wishes must count for something," said Lady Cecily.

Vanessa was unmoved by her ladyship's hasty speech. She knew that Sir Charles had never objected to his spouse's frequent and lengthy visits to friends, whether at their country estates or, more usually, up to London. What he had objected to and had refused to contemplate was the upkeep of an extravagantly fashionable town house that would have been occupied only during the height of the Season of any given year and otherwise been a useless drain on the estate. She reminded her mother of this. "You have always been at liberty to visit friends for months at a time."

Lady Cecily swept away the unwelcome reminder with a grand gesture. "It is not at all the same!"

"My father left Halverton and its concerns to me. As you are undoubtedly aware, several matters have cropped up since my father's death that demand my attention," said Vanessa.

"What care I for that?" asked Lady Cecily coldly.

Vanessa smiled. She had few illusions. "What, indeed?"

Lady Cecily shot a sharp glance up at her daughter. "What do you mean by that, pray?"

"Only this, ma'am. Quite beside our half-mourning, I shall not shirk my responsibilities at this juncture only to indulge your impatient whims. There will be time enough to consider a London Season when matters are satisfactorily in hand and I am confident that my agent can manage on his own for a time," said Vanessa.

"Halverton! That is all I hear. I do not know what Sir Charles was about, to place the estate and all the rents into your inexperienced hands when I could have managed everything very much better. I was bred to a greater position than this, after all!" Lady Cecily shook her head, her lips thinned. "But it is all of a piece. Sir Charles never once considered my wishes, nor even my advice."

Vanessa held her peace, though she very much wished to respond. She knew what it had cost her father to redecorate and refurnish the entire manor to his new bride's extravagant taste. She had seen the figures in the books, recorded in Sir Charles's own firm hand, and how such expenditures had proven to be a charge upon the estate. But she knew also that no good purpose would be served in reminding Lady Cecily. It would only lead to further strife between them, for she would not stand meekly by while her mother abused her father's memory.

Lady Cecily threw a glance of dislike up at the portrait of Sir Charles. "He insisted in his stupid obstinate fashion to rear you as though you were his true heir and see what has come of it! You think more like a man than a female."

Vanessa had not been enjoying the interview, but she laughed then. Her somber expression lightened and her eyes sparked with the light of affection. "Perhaps that is true. However, I do not regret it in the least. Papa's training and influence has disciplined me to know my own mind, and for that I am truly grateful!"

Upon uttering those words, Vanessa gracefully exited the drawing room. Outside the closed door, she turned toward the back of the house. Her ride had been delayed by the interview with her mother, but it was not so much a matter of urgency as it was the desire to remove herself from the house that set her walking quickly down the wide hall.

Before she had traversed much distance, an elderly gentleman emerged from a doorway. Vanessa stopped, a smile coming at once to her face. "Good morning, Howard. I see that you are better."

"Aye, Miss Vanessa. I am quite capable of resuming my duties," said the elderly gentleman, resting his weight on the cane. "Shall you require correspondence to be written later this morning?"

As a young man of scarcely twenty years of age, Howard Tremaine had taken service with Vanessa's grandfather and then had acted as her father's secretary. Vanessa had inherited his loyalty along with Halverton. Though bent with age and in fragile health, Howard Tremaine was still an astute and able secretary. He was also very much a part of the fabric of life at Halverton. He had gained the status generally enjoyed by distant relations, often sitting at table with the family and being included at their entertainments.

Vanessa had known him all of her life and she trusted him implicitly. She smiled warmly at him. "Yes, after luncheon. I will be out for the remainder of the morning. I intend to ride down to visit with the tenants, particularly Tommy Whetton. I wish to judge the man for myself."

Tremaine nodded. "Whetton's father was a good solid man. I believe that his son will prove to be equally trustworthy once he is back on his feet."

"As do I. I hope to offer him a bit of encouragement," said Vanessa. She pulled her whip through her fingers as she spoke.

Tremaine noticed the gesture. "Very good. I shall not delay you longer, Miss Vanessa. I know well that you prefer to be away before her ladyship is about," he said with the glimmer of a smile.

"I have already been closeted with my mother this morning," said Vanessa. Her brows creased, she said, "Lady Cecily is extremely restless, Howard."

"Ah." The old man instantly understood. He raised his white brows. "Shall I speak with Lady Cecily?"

"You may do so, of course," said Vanessa. "But I doubt that any word you say would do the least good, unless you were to tell her ladyship that we were removing immediately to London."

"No doubt," said Tremaine dryly. "However, railing at a third party is often beneficial to one suffering from an excess of emotion."

Vanessa impulsively put out her hand to him. "My dear old friend! You would do that for me, I know. But I do not wish you to subject yourself to her ladyship's uncertain temper. It would not be right to expect it of you."

"However, you do not expect it of me," said Tremaine quietly.

"No, I do not," said Vanessa emphatically. She smiled again. "I must be off now or I shall not return in time to change for luncheon. Take care, dear friend." She walked swiftly away.

Chapter Two

Tremaine looked after Vanessa thoughtfully, then he turned back to continue his slow progress. Outside the drawing room, he signaled the footman to open the door.

"Begging your pardon, sir. But ye'll not be wishing to go in there. Her ladyship is in a rare nasty temper," said the footman quietly.

"That is precisely why I must go in," said Tremaine on a sigh.

The footman bowed respectfully and opened the door. The old man passed through and the door slowly closed behind him.

Seated in her ornate chair, Lady Cecily looked around upon hearing the door open. "I do not wish to be disturbed," she snapped.

Tremaine advanced. "Forgive me for this intrusion, my lady. I have just spoken with Miss Vanessa. She is concerned on your behalf."

When Vanessa had exited, Lady Cecily had been left prey to seething emotions. The old man's quiet statement acted like a torch on her. "Do not speak to me of her! I am most displeased, Tremaine, most displeased!"

"So it is seen, my lady," said Tremaine. He indicated a chair. "May I?"

Lady Cecily irritably waved her permission, her thoughts still churning on her daughter's refusal to accommodate her. She suddenly burst out with a confidence, just as Tremaine had known that she would. "Vanessa has once again proven every bit as obstinate as I could have expected, Tremaine. I shall not acknowledge defeat, however. There has to be some way that I can get to London for the Season."

"Perhaps a visit to one of your dearest friends?" suggested Tremaine quietly.

Lady Cecily toyed with the appealing idea of importuning some friends in putting her up, but she swiftly discarded it. "Lady Simmons is bringing out her second daughter this Season, as well as preparing for the nuptials of her firstborn. She would be extremely reluctant to extend the hospitality of her house at this time," she said.

"Ah. What of Lady Daphne or Mrs. Peckam?" asked Tremaine.

Lady Cecily thought about her other two bosom bows. She had quarreled with both when she had last seen them. Lady Cecily knew that both ladies would still be holding a stupid grudge against her and that it would delight them to no little end if they were able to, regretfully, of course, indicate that having her as a guest was not at that time possible. However, that was not for Tremaine to know.

Lady Cecily made a sharp gesture of dismissal. "That will not answer the purpose, Tremaine, as well you know! The true problem will still exist. It will not be resolved by simply finding a welcoming domicile for myself over the Season. No, the answer lies in seeing to it that my daughter is wed, so that wretched codicil to the will can be met and I will at last have control of the income that I deserve."

"It is naturally the dearest wish of every mother to see her daughter well wed," said Tremaine quietly.

"Yes, indeed! However, it is beyond my understanding how Vanessa is to attach an eligible parti if we remain in these remote parts," said Lady Cecily.

"I cannot offer you a swift solution, my lady. I can only assure you that I will do my utmost to clear away the remaining obstacles inhibiting Miss Vanessa's sojourning in London," said Tremaine.

"Do so!" snapped Lady Cecily sharply. "You may go, Tremaine. I had hoped that perhaps you might bring light to my dilemma, but you have done nothing but mouth mealy assurances."

The old man levered himself out of the chair, using his cane for a brace. He bowed, but Lady Cecily was already turned away from him. Tremaine shook his head and walked across the drawing room to the door. He opened it and went through.

Lady Cecily scarcely heeded the quiet click as the door closed. She continued to brood, her thoughts going around and around. Eventually she came up with what she persuaded herself to be an acceptable solution. If Vanessa would not go up to London and take advantage of all the opportunities that might be had in a larger, more glittering society, then the girl would simply have to be pawned off on some local rustic. It was not what Lady Cecily might wish for a daughter of hers, of course. However, Vanessa was willfully choosing to over-throw all of her mother's good intentions and so the girl must live with the consequences.

Her decision made, Lady Cecily began to review the gentle-men of her acquaintance. It was a small list. There were few that she could call to mind who were in the slightest way eligi-ble. Besides the dearth of possibilities, there was the hurdle of lack of acquaintance to be gotten over. Naturally she could not simply invite the gentlemen to court her daughter. One must be subtler than that. One first had to court the gentlemen's families and come to be on an intimate footing with them.

For the first time Lady Cecily almost regretted that she had not formed very many close connections in the neighborhood. Then she shrugged, brushing aside the obstacle. What matter? She was still Lady Cecily Lester. However much she was dis-liked, her consequence must still carry weight with less ex-alted personages. If she summoned the neighborhood to a gathering at Halverton Manor, she was confident that the ma-jority would come.

Her daughter could scarcely object, either, for Vanessa had herself agreed that a few quiet parties would be unexceptional. Naturally, their neighbors would wish to return the favor of hospitality and so there would be invitations proffered to other entertainments.

Lady Cecily's mind was already hatching and evolving vari-ous amusements that would bring her daughter into proximity with the eligible bachelors in the neighborhood. Regrettably, there were only three, once Lady Cecily had eliminated the young sprigs who were younger than Vanessa herself and a widower who was too elderly. The reverend could conceivably be considered a shade too old for a nineteen-year-old miss, himself being a widower every day of forty. He had a trio of hopeful children on his hands, as well. But Vanessa was mature and capable for her years and Lady Cecily did not think it outside the realm of possibility that Vanessa might well like such a challenging situation.

Reverend Haversaw had the advantage of having a handsome living, given to him by Sir Charles. The two had been distant cousins, so it was not as though Vanessa would be precisely marrying beneath her. Reverend Haversaw was at least a gentleman born.

The other two eligibles were Mark Nashe and Howard Pemberton. They were both esteemable young men of adequate if not good birth.

Lady Cecily dispassionately thought of Mark Nashe's unimposing person. He was unremarkable in face or form, being several inches shorter than Vanessa. But there was nothing to really object to in that, thought her ladyship. It was perhaps unusual for a man to be shorter than his wife, but certainly not unheard of. Mr. Nashe's position was secure as the scion of the neighboring estate. There would be an advantage in promoting the match with the Nashes, Lady Cecily knew, for the prospect of adding Halverton to their own holdings through a marital alliance could not but appeal to them.

Lady Cecily made a mental note to begin cultivating a better and warmer acquaintance with Lord and Lady Nashe. It was fortunate that they were still out of circulation due to their long recuperation from illness. She would be able to make a sympathy call. Lady Cecily decided to do so the following morning and then turned her thoughts to the next eligible on her mental list.

Howard Pemberton. Lady Cecily involuntarily grimaced. As she recalled, the young man had seemed to be a coming sort as a boy, full of high spirits and mischief before he had been sent off to school. It was a pity that such promise had not been fulfilled in the man.

Not much had been seen of the Pembertons for some years. They had inherited a tidy estate somewhere in the north, it was

said, and had quite abandoned their former place. Then
Howard Pemberton had returned to reopen the house with a
maiden aunt as his hostess and to take charge of his domestic
staff. It was quietly said that the lady was probably his keeper,
too, for a duller young man it would be difficult to find. He
was kindly enough and well-liked, but was unfortunately
rather slow-witted.

However, Lady Cecily was prepared to welcome even such
a dullard as Howard Pemberton as her son-in-law if it would
enable her to receive possession of her allowance and leave
Halverton.

With the exception of Mr. Pemberton's slow thought
processes, Lady Cecily saw little reason for Vanessa to take
exception to him. The gentleman was tall and would comple-
ment Vanessa's own inches. His countenance was pleasant,
even to a degree handsome if one discounted the lack of spon-
taneity in his expression. He was well-set up, having a breadth
of shoulder much envied by men less blessed. Lady Cecily had
heard in passing that the gentleman was something of a sportsman, being particularly skillful on horseback. That should appeal to Vanessa, at least, for she was a notable horsewoman in
her own right.

Each of the three eligibles had their drawbacks, but none
were so severe as to be insurmountable, reflected Lady Cecily.
All in all, her ladyship thought that she could very well bring
something about for her daughter. Vanessa was nineteen. It
was past time that she made a push on her daughter's behalf,
and certainly next Season must be considered too late. Indeed,
the more Lady Cecily reflected on the matter the more certain
it appeared to her that her daughter would have had no more
than a slim chance at a credible match, even in London. The
girl was simply too old. Really, Vanessa should thank her for
looking out for her interests so well, she thought virtuously.

Lady Cecily left the drawing room and went upstairs, seek-
ing the privacy of her own dressing room. Her maid was in attendance but Lady Cecily dismissed the woman. She sat down
at her satinwood writing table and pulled out paper and pen
and ink. She had several lists to make for the planning of the
various entertainments that she had in mind.

Lady Cecily was almost cheerful. Another winter at Halverton would be worth it if she could engineer a match for Vanessa. She would then be able repair to London, ensconcing herself in her own residence rather than making a stay as a guest in someone else's town house. She would never be obliged to return to Halverton.

That evening Lady Cecily presided at her usual place at the end of the elegantly set dining table. As was her custom even when dining *en famille,* Lady Cecily had attired herself in an elegant gown and jewels. Her ladyship was noticed by the serving men to be in spirits, for unlike her usual habit she voiced few criticisms of the excellently prepared dinner. The veal and fish, removed by several side dishes, were pronounced to be for once quite edible.

Vanessa, seated at her mother's right hand, was also surprised by her mother's affability. She had dressed carefully for dinner that evening, having kept in mind that Lady Cecily would be quick to censure any perceived carelessness of attire. The ruched crepe gown she wore was lavish for a private setting, but it had the advantage of having once earned Lady Cecily's approval as being very pretty. Now it seemed that her precaution had been unnecessary.

Tremaine sat below Vanessa at the table. He said little, but his keen old eyes rested often and thoughtfully upon Lady Cecily's almost benign countenance. He did not think any words of his could possibly have led to this unusual amiability in Lady Cecily. He had been at Halverton when Lady Cecily had come as a new bride and he had had many years in which to become familiar with her character. He had seen this phenomenon before, and always it had heralded some scheme that her ladyship had hatched to get her own way. Tremaine awaited events, alert for any clue to what was in her ladyship's mind. All of his loyalty and concern were for Miss Vanessa, for whatever Lady Cecily had in mind would most nearly concern the mistress of Halverton.

Vanessa had steeled herself for more argument or a meal endured in cold silence with the exception of a few exchanges with Tremaine, but neither of these circumstances was forthcoming. Lady Cecily seemed almost mellow. Her ladyship even unbent enough to inquire how Vanessa's day had progressed.

Vanessa answered willingly enough but with sparing words. Past experience had taught her that her mother had no interest in the affairs of Halverton, or indeed, in anything that did not directly impact upon her ladyship's comfort. She touched briefly on her visits with the tenants and ended with the matter that had most absorbed her afternoon. "There was a bit of a dilemma over the flooding in the west end. Papa had meant to secure the services of an engineer who had experience in draining bottomlands. Mr. Travers agreed with me that we should go forward with Papa's intentions."

Lady Cecily nodded. "Sir Charles always gave great thought to whatever he did with Halverton. I do not doubt that you have made the correct decision, my dear."

Vanessa regarded her mother with a faintly amazed look. She glanced at Tremaine and saw the same emotion mirrored in his own eyes. This shallow praise of Sir Charles was virtually unparalleled.

Vanessa wondered what was the nature of this new tack that Lady Cecily had undertaken. Deliberately, she tested the waters. "It will take some weeks before the engineer arrives. I shall myself interview him. If he is able to accomplish the task, we shall end with several acres more of tillable land. That will eventually mean a considerable profit to us."

"Excellent, my dear. I am glad that it is in a fair way to being decided," said Lady Cecily, but with a somewhat bored air. She waved away the footman who would have replenished her wineglass. Glancing at her daughter as she set aside her napkin, Lady Cecily announced, "I am going up early to my rooms, Vanessa."

"Very well, Mother." Vanessa was not surprised. Lady Cecily had always indicated a clear preference for her own company over that of the baronet or her daughter after dinner. Her ladyship's habits had not changed overmuch since Sir Charles's untimely death.

Truth to tell, Sir Charles and Vanessa had both preferred to have the evenings reserved for their own easy conversations. Tremaine had generally respected their privacy, excusing himself at an early hour unless it was insisted upon that he was to remain. On those occasions, he and Sir Charles had enjoyed playing cards for mild stakes and Vanessa had occupied herself with embroidering. Lady Cecily's rare presence had always brought tension into the drawing room.

Leaving Tremaine to his after-dinner wine, Vanessa exited the dining room with her mother. She said good night in the hall as Lady Cecily parted company with her to go upstairs.

Vanessa retired to the drawing room, where coffee would shortly be served to her. She sat down in a comfortable chair in front of the warm hearth and took up her embroidery. This was the hour of the day that she had looked forward to most. It had always been a peaceful, informal time. Sir Charles had encouraged open discussion between them upon all manner of topics. As a consequence, Vanessa had never felt restraint in her father's company. He had come to know her hopes and dreams and goals.

Now there was only herself to rely on. Tremaine was a dear soul and devoted to her, but he had never presumed to put his own wishes or opinions above hers. Vanessa glanced up at her father's portrait. "Oh, Papa. I wish you were here now. I feel somewhat alone these days," she said on a sigh.

After a moment, during which she reflected with a quiet smile on her father's last stricture to her, Vanessa bent her head and set her first stitches of the evening. Between the circumference of her embroidery hoop grew a lavish creation of satin stitchings.

However much Lady Cecily deplored her daughter's steady temperament and her unfortunate knack for managing a man's estate, her ladyship could say nothing against Vanessa's most feminine accomplishment. Vanessa enjoyed embroidering and in fact had with her own hands stitched covers for many of the chairs and pillows scattered throughout the manor. The linens in the linen closet also bore testimony of her exquisite talent.

The door opened and Tremaine entered. Behind him, the butler and a footman carried in the coffee urn and a tray of biscuits and nuts. "I thought that I might join you this evening, Miss Vanessa," said Tremaine.

Vanessa smiled at the old man. "Pray do. I have been

melancholy these last few minutes and I was just wishing for
company."

The old man lowered himself into a chair. He carried a
Bible with him. "You will not mind if I read for a time?"

"Of course not. I well know the quiet delight that one may
find in the Scriptures," said Vanessa.

Nearly an hour passed by the clock. Coffee had long since
been finished. Vanessa and Tremaine had each pursued their
individual entertainments. It had been a companionable time.
Vanessa glanced over at her secretary, a smile just touching
her lips. The old man's head had begun to droop as he fell into
a light doze, his book still resting open on his knee.

The door opened. The butler entered, cleared his throat before announcing, "Lieutenant Copperidge and his sergeant of
the Excise, miss."

Tremaine woke at once. There was a momentary haze of
disorientation in his eyes. His voice quavered slightly.
"What's this?"

"We have visitors, dear sir. Pray send them in, Sims," said
Vanessa.

Chapter Three

The butler stood aside to allow the late visitors to pass into the room. The lanky lieutenant stepped over the threshold, his sergeant close behind him. Both men were in uniform. The sergeant took up a station just inside the door, his stance that of a stolid statue.

Vanessa set aside her embroidery on the marble-topped occasional table that stood beside her chair. She rose gracefully to her feet and held out her hand. "Lieutenant Copperidge? I am Miss Lester and this is my secretary, Mr. Tremaine."

Lt. Copperidge made a correct bow to the lady and the elderly gentleman. His physical grace would have done homage to any gently born lady's drawing room.

Tremaine had snapped quickly back to his usual shrewd state and he exchanged polite greetings with the excise officer. Vanessa watched as the two men took measure of one another. Later, she would ask her secretary what had been his initial opinion of the young exciseman. Tremaine's discernment of character had always been uncannily certain. She glanced at the large ormulu clock on the mahogany mantel. "This is an unexpected call, Lieutenant."

Lieutenant Copperidge nodded. "I am aware of it, Miss Lester. Forgive me for visiting Halverton at such a late hour this evening. I was in the neighborhood and hoped that I might catch you at home. I had hoped to find Lady Cecily at home, as well." There was a look of inquiry in his eyes.

Vanessa knew very well that proper etiquette required her to send a message up to her mother. However, she knew, too, that Lady Cecily would not consider a visit by an exciseman to be of sufficient importance to warrant disturbance of her solitude.

Dryly, she said, "Her ladyship does not receive visitors except those who come at her invitation."

Tremaine's lips twitched, but he gave no other indication of his appreciation for her honest assessment.

The lieutenant looked a little disconcerted at the bald statement, but then his expression cleared. His deeply tanned face eased into the fraction of a sympathetic smile. "Ah. I understand, of course. You are still in black gloves here at Halverton."

"Yes," agreed Vanessa. She did not bother to correct the lieutenant's apparent misconception that Lady Cecily had been made so distraught by her husband's death that she preferred to see only her closest acquaintances.

"Pray be seated, Lieutenant," said Vanessa, seating herself. She waited until her secretary and the lieutenant had taken a chair, then gestured toward the sergeant questioningly. "Perhaps the sergeant would care to join us?"

Lieutenant Copperidge smiled. "My sergeant would feel himself extremely uncomfortable to be seated in a lady's drawing room, ma'am. Isn't that right, Higgins?"

"Indeed it is, sir."

Vanessa smiled. She asked curiously, "What may I do for you, Lieutenant?"

Lieutenant Copperidge crossed his legs. He was obviously from good family and was completely at ease in his surroundings, unlike his sergeant who stood stiffly at attention in the background. "I have been visiting with each of the landowners in the vicinity, Miss Lester. My purpose has been not only to introduce myself, but also to assure you and others that my troops and I are at your disposal whenever you should have word of illegal activities in these parts," he said.

Vanessa knew instantly what some of her neighbors had thought of the young lieutenant's declaration. She shared a glance with Tremaine, knowing that he, too, was aware of the likely reactions. Many in the county felt and frequently voiced deep reservations about the heavy penalties imposed against those involved in free trade.

Vanessa hoped that most had kept those opinions to themselves. The poor lieutenant had a difficult enough task as it was, she thought, without coming face to face with rude opposition. The oft-expressed justification for the smuggling trade was one she had heard all of her life. Her own father had laid down in his cellars several casks of prime French wines. But that was not something that she would confide to this earnest young man.

"Thank you, Lieutenant Copperidge," said Vanessa quietly. "It will be a comfort to all of us, I am certain."

"Now as to that, Miss Lester, I must wonder," said Lieutenant Copperidge with a sudden smile.

Not a fool, then, thought Vanessa, and she smiled at him. She could only respect an individual of conviction who, though aware of obstacles, nevertheless was determined to carry through with his duty. Certainly Lieutenant Copperidge gave every appearance of being just such a man.

"You are to be commended, Lieutenant. It is not an easy task that you have embarked upon," said Vanessa. "Smuggling has been a long-standing tradition in these parts."

The lieutenant's lean face flushed under his tan. "Thank you, Miss Lester. I trust that I am successful in the performance of my duty. I would be derelict indeed if I did not stress to you that it is not only the illegal freebooting that I have been commissioned to counter, but any possible spy activity."

Vanessa was deeply startled. "Spy activity?"

Tremaine stiffened in his chair. His eyes had taken on a startlingly penetrating alertness. He murmured something under his breath that was not quite audible.

"Yes, ma'am." Lieutenant Copperidge glanced at the old man, his square jaw tightening at what he interpreted to be criticism. "We have it on excellent authority that French spies have been making good use of the smuggling routes in their traitorous trafficking." His eyes flashed suddenly. "As you may imagine, Miss Lester, that is particularly abhorrent to me. The security of our country must be maintained."

"Yes, indeed!" Vanessa shook her head in wonder. "Of course I have seen the watchfires built up on the cliffs in readiness if ever there should come an invasion, but I never considered anything of this sort to be taking place. It is dastardly."

"It is an insidious threat, indeed. I hope that I may count on you and Lady Cecily and all of your household at Halverton to pledge your allegiance to support my efforts to stamp out this threat," said Lieutenant Copperidge, his gaze touching again on the elderly gentleman.

Tremaine's lips tightened. Otherwise his seamed face was expressionless. What his thoughts might be over the excise officer's revelation could not be read.

"But of course! There can be no question," said Vanessa. She had noticed that glance at her secretary and she wondered at its import. Surely the lieutenant could not suspect Tremaine or any of the rest of her retainers to be embroiled in such an ugly business.

"Thank you, Miss Lester." Lieutenant Copperidge stood up. "Then I shall not impose upon your good nature any longer. I give you good night, ma'am. Pray convey my regards to Lady Cecily. At a more opportune time I hope to make her ladyship's acquaintance."

Vanessa had risen and she now gave her hand to the exciseman. "Thank you, Lieutenant. I shall do so. You may be assured of a welcome at Halverton whenever you chance to come this way."

The lieutenant's rather severe countenance eased into another smile. He honored her with a graceful bow. "I appreciate your kindness more than I can say, Miss Lester."

Vanessa gathered the distinct impression that he had not been accorded the same courtesy by some of her neighbors.

He exited then, taking with him his silent sergeant.

When the door had closed behind the excisemen, Vanessa turned to her secretary. "What do you make of it, Howard?"

"It is something indeed when good English folk are suspected of consorting with traitors," said Tremaine. Unusual color tinged his face. "That puppy actually had the gall to require an oath of loyalty from you and all of Halverton. 'Tis an insult!"

"I took it to be a mere request for assurance," said Vanessa quietly. "You are deeply exercised, my dear friend. What is it that has put you into such a heat?"

Tremaine grasped his cane and levered himself out of the chair. "Naught but an old man's lack of patience, Miss

Vanessa. When that officer first mentioned spy activity, I knew instantly what was on his mind. This Lieutenant Copperidge suspects everyone and he is patently of a zealous bent. He will undoubtedly see bogies where there are nothing but shadows. I do not wish to see our peace at Halverton cut up. You have too many burdens already."

Vanessa was touched. "Thank you, dear sir. However, I assure you that I am perfectly capable of handling an excise officer, even one so dedicated as Lieutenant Copperidge has expressed himself to be. I shall not allow him to upset us here at Halverton. Of that, you may be assured."

The old man sighed. "Very well, Miss Vanessa. I shall trust in your judgment. You may rely upon me in any capacity, of course."

"How well I know it! Let me ring for a pot of tea. I believe that we both need a soothing restorative after such an astonishing visit," said Vanessa, going over to pull the bell rope.

When the butler entered, she gave her quiet order. Then she looked over at her secretary, regarding him rather anxiously. Tremaine had slumped back down into the chair and he appeared to be brooding at the fire.

Vanessa reseated herself and took up her embroidery again. Slowly she set a stitch. After a moment, she said, "Naturally I have heard rumors now and again of smuggling activity. I know for a certainty that my father, like many of our neighbors, enjoyed a tacit understanding with the smugglers."

"Not in the sense that you mean, Miss Vanessa," said Tremaine, roused out of his reverie. "Unlike his father before him, Sir Charles never actively pursued a relationship with the smugglers. He simply did not question the appearance at his table of the expensive French wines that have all but disappeared from the wineshops because of the trade embargo. Nor did he ever question the occasional use by strange pack strings of the abbey."

"The abbey!" Vanessa looked at her companion in surprise. The ruined abbey that stood on Halverton lands had over the years become well-hidden by forest overgrowth and was all but forgotten by most people. She herself had not thought of it in years. "I didn't know anyone was going there."

Tremaine shook his head. "I should not have mentioned it. I thought you knew, but obviously that is not the case. The less known about the gentlemen of the night, the better it is for all around."

"Howard, pray tell me the truth. Is the abbey presently being used by smugglers?" asked Vanessa.

Tremaine hesitated. There was obvious reluctance in his expression to answer her question. But his loyalty was such that he could not hide anything from her. "I do not know for certain. I suspect that infrequent stops are made. I have overheard certain rumors." A smile flickered over his countenance. "I am an old man. Once I would have been in the thick of such goings-on, but no more. I have lost touch since Sir Charles chose to distance himself from the smuggling. You see, he had thought more of his reputation, his heritage, and his family than he did of the advantages of maintaining his contacts. He would not have blatantly endangered any of those things for all the wine in France."

"I see. Of course I understand," said Vanessa slowly.

Obviously Sir Charles had from time to time done business with the gentlemen of the night, but he had not encouraged their commerce with him and had protected his family from their stealthy contacts. Therefore as a child Vanessa had heard much about the freebooters, but she had never actually had personal contact with them.

Vanessa had long suspected that her state of ignorance was not shared by certain individuals of her household. Astonishingly enough, she had never thought of her secretary as being one of them. But of course Tremaine, with his long residence at Halverton, must have been involved. Now he had inadvertently indicated that some of the staff were almost certainly tied to the gentleman's trade themselves or had kinsmen involved.

She found herself therefore in a delicate situation. On the one hand Vanessa sympathized with Lieutenant Copperidge and others like him, who were merely attempting to do their duty and put a stop to a hundred-year tradition.

Vanessa felt that to be a hopeless task, in any event. But compounding the problem was her certainty that she and her neighbors were probably intimately acquainted with many who were hand in glove with the smugglers. She did not honestly see how she or anyone else could turn information on a person they knew, even after becoming privy to such information.

"I hope that I have not overburdened you?" asked Tremaine anxiously.

"No, of course not. I was merely assessing the situation," said Vanessa. "What make you of Lieutenant Copperidge's alarming assertion that spies are making use of the smuggling routes?"

The flicker of a smile crossed Tremaine's face. "We are both realistic enough to realize that patriotism could be sacrificed for profit."

Vanessa nodded. Thoughtfully, she said, "The smugglers no doubt demand a high price to ferry that sort of cargo." In fact, she would scarcely be surprised if the shadowy figures and the vital information they carried were not more profitable to the smugglers than all the rest of the goods that were carried back and forth across the Channel. Certainly there was more risk involved in providing passage for such personages than there would be in trading English woolens and leather goods for French wines and barrels of laces, silks, and velvets.

Vanessa snipped her silk and chose another color to thread on to her needle. "We need not concern ourselves too closely," she said. "I believe that I know my own household and tenants too well. No one of Halverton could possibly consider giving aid to the French cause."

"I concur. Spies and high treason are very far from the quiet waters of Halverton's existence," said Tremaine, nodding.

"However, I do pity poor Lieutenant Copperidge. No doubt he will do his best to catch out the smugglers. Perhaps in the process he will manage to snare a desperate and dangerous spy," said Vanessa. She almost hoped that the lieutenant would have the opportunity to do just that. It would serve to guarantee a promotion for him in a rather despised branch of the military and she had rather liked the stern young lieutenant.

"The less traffic Halverton has with that one, the better," said Tremaine firmly.

"Actually, I was thinking of inviting Lieutenant Copperidge and his taciturn sergeant to dinner some evening," said Vanessa coolly, but with a hint of mischief in her eyes.

She laughed outright at her secretary's expression. "You are naturally thinking that in some quarters it might be thought odd of me to do so, but I care little enough for that. My father did just as he pleased and he was well respected. I think that I could do worse than to follow Sir Charles's example."

"No, Miss Vanessa, that was not what I was thinking," said Tremaine, barely controlling his emotions. "Have you thought of the possible consequences if you pursue this course?"

Vanessa knew perfectly well what her companion was referring to, but she chose to pretend that she had misunderstood him. She rather thought that keeping an overzealous excise officer underfoot and under close observation might prove more advantageous than otherwise. However, she did not wish to debate the issue with Tremaine. "There is my mother to be considered, naturally."

"Lady Cecily?" repeated Tremaine, startled. "I fail to see how her ladyship figures in, Miss Vanessa."

Vanessa laughed again and shook her head. "Why, Howard, do you not see? Lady Cecily will undoubtedly freeze up alarmingly at the prospect of having two lowly excisemen welcomed to Halverton Manor. But no doubt her ladyship can be brought round when she is casually informed that the lieutenant is young and obviously well-bred. I anticipate that Lady Cecily will instantly want to know whether the lieutenant is married. If Lieutenant Copperidge is not supporting a wife, I imagine that Lady Cecily will be very pleased to think that I have acquired a beau."

Tremaine was thrown firmly off track by this rabbit trail. His voice tinged with sympathy, he murmured, "I am more sorry than I can say, Miss Vanessa."

Vanessa was instantly ashamed of her flippancy. "No, I am sorry, dear sir. It is perfectly horrid of me to expose my cynicism. One would prefer to be unaware of one's mother's machinations, of course, but there it is. I cannot pretend otherwise."

"Sir Charles told me that he had revealed to you in plain terms his understanding of Lady Cecily's ambitions and what the probable result would be of the condition that he had set forth in his will. I had hoped that the shock would not grieve you," said Tremaine.

Vanessa ignored the last of his statement. She truly had no response that she could make that would not sound rather self-pitying, and self-pity was something that she despised. "I had already surmised that my mother would not wish to remain at Halverton a moment longer than was deemed necessary and so my father's explanation scarcely came as a surprise to me," said Vanessa. "I have always been aware of Lady Cecily's dissatisfaction with Halverton, but I never understood it. I have always loved the place."

"Aye, and your content was balm to Sir Charles's lonely heart," murmured Tremaine.

Vanessa smiled at the old man with misted eyes. "Thank you, Howard. You could not have said anything better to me."

A short silence fell as both turned to their own thoughts. Vanessa's reflections were not altogether pleasant. She knew that as soon as she was well wed, Lady Cecily would acquire what her ladyship had always desired. Lady Cecily would have an independence of a size that would support her in London in the custom to which her ladyship believed she was entitled. Naturally, Lady Cecily's every waking thought would be turned to the matter of getting her daughter to the altar.

"I spoke to Lady Cecily earlier today. I made the suggestion that her ladyship might wish to visit friends," said Tremaine suddenly.

"You should not have put yourself in the fire, Howard. But nevertheless I do thank you," said Vanessa. She paused, then asked, "And will she?"

"Unfortunately, her ladyship did not seem to feel that was a viable solution for her *ennui*," said Tremaine.

"I see," said Vanessa, thoughtfully pulling free a knotted stitch. It had always been pleasanter at Halverton Manor when Lady Cecily was away. Certainly it would be more comfortable at this time if her ladyship would decide to go on an extended visit somewhere.

Vanessa gave a soft sigh. She had stood firm against all of her mother's arguments and importunities, but she had not enjoyed it. She harbored no illusions, either. Lady Cecily would approach her again in a matter of days or weeks and there would again take place one of those antagonistic interviews. Unless Lady Cecily decided to make one of her lengthy visits to friends, however, she knew that she would simply have to make the best of the uncomfortable circumstances.

"It is a pity that Sir Charles did not provide better for you," said Tremaine with unwonted force.

Vanessa lifted her gaze from her needlework to stare at her companion in surprise. "Not provide for me?" she repeated.

Tremaine waved his hand. "I do not speak of materially. Sir Charles left you Halverton and it is well that he did so. But he did not provide for your personal future."

"Do you mean by contracting my hand?" asked Vanessa, somewhat amused by the old-fashioned idea.

"Precisely," said Tremaine. He smiled. "You will think me an old doddering fool, Miss Vanessa, but I should like to see you wed before I die."

"Then I have many more years in which to accomplish that goal," said Vanessa, returning his smile.

"Do you not wish to wed, Miss Vanessa?" The old man's question was soft.

"Of course I would like to wed." Vanessa turned her head to look into the crackling yellow fire. She did not want her old shrewd friend to read her thoughts in her eyes.

It was the hope of every young woman to entrust her heart to a like-minded gentleman. Since Vanessa had emerged from the schoolroom she had naturally attended all of the assemblies and private parties in the county, so she was not quite without exposure to male admiration. But Vanessa had yet to be introduced to any gentleman who could sweep her off her feet.

Vanessa returned her gaze to the old man who sat watching her. A smile touched her face. "It is melancholy to admit it, but I am of a rather romantic bent. Such a trait is to be deplored in one who has been reared to manage a man's portion, do you not think?"

"On the contrary, I suspect that it is the making of you," said Tremaine unexpectedly. He got up out of the chair. "I am feeling the hour, I fear. I trust that you will not be offended if I take myself off to bed?"

"Of course not. I wish you a good night, dear friend," said Vanessa.

Tremaine slowly crossed the floor and let himself out of the drawing room.

Chapter Four

Vanessa was left with much to think about. Her old friend's quiet query had set her to pondering her own nature and situation. She knew herself to be a fool for harboring the hope of one day finding the one man who would set her heart on fire, but she could not deny that it existed. And so she had resisted the temptation to persuade herself that just any eligible gentleman would do.

There had been one or two gentlemen who had shown a flattering attention toward her and who had kindled a lukewarm interest in her breast. But Vanessa had recognized that what she felt was not a strong enough attachment upon which to form a basis for marriage.

Vanessa and her father had discussed the possibility of her marriage on numerous occasions. Sir Charles had given his daughter valuable advice. Out of the wealth of his own experience, he had adjured Vanessa to become thoroughly acquainted with whatever gentleman struck her fancy.

"Then you will be in a better position to judge their character, my dear," he had said with a rather twisted smile. "It is vital that you have some notion of what they are like under what may appear on the surface as a well-formed face and figure. You will avoid later disillusionment."

Now recalling that conversation, Vanessa again shook her head. Quite dispassionately, she thought about her mother. She knew well of Lady Cecily's driving determination. Until there was no longer the least hope of setting up residence in London for this Season, Vanessa anticipated a battle of wills over the matter. If she gave way on that point, then there would be no avoiding Lady Cecily's ruthless efforts to set her up as a matrimonial prize ripe for the plucking. Vanessa hoped that she was levelheaded enough to profit from her father's dearly-won experience and did not allow herself to be driven into a corner.

London was the natural choice for a young lady who was interested in looking about her for a suitable spouse. Vanessa intended to go up to the metropolis with her mother for the following Season. She had already had Tremaine send out inquiries to leasing agents for a suitable town house to be found for next spring. However, she had not informed Lady Cecily of that fact because she knew her ladyship would step up the intensity of her strident and wearying efforts to make her daughter comply to her wishes at once.

Vanessa's discretion was a form of self-survival. As she had patiently explained several times to her mother, there were good reasons for remaining at Halverton for yet a while. She would be derelict in her duty, indeed, if she did not first see to it that the day-to-day operations of Halverton would continue to run in a smooth manner.

Vanessa's thoughts ticked off the numerous responsibilities that she shouldered. There were tenants to think about and crops. Some of the older cottages required repair and there were two new tenant families that had to have housing. She had ordered the cutting of lumber for that purpose and for selling. The oats and barley had been cut and the fields were being seeded with winter clover. The orchards had yielded a good crop of apples, pears, peaches, and plums. The jellies and jams and dried fruits had been put up, but the ciders and fruit wines were in the making.

There was also the livestock. Her agent, Mr. Travers, had suggested that she purchase a new stud bull to increase the herd of milk cows and calves. She was already negotiating with the squire for one of his big brutes.

The swine and sheep pens had to be readied before winter. Later, as the weather grew cooler, the butchering would need to be supervised. The salting down of hams and bacon could not be rushed.

In the early spring there would be the calving and lambing. When it grew warm again, it would be time for the shearing and carding of the wool. It appeared that Halverton would have a good crop of wool that year that could be turned for a profit.

It would take time for Mr. Travers to understand all of his duties and become thoroughly versed in all of Halverton's business. Halverton was very nearly a self-sufficient estate, becoming unencumbered at last under her father's prime management and now beginning to enjoy a healthy profit under Vanessa's careful hand. Vanessa was not willing to give over the reins into her agent's hands until he had seen and been involved in the entire cycle of life at Halverton. It would also take time for the bailiff and the tenants to learn to trust in Mr. Travers's judgment.

When the agent was thoroughly established in his role, Vanessa felt that she would be able to turn her thoughts to herself and her own concerns. In short, fashionable dresses and beaux and lavish parties would simply have to wait another year.

Vanessa grimaced to herself. She readily acknowledged the validity of Lady Cecily's argument that her age was against her in the eyes of most gentlemen looking out for a bride. That consideration had occurred to her more than once. Every year that she remained unwed only added to that detriment. Many young misses emerged out of the schoolroom at sixteen or seventeen years and were married within months of making their social debut.

Vanessa chuckled to herself suddenly. She would definitely find herself out of place among such youthful company. While the other young ladies would have nothing on their minds but attaching the eligibles, she would be wondering whether or not the new drainage system was working as it should.

She set another deft stitch in her embroidery, still smiling. Undoubtedly her style of conversation would have to be amended. She would have to remember to be airy and frivolous in her observations and never allude to the price of feed corn.

Sir Charles had offered to send Vanessa up to London when she had turned eighteen and her governess had been released. Sir Charles had said that it was time that she try her wings. But Vanessa had declined. She had already seen the toll that ill health had taken upon her father in the year and a half since a near-crippling riding accident. She had not wanted to leave him.

Sir Charles had not pushed the matter, sensing himself that his time was shortening. He had been selfish enough to want to spend that time with the one person in all the world who had unconditionally loved him. It would have been a bleak prospect indeed to step through the twilight with no one nearby except the wife who had so thoroughly rejected him. He had said only, "I have confidence in your judgment, Vanessa. You must do as you think best."

Now indeed Vanessa was abiding by her own judgment with none to guide her. Certainly, she had those who advised her. Tremaine was always willing to impart the wisdom of his years. The family solicitor and her neighbor, the squire, had also given her solid counsel. More than once Reverend Haversaw had helped her over a difficult trial with common sense and a compassion for which she would always be grateful. Perhaps even more than her most intimate female friends, these four gentlemen had realized the deep-felt loss and burden that she had operated under since Sir Charles's death.

Vanessa was not one to wallow in self-pity and grief, however. She recognized that her life must continue to march forward, and to that end she had given serious consideration to spreading her wings a little beyond the boundaries of Halverton.

Once she was completely out of black gloves and the most pressing estate matters had been resolved, she would be at liberty to set into motion the next steps in her life. She would go to London for a Season and allow her mother to launch her with all pomp and ceremony. She would enter into every amusement wholeheartedly and she would become acquainted with every eligible gentleman who was brought to her notice.

The inherent romance of her soul hoped for a fairy-tale ending. But Vanessa had a prosaic streak, too. She had promised herself that she would not settle for less than what she desired. If she did not discover that one very special gentleman she felt was meant for her, she was prepared to return home and remain Miss Lester, mistress of Halverton.

The clock struck midnight. Vanessa was startled at the amount of time that had elapsed. Her thoughts and her embroidery had made it pass swiftly. On the echo of the chimes, the door opened. The butler entered. "Will you be wanting anything else this evening, miss?"

"No, thank you, Sims. I believe that I shall retire in a few moments," said Vanessa. She began putting away her embroidery. Her maid would still be waiting up for her and would scold her for keeping such late hours when she would no doubt rise at her usual predawn hour. However, Vanessa never felt fatigued no matter what hours she kept. She had been blessed with a reserve of energy that had never failed her.

"Very good, miss." Sims advanced in a stately manner to the fireplace. He bent down to begin the task of bedding the log in the ashes for the night. He glanced around. "It is good to see Mr. Tremaine up and about again, miss."

"Indeed it is," agreed Vanessa. "I have missed his fine hand these last few weeks. My copperplate is rather indifferent, I am afraid. I do not know how I shall go on when he retires."

"Oh, I don't think you need be anxious on that account, miss. Mr. Tremaine isn't one to give up his duties until the very hour he is called home to heaven," said Sims comfortably.

"You are right, of course," said Vanessa, smiling. Having tucked away all of her fancywork, she closed the lid of her sewing basket. She started to rise out of her chair.

"Miss, if I may be so bold, I should like to ask a question."

"Of course, Sims," said Vanessa, turning toward the butler. "What is it?"

The butler straightened, holding the poker in his hand. "Those excisemen. What was it that they wanted?"

Vanessa was surprised. She had anticipated a query regarding some working of the household. At once, she knew that the butler's curiosity was not idle. "Why, nothing very much. Lieutenant Copperidge was merely introducing himself around the neighborhood and offered his services if we should ever have any information regarding smuggling."

"I see." The butler bent down again to poke the log.

"Sims, the gentleman was also interested in anything that

might lead him to anyone who is in league with the French,"
said Vanessa quietly.

The butler's head snapped around. He wore a shocked expression. "French spies, miss? Here? No, miss, I would stake
my life on it!"

Vanessa was satisfied that her suspicions had been correct.
The butler did know something about the gentlemen of the
night. She smiled reassuringly. "Oh, I don't think that the lieutenant was particularly implying that we at Halverton harbored
such desperate ruffians. Mr. Tremaine and I differ in that opinion, however."

"Indeed, miss?" The butler was staring at her fixedly.

"Yes. Mr. Tremaine felt that Lieutenant Copperidge was
the sort who suspects everyone and everything, and therefore Halverton falls naturally under suspicion," said
Vanessa. "Even if that is so, I do not believe that was Lieutenant Copperidge's intended message. He was simply re-
laying a cautioning word that there has been such activity
discovered hereabouts."

"Mr. Tremaine is a knowing one, miss. If he says that excise
officer suspects Halverton of evil doings, then it's likely true,"
said the butler. "It's not what I like, miss."

"Nor I," said Vanessa. Her eyes did not leave the butler's
face. "Lieutenant Copperidge said something else, Sims. He
said that it is suspected that those involved in such treasonous
traffic are making use of the smuggling routes."

"Never, miss!" exclaimed Sims.

Vanessa was silent a moment, her thoughtful gaze on the old
butler's troubled countenance. Quietly, she said, "I imagine that
it could be quite profitable to transport such individuals back
and forth across the Channel."

"No doubt, miss. However, I am positive that no true-
blooded Englishman could stomach such, even for a price,"
said Sims, his face set rather more than usual.

"That is precisely what I have told Lieutenant Copperidge.
We at Halverton could not possibly have connections of any
sort to treason," said Vanessa.

She curiously noted the butler's suddenly distracted expression. She had never been certain who at Halverton might be

involved with the freebooters, nor had she ever inquired, but she rather thought that the butler might have a few shrewd notions of his own.

In any event, she had conveyed her oblique warning. She was confident that it would be carried to the proper ears. Hopefully, those who heard it would react in the same way that the old butler had done.

Vanessa gathered up her skirts and started toward the door. "Good night, Sims."

The butler appeared to make an effort to gather himself together. He quickly preceded her to the door and opened it, bowing slightly. "Good night, miss."

Vanessa left the drawing room, crossed the empty entry hall, and started up the winding stairs.

The butler recrossed the drawing room to the hearth. He thoughtfully finished banking the log and then snuffed the candles before he, too, exited the drawing room.

It was his custom each night to make certain that all the windows and doors of the manor house were locked before he sought his own bed. After performing this necessary duty, however, he did not at once retire to his own quarters.

Instead, he wrapped himself in a heavy woolen cloak and stole out of a side door of the manor, carrying with him a shielded lantern. He fit a large key into the door and securely locked it behind him. Then he walked swiftly toward the stables.

Chapter Five

Vanessa's morning was spent in her study wrestling with her financial records. When at last she had gotten the columns to make sense, she went out again on her mare to inspect the orchards and to visit with some of her tenants. When she returned to Halverton that evening, wearied and mud-splattered, she was well-satisfied. For the first time in months she had accomplished all that she had set herself to do.

When the Sabbath bell began ringing the next morning, Vanessa and her mother rode in the carriage the short distance to church. Exchanging nods and words of greeting with their neighbors, they crossed the old church porch and entered the sanctuary.

Lady Cecily led the way to the front of the church to their pew. Her ladyship acknowledged nods of recognition from various prominent landowners and professional men, but she virtually ignored the prosperous shopkeepers, pub keepers, and farmers. It was not her custom to extend recognition to those so far beneath her in the social order.

Vanessa had no such false pride. She returned all greetings made her, including Mr. Rutherford's genial smile and wave. The gentleman might be only a farmer, but he was a good man and a good neighbor. She showed a slight reserve, however, to Mr. Nashe, who had recently returned to the neighborhood. Vanessa had known him all of her life, but she had no fond memories of their childhood association.

It was a rather dreary day, a light rain having fallen since dawn, and attendance at the service was sparser than one might have expected in a countryside known for its deeply in-grained devotion. Nevertheless the rector gave a sound sermon as though the house was full, taking as his text the familiar lesson on loving one's neighbor as oneself.

Vanessa was reminded by the sermon of her critical reflections about Mr. Nashe. She felt guilty for harboring what were plainly childhood prejudices and she decided to make amends for her slightly chilly manner toward him the previous day.

When the service was over and the parishioners were leaving their pews, Vanessa offered a friendly smile to Mr. Nashe. Mr. Nashe responded by graciously offering his escort. Vanessa accepted his arm for the length of the aisle toward the north door of the church. It must have looked a little ridiculous to some of her neighbors since she was several inches taller than Mr. Nashe. But such considerations rarely registered with Vanessa.

Lady Cecily knew that Vanessa was unlikely to pay heed to the mockery of others, but Mr. Nashe was altogether a different thing. It was obvious to the meanest intelligence that the gentleman had his pride. He bore himself with almost a strut in his stride. One must be realistic and recognize that Mr. Nashe could well shy off from courting Vanessa if he discovered himself to be the butt of jokes.

Mr. Nashe was an eligible party, which must never be forgotten. Definitely Vanessa must be warned to be careful of her choice of footwear. Perhaps, too, Vanessa might learn to droop a little when she stood or walked, mused Lady Cecily.

Unaware of the astonishing turn of her mother's thoughts, Vanessa exchanged commonplaces with Mr. Nashe. They made their slow way to the front of the church where the rector stood under the heavy stone arch of the porch to greet each of his parishioners before they left. Carriages were brought around to the porch steps with unerring precision and the ladies were handed up inside to escape the still-falling rain. Their escorts called a final farewell to the rector before swinging up into the carriages and giving the office to their drivers.

Vanessa glanced toward the local squire. She wanted to be certain to exchange a few words with Squire Leeds, for he was quite one of her favorite people. When she saw a certain large tall gentleman talking quietly to the squire, Vanessa was startled, for she instantly thought that she recognized the younger gentleman.

"Why, isn't that Howard Pemberton with the squire?" she asked, surprised.

The Pembertons had not lived in the county for many years. Since their departure Pemberton Place had been shut up, occupied only by an elderly caretaker and his spouse. There had not been any word of the family since they had left, though Vanessa had heard that the house was going to be reopened. It was therefore astonishing to suddenly see a Pemberton standing in the church after so many years.

"Is it?" Mr. Nashe glanced casually around. "Oh, yes, so it is. I did not immediately recognize him in that plain coat."

Ignoring Mr. Nashe's drawled slur, Vanessa turned aside to speak to the squire and his companion. Her reluctant escort accompanied her. She felt gladness at the prospect of greeting Howard Pemberton, who had been an old childhood playmate. He and Benjamin Nashe had teased all of the neighborhood girls unmercifully, but they had also been good friends. Many of Vanessa's happiest memories included the boy, Howard Pemberton.

Vanessa greeted the squire and inquired after Mrs. Leeds and their daughters. "Is it not this week that they will be returning from their visit to Mrs. Leeds's relations?"

"Aye, and glad I shall be of it. I have missed them all. It is difficult for an old gentleman such as myself to adjust to bacheloring," said Squire Leeds gruffly.

Vanessa laughed and agreed. She then drew his attention to Mr. Nashe. "Squire, I am certain you must recall Mr. Mark Nashe?"

The squire stared at Mr. Nashe with a penetrating look from under white craggy brows. He nodded. "Aye, I recall you well. A more finicky boy I never saw. How are Lord and Lady Nashe? I have not seen them in some time."

"They are doing well, sir," said Mr. Nashe politely. "I hope to see them completely recovered before many more weeks."

The squire was not to be satisfied with such brevity. "Do you now? That is good news indeed. But tell me, what of Lord Nashe's gout? He was complaining bitterly of it before he was thrown down ill. And that nervous tic of her ladyship's? It was troubling the good lady a good deal, so I heard."

As Mr. Nashe was firmly caught by the squire's solicitous inquiries, Vanessa turned to Mr. Pemberton, the tall gentleman who seemed to be trying to edge past them and had already half turned away. She was surprised, for surely he could not feel that he was in any way intruding upon them. He might have been gone from the county for many years, but he was still to be considered a neighbor.

Vanessa stayed him by calling him by name. "Mr. Pemberton?" It seemed to her that he hesitated a bare second before he turned around.

Expecting the warmth of recognition, Vanessa was taken aback by the completely bland expression on Howard Pemberton's face. It had never occurred to her that he might not recognize her as readily as she had him. She said with a smile, "Surely you must recall me, Mr. Pemberton. I am Vanessa Lester of Halverton."

The blank look slowly dissipated, leaving a wide, somewhat uncertain, grin. "Of course I do. You are Miss Lester of Halverton."

Mr. Nashe had observed the exchange and he looked faintly contemptuous. Cutting off the squire's gruff discourse, he said, "Pemberton, surely you recall Miss Lester. She was one of several friends from both of our childhoods."

Mr. Pemberton stared hard at Mr. Nashe. "You're Benjamin's brother," he discovered. He seemed inordinately pleased with himself for his feat of memory.

Vanessa was shocked. She stared up at the gentleman who had answered to Howard Pemberton's name and possessed his features, but who bore not the remotest resemblance to the clever boy she had once known.

The squire shook his head. "Poor lad," he muttered. He patted Mr. Pemberton on the shoulder.

"At last the light dawns," murmured Mr. Nashe.

Her companion's rather malicious tone galvanized Vanessa out of her appalled paralysis. She hurried into speech. Holding out her gloved hand to Mr. Pemberton, she said, "In any event,

I am happy to renew my acquaintance with you, Mr. Pemberton. I hope that I shall see more of you, sir."

Mr. Pemberton retained her hand for a moment longer than necessary, gazing down at her. If any other gentleman had done so, Vanessa would have suspected him of flirting with her. But there was nothing of that in the tall large gentleman standing before her.

Pemberton wore an expression of slightly bovine amiability. With the dignity of ingrained manners, he said, "Thank you, Miss Lester. I am honored."

Vanessa gently withdrew her hand, pitying the gentleman. She felt almost an inclination to weep. She nodded as she lightly placed her gloved fingers on Mr. Nashe's extended arm. "Good day, Mr. Pemberton."

The squire captured Mr. Pemberton's attention with a simple query and Vanessa and Mr. Nashe were able to make a graceful exit.

When they were well out of earshot, Vanessa said, "I would not have believed it had I not seen it for myself. In fact, I had not given credence to the reports that we heard at Halverton. Never would I have taken that to be Howard Pemberton, except that he looked quite the same in features and figure."

"Quite dull-witted, is he not?" said Mr. Nashe.

He spoke in a distasteful tone that set Vanessa's teeth on edge. She had always had a soft heart for hurt and abandoned creatures. It had shocked her that Howard Pemberton had changed so drastically, but at the same time her innate compassion had been aroused toward him. She did not care at all for Mr. Nashe's casual dismissal of the unfortunate soul. "I trust that I would never use a term that must give the poor man pain," she said.

Mr. Nashe glanced quickly up at her face. He smiled and shrugged. "You think me cruel, then, Miss Lester? On the contrary. I am still confounded that our friend has sunk to such levels. I met him last week in the village. It came as much a shock to me as it has to you. The gossips have it that he suffered some sort of putrid fever as a child that permanently incapacitated his intellect. His aunt, Mrs. Dabney, returned to the county with him just short of a month ago and they have opened the old Pemberton place. Mrs. Dabney is officially Pemberton's hostess, but I suspect that she is more caretaker than otherwise."

"How horrid it all is," said Vanessa feelingly.

"Yes, isn't it?" Nashe's drawling tone expressed more indifference than otherwise. "Ah, here is Lady Cecily and the good reverend."

Mr. Nashe greeted both while Vanessa could only wonder at his callousness.

Lady Cecily had walked past as Vanessa was reestablishing her acquaintance with Mr. Pemberton. She was mildly curious what her daughter would make of Mr. Pemberton, but she had not paused to listen. Now as she responded to Mr. Nashe, her ladyship cast a glance at her daughter's unusually shadowed expression.

Her ladyship still considered Mr. Nashe to be her primary candidate for a son-in-law. However, she would not totally discount Howard Pemberton. One must keep an open mind, after all. As for the rector, Lady Cecily had already decided that it was time to begin cultivating him on Vanessa's behalf. She had therefore taken pains to speak to the man at greater length than was her usual custom. She even went so far as to remind the gentleman of their loose family connection.

When Vanessa and Mr. Nashe had come up, Lady Cecily was in the process of inviting the rector to tea. "You must come, Reverend Haversaw. I simply insist upon it, for I have been thinking for some time that I should establish a better understanding with you and I am not one to put off the performance of my duty," said Lady Cecily.

"An esteemable quality, my lady. Very well, I shall come to tea this afternoon. I am truly honored by the invitation and the gracious thought behind it," said Reverend Haversaw.

Lady Cecily smiled and nodded in a regal way. Seeing her daughter on Mark Nashe's arm, she gave a satisfied nod. "And here is my daughter and Mr. Nashe! Vanessa, you will be glad to hear that the good reverend has condescended to join us for tea."

Vanessa wondered what had gotten into her mother, for Lady Cecily was not in the habit of extending such courtesies.

If the invitation had not been issued to the rector, she would have suspected that her mother was attempting to put into place a matchmaking ploy. But that was a nonsensical thought in this instance. Vanessa smiled at the rector. "I shall be glad to have you at Halverton, Reverend Haversaw. It has been a long time since your last visit to us."

"Yes. Unfortunately it was a sad occasion then," said Reverend Haversaw sympathetically.

"Mr. Nashe, I trust that you will also make one of our little party?" inquired Lady Cecily, turning her head. She had no patience for sentiment. Life was for the living. She meant to see to it that her daughter was settled as quickly as possible into marriage so that she could begin living her own life again just as she wished.

Mr. Nashe expressed himself most happy to be included in such a comfortable party. "However, I fear that I must decline. I never know from one moment to the next whether I shall be called to one of my parents' bedsides as they succumb to yet further crises. May I take the liberty to consider the invitation to be an open-ended one, my lady?"

"Of course, Mr. Nashe," said Lady Cecily, almost visibly purring. "You will be welcome at Halverton whenever you should choose to come over. And certainly we would be most glad to hear the latest tidings on Lord and Lady Nashe. I trust that they are not at present in crises?"

"I would not have been so bold as to have come to morning services if it had been otherwise, my lady," said Mr. Nashe, the faintest curl to his lips. "However, as I have said, that may well be subject to change at a moment's notice. My father in particular is not a cheerful or robust patient. His fretful crotchets tend to wear upon him and the entire household. I am patently the only one whose ministrations will satisfy him."

"Very natural, I am sure," said Reverend Haversaw. "You are dutiful, indeed, to bear so patiently with a difficult situation, Mr. Nashe."

Mr. Nashe flashed a thin smile. "Am I not? Perhaps I shall request canonization after all is said and done."

The rector's expressive gaze registered a hint of disapproval and trouble, but he smiled nevertheless. "I shall call on Lord

and Lady Nashe in the next day or two, Mr. Nashe. I should
like to sit with them for a few moments."

Mr. Nashe uttered a short laugh. "I wish you merry, sir."

Vanessa felt that it was time to take her leave. Once again
she had become annoyed by Mr. Nashe's seeming callousness
and she felt a distaste for remaining in his company. She was
relieved to see that the crested Nashe carriage was drawing up
in front of the church steps.

Vanessa withdrew her fingers from Mr. Nashe's elbow and
stepped back so that she was able to offer her hand to him. "I
shall bid you good day here, Mr. Nashe. Perhaps we shall see
you later at tea. Regardless, pray convey my respects to Lord
and Lady Nashe," she said.

Mr. Nashe took her hand and carried her gloved fingers to
his lips for a brief salute. "I shall do so, of course. It is good of
you to remember them," he said formally. He bowed to Lady
Cecily and took leave of Reverend Haversaw before saunter-
ing down the front steps of the church. The driver had stepped
down from the box to open the carriage door and Mr. Nashe
climbed inside it.

Lady Cecily looked after the departing carriage with an approving expression. "Mr. Nashe has quite a distinctive air
about him. It is a pity that some of our local blades do not em-
ulate his manners."

Vanessa's eyes met the rector's, quite by accident. She recognized the same expression in Reverend Haversaw's face as
she was certain was on her own. She could not think of a
worse person for the younger set to imitate than Mr. Nashe.
"For my part, I think that Mr. Pemberton demonstrates more
the ways of a gentleman," she said quietly.

"How can you say so, Vanessa? The man is a perfect dolt,"
said Lady Cecily brusquely.

"Kindness and consideration are not rooted in one's intelligence, but rather, in the heart," said Reverend Haversaw gently.

Lady Cecily smiled, but tightly. She disliked being corrected by anyone. She determinedly mastered the impulse to
give the rector a well-deserved setdown. After all, she had invited the man to tea. She did not wish to offend his sensibili-

ties at this juncture. "As you say, sir. We shall see you at tea, then?"

"Yes, of course, my lady. My housekeeper will be well able to watch over my children during that time, so that I shall have a free hour or two," said Reverend Haversaw. "It is generally the quietest part of the day since I insist upon a nap for each of them then."

Lady Cecily nodded. She was supremely bored by the explanation and her smile was perfunctory. "Come along, Vanessa. I see that our own carriage has come at last. We must let the good rector attend to his affairs now."

"Of course, ma'am." Vanessa held out her hand again. "Good-bye for now, sir. I look forward to your visit later."

Reverend Haversaw inclined his head in acknowledgment, a faint tinge of color coming into his face. He had heard the sincerity in Miss Lester's voice and he appreciated it. Many times invitations were issued to him simply as a matter of form, as he believed was most certainly Lady Cecily's motivation. At other times appeals were made for his presence at the bedsides of the sick or dying. It was a rare pleasure to be wanted simply for himself. "Thank you, Miss Lester. I, too, look forward to it."

Chapter Six

That afternoon it was confirmed that the rector would be the sole guest to tea, for Mr. Nashe sent around his regrets. Lady Cecily frowned over Mr. Nashe's note. "I had hoped that Mr. Nashe would think better of his refusal," she said disapprovingly.

"I am certain that Mr. Nashe feels just as much regret as you could wish him to, Mother," said Vanessa, her words reflecting her private thoughts. She felt that she had drawn a fairly accurate notion of Mr. Nashe's dedication to his convalescing parents. No doubt the gentleman disliked above all things to be kept kicking his heels at Nashe Hall in the name of filial duty. Surely even taking tea with two ladies would have been preferable to Mr. Nashe's way of thinking.

Lady Cecily nodded. "No doubt you are right, Vanessa. Naturally Mr. Nashe would have come if circumstances were different. We shall hope that Lord and Lady Nashe make a speedy recovery so that Mr. Nashe may avail himself of our hospitality in the future."

Vanessa murmured a vague assent, but in reality she was not disappointed by Mr. Nashe's defection. Despite her good intentions, she still could not like the gentleman. Mr. Nashe's attitude toward the unfortunate and infirm was utterly foreign to her. His unfeeling comments regarding Mr. Pemberton's situation had not endeared him to her. Quite the opposite, in fact. Vanessa had had quite enough of Mr. Nashe for one day.

Vanessa could not help but contrast Mr. Nashe's attitude with Reverend Haversaw's. She had never known the rector to speak an unkind word or to display dissatisfaction with his circumstances. She said as much to her mother, then commented,

"I count him as one of those rare people upon whom one may always depend."

Lady Cecily glanced at Vanessa, her brows a little raised. "I am happy to hear that the rector stands so high in your estimation, my dear. Certainly Reverend Haversaw has many admirable qualities that perhaps have not heretofore been so readily apparent to me."

Vanessa regarded her mother with slight surprise. "How do you mean, ma'am?"

Lady Cecily was unable to reply, because at that moment Reverend Haversaw was shown into the drawing room. Lady Cecily rose to greet him, holding out her hand. "Reverend, how good of you to come," she said cordially.

Lady Cecily raked a critical glance over the rector's attire and was not entirely displeased. Reverend Haversaw's brown coat was too loosely fitted to be fashionable and his square-cut single-breasted waistcoat was entirely too plain for her ladyship's taste. His starched white cravat was tied in a simple bow, but its folds were fixed with a particularly brilliant diamond stickpin. There was nothing at all to be faulted in his tan breeches and highly polished boots.

Lady Cecily offered a thin smile to the rector. "Pray be seated, Reverend Haversaw. Sims, you may begin serving now. Our most welcome guest has arrived."

Vanessa quietly exchanged greetings with Reverend Haversaw. The man appeared overwhelmed by his reception and no wonder, she thought. Vanessa could not recall that Lady Cecily had ever extended such amiable courtesy toward the good rector.

Again it fleeted through Vanessa's mind that there must be something ulterior behind her mother's change of front. However, Vanessa was content for the moment to allow things to go on as they were. Whatever Lady Cecily had in mind did at least have the advantage of providing a friendly atmosphere over the tea.

Lady Cecily was on her best behavior as hostess. Reverend Haversaw was plied with hot sweetened tea and biscuits and was pressed into accepting a helping of a heavy fruitcake. Vanessa was amazed at how her mother was drawing the rector out of his natural reserve and causing the man to feel comfortable. The most astonishing thing was that Lady Cecily was actually going to the effort of doing so.

Soon Reverend Haversaw was confiding to his hostess some of the cares that had been laid upon his shoulders since he had become a widower two years past. "It is difficult to properly raise three young children on one's own. Of course, my housekeeper is good and kind to them and she does as much as she can, but it is not the same as having a mother," he ended on a sigh.

"Of course it is not. I feel for you, indeed, sir. The care of a servant is all very well, but children naturally need a mother," said Lady Cecily. Her expression seemed to be permanently etched in lines of sympathy. As she turned away to set aside her own teacup on a small occasional table, however, she smothered a yawn.

Catching her mother's subterfuge, Vanessa was amused. This tea was not Lady Cecily's preferred style of things. She wondered whatever had possessed Lady Cecily to suggest it. Vanessa turned to address the rector. "Did you not say that the youngest boy, Timothy, is still greatly affected by the loss of his mother?"

A shadow crossed Reverend Haversaw's face. "Indeed, Miss Lester. He has seemed to close in upon himself. I have tried valiantly to reach him. But nothing that I have done has made the least impression."

"I do not wish to put myself forward, for I am very ignorant of such matters as childrearing," said Vanessa. "However, I have frequently observed that when an animal sustains the loss of an offspring, it goes into just such an uncaring state as you have described. But if an orphan is presented to it, the animal many times accepts it as her own and completely recovers. I wonder whether Timothy's case might be helped in a similar fashion?"

Reverend Haversaw's eyes were fixed on her with almost painful intensity. "How do you mean, Miss Lester?"

"Perhaps if Timothy had some creature to care for, to love, his own interest in life around him might be revived," suggested Vanessa.

"Yes, I certainly can see the wisdom in that," said Reverend Haversaw slowly. "Caring for a fellow creature, one that demands nothing of him but which simply extends its own affection, may touch his heart in a way that I cannot." A gleam had come into the rector's eyes. "Why, it could very well answer the purpose. Certainly I should like to give it a try. What sort of creature would you recommend, Miss Lester?"

"Actually, if you have no objection, I was thinking of giving the children a pony that we have here at Halverton. It is getting on in years and is no longer capable of work. I should like to see it live out the remainder of its life well-loved and well-cared for," said Vanessa.

"No, no, I have no objection! That is very generous of you, Miss Lester," said Reverend Haversaw.

"Then I shall make arrangements for one of the stablehands to deliver him to you in the next day or two. Naturally the man will stay to instruct the children in how to care for the pony," said Vanessa. "Is that convenient to you, sir?"

"The sooner the better, Miss Lester. We have a small barn and a meadow behind the rectory that I deem to be perfectly suitable for a small pony. I cannot tell you how grateful I am for your thoughtfulness and kindness," said Reverend Haversaw.

"I only hope that it answers the purpose," said Vanessa. "I will myself call on you later to see how things are progressing."

"You will be most welcome at any time, Miss Lester. My children will wish to thank you in person for such a wonderful present as you are making to them," said Reverend Haversaw. He asked several eager questions about the pony, to which Vanessa replied with all good humor.

A few minutes later, Reverend Haversaw caught sight of the clock on the mantel. "Oh my, is it indeed so late?" He slipped his pocket watch out of the crescent-shaped pocket in his waistcoat and checked the time. "I see that I have quite overstayed my welcome," he said, smiling.

"Not at all, sir," said Vanessa. "My mother and I have enjoyed your conversation."

"You are kind to say so, Miss Lester," said Reverend

Haversaw. "However, it is time that I returned home." He took his leave of both ladies, but his excuses were particularly warm toward Vanessa.

Lady Cecily had murmured a perfunctory protest over the rector's leavetaking, but she had also pulled the bell to call for the gentleman's carriage. When the butler entered, it was found that he had anticipated the summons. Sims informed the rector that his gig had already been sent for from the stables. He held the rector's low-crowned beaver, gloves and umbrella in readiness.

Reverend Haversaw smiled. "It seems that I am well provided for, indeed. I shall say good day now, my lady, and to you, Miss Lester."

When the rector was gone, Lady Cecily turned to her daughter with a satisfied visage. "I am most pleased with you, Vanessa. You have acted in a manner quite complimentary to yourself. Reverend Haversaw was suitably impressed by your concern and by your offer of the pony for his children."

"That is not why I did it, ma'am," said Vanessa, picking up her embroidery. "As well you know, I hope."

"Of course you did not. But as it turns out, nothing could have been more fortuitous than your recalling that pony. You will naturally wish to satisfy yourself that the children are caring properly for it, so I expect that you will make several visits to the rectory," said Lady Cecily.

Vanessa leveled a straight look at her mother. "What is this about, Mother? It is not like you to concern yourself with such simple matters. Why are you so anxious about it all?"

"Why, if I seem anxious, my dear, it is only because I wish you to be sure to take your groom with you on these charitable calls. I would not wish anyone to begin gossiping about you and Reverend Haversaw. The man is a widower, after all," said Lady Cecily.

"Gossip about me and Reverend Haversaw? Why, the man is all of forty and a sort of cousin besides! Surely no one could think anything of it at all," said Vanessa, surprised.

"I know the world a good deal better than you do, Vanessa. And forty is not a great age, after all. The rector is a good-looking man in his own fashion, though I do not care for his taste in waistcoats. Too dull by half. I should like to see a smarter crop to his head as well, but I suppose that a man of the cloth cannot be a pattern card of the fashionable," said Lady Cecily.

Her ladyship's acid observation sounded much more in character and Vanessa laughed. "No, indeed! It would set the whole congregation on their ears if the rector were to stand up in the pulpit tricked out like some dandy."

"Really, Vanessa! How you do take one up. I merely voiced regret that Reverend Haversaw does not present himself to better advantage. A wife would undoubtedly prove to be a beneficial influence upon him, as well as on those children. Perhaps I shall turn my mind to providing a suitable partner for him," said Lady Cecily.

Vanessa was alarmed. She had suspected that her mother had some game that she was playing regarding the rector. Lady Cecily's statement merely confirmed her suspicions. "Pray do not even think it, ma'am. I am certain that Reverend Haversaw would much prefer to order his own affairs."

"We shall see," said Lady Cecily, a small smile playing about her mouth.

Vanessa suddenly wondered again whether she herself could be her mother's candidate. Then she rejected the notion as being too incredible. Lady Cecily might fervently wish to see her wed, but not to a gentleman of the cloth, especially one whom her ladyship had practically stigmatized as tasteless in his dress. Lady Cecily was proud, even vain, as Vanessa readily acknowledged. Her ladyship would not tolerate such a humble connection even though Reverend Haversaw was gently born and a distant cousin.

"Whom did you have in mind, ma'am?" asked Vanessa, setting a stitch.

"What?" Lady Cecily stared, taken aback by the blunt question.

"As a fitting bride for Reverend Haversaw," said Vanessa, clarifying herself. "Have you already someone in particular in your sights?"

Lady Cecily played with her bracelets. "I have not spent any great thought upon the matter, Vanessa. Why do you ask?"

"I was merely curious, for I consider Reverend Haversaw to be a particular friend. Whoever your choice falls upon must have a love for children as well as possess a charitable nature," said Vanessa. "The rector is such a good man himself that I should dislike seeing an archwife thrown in his way. In that event, I would consider it to be my duty to warn him about any such scheme."

Lady Cecily gave a thin, amazed laugh. "My dear! I had no notion that you held such a very high opinion of Reverend Haversaw. It is quite startling, I must say."

Vanessa glanced at her mother. "Reverend Haversaw has been a good friend to us at Halverton, especially during the months that Papa was ill. Naturally I wish only the best for him."

"Of course, Vanessa. If the matter should ever arise, I shall inquire whether the female meets with your approval. There! I trust that satisfies you?" asked Lady Cecily with a tinge of sarcasm.

Vanessa allowed a small smile to play about her lips. "I suppose that it must."

"It seems to me that you share that same quality of compassion that you have remarked in Reverend Haversaw," said Lady Cecily. "I observed it most particularly when you spoke to him about the boy, Thomas."

"Timothy," corrected Vanessa.

"Thomas, Timothy. It matters little," said Lady Cecily, waving her hand in a disinterested fashion. "They are both biblical names, are they not?"

"I imagine that it matters to the boy," said Vanessa dryly.

"That is neither here nor there. I am more intrigued by Reverend Havesaw's personal circumstances. He is in need of a wife. The proper sort, of course," said Lady Cecily.

Vanessa lowered her embroidery. "I beg of you, ma'am. Allow the poor gentleman to address his own situation in his own way."

"That is my full intention, Vanessa," said Lady Cecily. "One cannot simply order a gentleman to make an offer for a particular lady, after all."

"I am relieved to hear you say so," said Vanessa, resuming her stitchery.

"What a very odd notion you have of me, indeed," said Lady Cecily. "While it is true that Reverend Haversaw is a minor cousin of Sir Charles's, and also true that he owes his comfortable living to Sir Charles's generosity, I would not dream of inserting myself so crudely into his affairs."

"That is comforting to know, at least," said Vanessa with a quick smile.

Vanessa had not wanted to fall into an argument with her mother over the rector, but at the same time she had felt compelled to speak up on the gentleman's behalf. She herself knew well Lady Cecily's hard determination once her ladyship became obsessed with some notion. Therefore Vanessa had wanted her own position to be quite clear. She disapproved so strongly of Lady Cecily's stated intent to mix into the rector's affairs that she would warn the gentleman of such scheming if it became known to her.

"I must say, Vanessa, that you are provoking my temper," said Lady Cecily, her color heightened.

"It is a pity that we do not agree well with one another's company," said Vanessa. She set aside her embroidery. "In light of that, I am certain that you will not mind it if I leave you to make the proper arrangements with the stables for the pony."

"Certainly not. Far be it for me to stand in the way of a charitable deed," said Lady Cecily virtuously.

Vanessa left the drawing room with only a single thoughtful backward glance.

After she had changed into a warm walking dress and put on a cloak over it, drawing the hood over her head, she headed out of the back of the manor. The wind had picked up and the rain was now blowing. It was going to be a muddy morning, Vanessa thought, as her half-boots skirted a puddle.

When she reached the stables, she called her groom to her and told him what she had arranged with the rector. The groom nodded his approval. He was plaiting a rope and had not paused in his task, only glancing up now and again as Vanessa had spoken. "That be the best thing for the little pony.

He is lonely being shut up away from his former mates as he is. It will give the poor old boy new life to be cozened, like."

"That is what I thought, too," said Vanessa, nodding. "Very well, then, John, have someone see to it tomorrow. I will be out in the morning, of course."

"O'course," said the groom matter-of-factly. He would not expect a bit of weather to affect Miss Lester's riding one whit.

Vanessa had turned to go when the groom stopped her.

"A word wit ye, miss," said John, lowering his voice. He looked around the stable, but none of the others seemed to be inordinately interested in Miss Lester's visit. The quiet talk still flowed as stalls were raked out and harness was repaired.

Vanessa glanced at the groom's face, then stepped closer to him. "What is it, John?"

The groom's strong agile fingers did not pause in plaiting the rope. "The abbey was used last night," he said quietly.

Vanessa looked sharply at her groom. "Are you certain? The abbey has not been used since a year or two before Sir Charles was taken ill."

"I'm certain of it, miss, and that is why I thought you should know," said the groom.

Vanessa stood for a moment, a troubled expression in her eyes. "I mistrust the timing, John," she said slowly. "The excisemen were at Halverton not a fortnight ago. What do you think it means?"

"I'm thinking that we must go warily, miss," said John, glancing up at her. "The gentlemen of the night dislike questions, but I've heard whispers. That Lieutenant Copperidge is a regular hound to the chase. He's flushed 'em now and again. Their old haunts are not so secure as formerly."

"And so they have begun to use the abbey again," said Vanessa.

"So it appears, miss," said John.

"I do not like it. Halverton has suddenly been put into the middle when I had been confident of our neutrality. But at this juncture I fail to see how I can put a stop to the nocturnal visits to Halverton lands," said Vanessa.

"Perhaps a word with Sims might be of some use," said the groom with another quick glance.

Vanessa took the point at once. "Thank you, John," she said slowly. "I shall have a word with Sims at once." She nodded her thanks and left the stables. The rain was coming down harder. Vanessa drew her cloak closer about her and ran across the yard to the manor house.

Chapter Seven

Lady Cecily announced that she had sent out invitations to a dinner party set for a week away. "The moon will be at its fullest then, so there shall be no difficulties attending the travel to and from Halverton. We shall be sitting down twenty people. It will not be a large gathering, but I believe it will be thought respectable, all the same," said Lady Cecily.

Vanessa heard her mother out with silent astonishment. "You astound me, Mother. It was not so very long ago that I reminded you that we are still in mourning," she said.

"We are in half-mourning," corrected Lady Cecily. She regarded her daughter's frowning expression with upraised brows. "Surely you can have no objections to me holding a dinner party. You did agree that a few quiet entertainments would be perfectly suitable."

"Yes, I do recall saying something of the sort," said Vanessa slowly. She gazed at her mother for a long moment. "Very well, ma'am, I make no objection to this small gathering. However, it must be understood that I shall not be so lulled and seduced by a taste of society that I shall overthrow my scruples and remove to London for the Season."

"Really, Vanessa, how nonsensical of you! As though this countrified party may be equated with a grand London function," said Lady Cecily disdainfully. "If you were to be dazzled by such small fare as this, I would not be able to trust you to a Season!"

Vanessa laughed at her mother's sarcasm. The wariness in her eyes disappeared, being replaced by a gleam of amusement. "No, indeed! You are quite right, Mother. I am such a backward noddy that I would disgrace you terribly."

"I do not think it, Vanessa. You are too well-bred not to realize what is due to your name," said Lady Cecily. "However, I trust that you will take your proper place in my efforts to bring us back into society. We cannot continue in the same isolation as we have done. It would be ludicrous to suppose that such sacrifice is proper at this juncture."

Vanessa nodded, her reflections thoughtful. She knew that her mother thrived on amusements and attention. It was only natural that Lady Cecily, frustrated in her attempts to remove them to London for the Season, would turn her thoughts to entertaining at Halverton.

"Perhaps it is time that we extend Halverton hospitality to our neighbors once more. We have been very quiet these past several months," conceded Vanessa.

"Quite," said Lady Cecily flatly.

"Whom have you invited, ma'am?" asked Vanessa.

Lady Cecily handed over a sheet of her letterhead. "You may see for yourself, Vanessa. It will be quite unexceptional. All of the more prominent personages of the county have naturally been invited. I have included Lord and Lady Nashe, even though I do not anticipate that they will attend. However, I am fairly certain that Mr. Nashe will do so. There will also be Squire and Mrs. Leeds and their whey-faced daughter and son. I trust that Reverend Haversaw will grace the gathering, as well."

Lady Cecily frowned. "I have also invited the Claridge sisters, both of whom will be certain to make it their business to entertain the bachelors. A more forward set of spinsters I have yet to meet. One assumes that they never married for that very reason."

"Miss Amanda was widowed, I believe," said Vanessa absently, her gaze still running down the list.

"It scarcely matters, does it? One must still wonder at their simpering ways," said Lady Cecily disdainfully.

"If you so dislike them, why did you invite them?" asked Vanessa, looking up from the sheet.

"One must make up one's numbers, after all," said Lady Cecily with a shrug.

"I see that you have invited Mr. Pemberton and his aunt, Mrs. Dabney," said Vanessa.

Lady Cecily nodded, her expression turning bland. "But of course. I could not very well ignore the heir of Pemberton Place. And even though Mr. Pemberton is rather dull-witted, his manners are more than adequate."

"I thought that you disliked Mrs. Dabney," remarked Vanessa, handing back the guest list.

"I am certain that I never said such a thing," said Lady Cecily stiffly. "I simply do not appreciate Mrs. Dabney's unfortunate tendency to attempt to dominate everyone around her."

"Of course. I quite understand your aversion," said Vanessa, straight-faced.

Lady Cecily glanced sharply at her daughter, but as Vanessa's expression was innocent of all but polite interest, she banished the suspicion that her daughter was somehow laughing at her. It was not possible that anyone could possibly lever gentle ridicule in her direction, in any event. "As I have already said, it will be an unexceptional gathering. Do you go into the village?"

"Yes, I have promised Cook to stop at the butcher's shop," said Vanessa.

Lady Cecily's face expressed her displeasure. "I wish you would allow the servants to run such mundane errands, Vanessa. It is really not at all worthy of your position."

"I had also meant to pay a visit to the rectory, but I suppose that also is to be considered beneath me," said Vanessa coolly.

Lady Cecily at once disclaimed. "Of course not! That is quite a different thing. An act of charity cannot be considered to be unworthy of one's time."

"Yes, Mother. So I thought," said Vanessa with gentle irony.

Lady Cecily smiled at her daughter. She was actually feeling quite in charity with Vanessa, what with this business of the pony with the rector and now her daughter's tacit agreement to the dinner party. "I know that you shall do just as you ought, Vanessa. Pray do not let me keep you from your errands. Since you are going into the village in any event, I shall ask my maid to give you a short list of items that I require from the apothecary's. The winter months always seem to be

hard to my lungs here at Halverton. It will be beneficial to
have a few remedies on hand."

"I shall be happy to attend to it, ma'am," said Vanessa.

Vanessa drove herself in the gig into the village. Three
weeks had passed since she had offered to give the pony to
Reverend Haversaw. It was a bright cold day, one in which all
problems seemed far away. Indeed, since her short talk with
her butler and the resulting assurances that Halverton would
not be involved in any smuggling activities, as well as the con-
tinuance of Lady Cecily's unusually benevolent mood,
Vanessa felt quite at ease with her world.

Vanessa discharged her commissions to the butcher and the
apothecary, then stopped to visit at the rectory. Vanessa had
always thought that the rectory was a handsome building, situated as it was near the village church and surrounded by trees
and lawns. It was a pity that most of the dozen or so bedrooms
were not in use, but a widower and three children and a handful of servants could not be expected to fill a house that had
originally been intended for a much larger household.

Vanessa had begun stopping at the rectory since the pony
had become a member of the rector's household to check on
its welfare and its progress with the children. She was surprised when she became a favorite visitor with the reverend's
three mop-headed children. However, she was their benefactor
and they saw in her easy manners and laughing eyes someone
that they could call upon to applaud their newest equestrian
exploits.

Reverend Haversaw was equally glad to welcome her to his
home. He had continued to be almost embarrassingly grateful,
telling Vanessa several times that the pony was already serving to good purpose.

"I cannot begin to convey to you the depth of my gratitude,
Miss Lester. If it had not been for your generosity, I am fairly
certain that little Timothy would still be sleeping badly and
spending his days moping about. Until he contracted the
measles, he was running and playing with his brother and sister just as he did formerly," said Reverend Haversaw.

"I am glad, sir. Indeed, I had hoped that having the pony
and riding and caring for it would capture Timothy's interest.

One observes that it is usually the way with caring for God's creatures. They ask so little of us and love us unconditionally," said Vanessa.

"Quite true. I think that is what has drawn Timothy so quickly out of his apathy. He pets and talks to the pony as though it understands every word, and perhaps it does. It is a gentle mount and playmate for the children," said Reverend Haversaw. He laughed suddenly and the lines that had been etched into his face with the passing away of his wife disappeared. "Timothy fusses and begs continually to be allowed to feed the pony a special treat. He has quite adopted it as his own."

"I hope that you have not been tried overmuch with wrangling over ownership," said Vanessa, smiling.

Reverend Haversaw shook his head. There was a rueful expression in his blue eyes. "There have been small instances and outbursts of argument, but I have explained that the pony belongs to each of them. On the whole, the children have been very good at sharing. It is a good lesson for them."

"I am glad that it is working out so very well," said Vanessa. "I trust that Timothy will quickly recover and will soon be running about again."

They had walked outside to the meadow behind the rectory to watch the two older children's antics with the old pony and now had turned to retrace their steps through the dormant garden to the handsome house.

"I am certain that he will," said Reverend Haversaw. "It was kind of you to think of him and to bring him a present. He will be more patient with his illness now that he has a new puzzle to work. Will you stay to tea?"

Vanessa shook her head. "I think not today, thank you. I have been to the butcher's and should not delay much longer in returning to Halverton or Cook will have my head. She would have sent one of the boys to the village except that I persuaded her that I could be back with tonight's entree so much quicker."

Reverend Haversaw chuckled. "Then I shall not keep you any longer. My own good cook can be very fierce, so I know precisely your position. Thank you for coming, Miss Lester."

"I always enjoy my visits here," said Vanessa, gathering her whip from the elderly butler.

"I am glad, for you are always welcome," said Reverend Haversaw.

Reverend Haversaw walked Vanessa out to the gig and handed her up into it. Vanessa exchanged a few words more with him before gathering the reins. The rector waved his farewell as she drove out of the yard.

Vanessa was just leaving the village behind when she saw Lieutenant Copperidge approaching on horseback. Slowing the gig, she lifted her gloved hand to hail the exciseman. "Good day, Lieutenant Copperidge."

He obligingly pulled up and bowed from the saddle. His habitually stern expression was lightened with a smile. "Good day to you, Miss Lester. I trust that I see you well?"

"Indeed I am, thank you. I had hoped that I would see you today, sir," said Vanessa.

The exciseman's dark brown brows lifted. His gaze sharpening, he asked, "Might I inquire why, Miss Lester?"

"It is nothing of great moment. Merely that I wished to extend an invitation to you and to your sergeant to a dinner party that my mother is holding on Thursday," said Vanessa. "I realize that it is rather sudden notice. However, my mother had no notion of your direction and as I was coming into the village this morning to discharge a few commissions, I appointed myself as her deputy."

"That is good of you, Miss Lester," said Lt. Copperidge slowly, examining her face closely as though he was attempting to decide what had prompted her solicitation.

Vanessa smiled at the exciseman, having little difficulty in discerning the trend of his thoughts. A young lady of quality did not extend invitations to single gentlemen who were scarcely known to them. However, she had previously had occasion to speak to Lt. Copperidge and so she knew him to be born of good family. With a short explanation, he would know this invitation for what it was. "I do hope that you shall be able to attend. I believe that many of the more prominent personages of our county have already accepted. You will find a vastly more congenial atmosphere under such circumstances than I suspect that you found upon your visits around about."

A gleam came into Lt. Copperidge's slate blue eyes, and the faint suspicion in his expression vanished. "I am honored, Miss Lester. Most assuredly I shall attend, and I speak for my sergeant as well."

Vanessa nodded. She gathered up the reins again between her slim fingers. "I shall tell my mother so." She knew that the lieutenant was not fooled over whom he had to thank for his inclusion in the dinner party. She said dryly, "Lady Cecily will express herself most volubly, I assure you."

Lt. Copperidge was surprised by a crack of laughter. He caught himself up almost immediately. But he was still grinning as he said, "Pray extend my appreciation to her ladyship for her kind invitation, Miss Lester."

"Until Thursday, then," said Vanessa, smiling at him. She thought that the light of humor set well on his stern features.

The lieutenant bowed and stepped his mount back from the gig. Vanessa lifted the reins and gave her team the go-ahead. As she drove away, she thought about what she had done. Lady Cecily would naturally be aghast and furious that she had invited a lowly exciseman to dinner at Halverton, but Vanessa thought that she could weather her mother's inevitable tirade. She had done the exciseman a good turn and that was what mattered most.

Naturally Lt. Copperidge was appreciative of the effort that had been made on his behalf. He was no fool. The invitation would open doors that almost certainly would otherwise have remained closed to him. However, once he was seen to be an invited guest of proud Lady Cecily of Halverton, other invitations would likely be issued to him and he would enter a society that he would not otherwise be privy. That position would give him access to conversations and relationships that would stand him in good stead in the dispatch of his duties.

Vanessa urged her team into a faster pace. The chill wind on her face felt good. She enjoyed the crisp feel of late fall, almost being able to smell ice on the air. Her thoughts were idle, an unusual state after so many weeks of intensive decision making and months of grief. But at last Vanessa felt herself beginning to relax and enjoy the small things of life again.

A horseman was coming toward her down the hedgerowed lane. The gentleman wore a riding coat of dark green with plated buttons, pale biscuit breeches, and shining topboots. He sat tall in the saddle, his left hand lying negligently on his thigh.

Vanessa recognized him, of course, but she was not intending to stop. A friendly nod would do for Mr. Pemberton, for he had shown himself to be rather ill at ease whenever he had found himself to be in her company. To Vanessa's surprise, Mr. Pemberton slackened his horse's smart clip and swung its head around as the gig came level.

"Good morning, Miss Lester," said Mr. Pemberton in a hearty voice, as he came alongside the gig and kept pace.

"Good morning to you, sir." Vanessa smiled up at him, slowing her own horse. It was the first time that Mr. Pemberton had voluntarily sought out her company and she was curious to see what came of it.

Mr. Pemberton was undeniably an attractive man and he sat his horse with all the grace of a born horseman. He scarcely seemed to notice his mount's sudden sidling, but controlled it with one strong hand on the reins. His lean features were pleasant and tanned, marred only by a certain vagueness of expression in his blue eyes and over-wide smile. His beaver was pulled down close over his close-cropped chestnut locks, serving to shade his face so that his expression was not readily discernible. But Vanessa was fairly certain that he was gazing at her with the simple pleasure that he seemed to regard everything and everyone around him.

Vanessa felt again a fleeting regret for the loss of the lively boy she still recalled so vividly. It had pained her each Sunday to acknowledge Mr. Pemberton's vague pleasure in their exchanged greetings. She felt that she had lost a vital link to her past, as indeed she had. Beside Cressy and Eleanor Nashe and their brother Benjamin, Howard Pemberton had been one of her most constant companions.

She wondered what that quicksilver laughing boy would have grown to have been like if it had not been for a putrid

fever. Certainly he would not have metamorphosed into this
genial, amiable, but somewhat dull creature.

Vanessa felt guilty and ashamed of herself for such uncharitable thoughts and she thrust them away. "I trust you are well,
Mr. Pemberton?"

He laughed as though at a huge joke. "Why, I am always
well. You may ask of anyone if I am not. My dear aunt says
that I have the thick head and the constitution of an ox, you
know."

Vanessa gave her head a shake at the repeated words. Surely
Mrs. Dabney had not meant to be unkind to her nephew when
she had told him that. Perhaps she had spoken out of exaspera-
tion and the poor man had never realized that it had not been a
completely complimentary description of himself. "I am glad
that you do not suffer from the more common ailments, Mr.
Pemberton. I am myself scarcely ever ill, but there are others
not so blessed. Lord and Lady Nashe, for instance, are recovering very slowly from a peculiarly debilitating illness. And I
have just been to visit with the rector to take a present to his
youngest boy, who has contracted the measles. He is utterly
wretched, poor boy, for he would much prefer to be out of
doors riding on his pony."

"I feel for the lad. I myself ride each morning," said Mr.
Pemberton.

"Do you indeed?" asked Vanessa politely.

"A good hard workout is a wonderful beginning to the day
and seems to blow the cobwebs out of my head," said Mr.
Pemberton with a laugh. "I do not think that I should like to go
without it."

"I, also, ride in the early mornings," said Vanessa. Her heart
was touched with his unwitting description of his infirmity.
Out of pity and compassion, she said, "Perhaps you will ride
with me one morning, Mr. Pemberton?"

Vanessa had the oddest impression that Mr. Pemberton was
startled and dismayed by the suggestion. But then she thought
it must have been a trick of her imagination, for his acceptance
was made with a wide, ingenuous grin.

"I would be honored to escort you, Miss Lester," said Mr.

Pemberton, bowing over his saddle. "Shall I call for you tomorrow around eight of the clock?"

"Please do, Mr. Pemberton," said Vanessa. "Shall we see you and your aunt on Thursday?"

Mr. Pemberton looked confused. Then his face cleared. "Oh, you are referring to Lady Cecily's dinner party. Of course, Miss Lester. My aunt was telling me only this morning that she was looking forward to it."

They spent a few moments exchanging polite observations about their surroundings. Then Vanessa gathered her reins to signal an end to their meeting. "Now I must be on my way or my mother will begin to wonder what is keeping me."

That was a bit of a bouncer, thought Vanessa ruefully. Lady Cecily would hardly notice her absence unless there was something that her ladyship wanted of her. But Vanessa did not think that the exaggeration would matter in this instance. Mr. Pemberton was not astute enough to realize that Lady Cecily's mothering instincts were scarcely worthy of the name, nor would he remember the true state of affairs since he had not even recalled Vanessa herself when she had reintroduced herself to him.

"Of course, Miss Lester," said Mr. Pemberton with his polite manners. "I understand perfectly."

Vanessa was quite certain that he did not and it was just as well. She was amused by her thoughts and she was smiling as she exchanged a few more broad pleasantries with Mr. Pemberton before taking final leave of him.

Mr. Pemberton put heel to his mount and set off in his original direction.

Once Vanessa was again free to continue on her way, she began to regret her generous impulse to include Mr. Pemberton in her morning ride. After they had spoken about the weather and the various crops in the fields, it had proven to be a challenge to sustain a conversation with Mr. Pemberton. That had led to Vanessa's rather broad excuse to take leave of him.

Vanessa could not imagine what it would be like to be in the gentleman's company for an hour or more on the morrow. But she resigned herself. She had issued the invitation and it had been accepted. It would not be right now to renege and send around her regrets simply because she was assured of an hour of boredom.

Certainly it would not hurt her to show this small kindness to a fellow creature, particularly one who had lost so much and who struggled so hard to please. If there was any one positive thing that could be said of Mr. Pemberton, Vanessa thought, it was that his manners were exquisite.

Chapter Eight

True to his word, Mr. Pemberton arrived promptly at eight o'clock the next morning. Vanessa had almost hoped that he would forget their assignation, but when he did not, she was ashamed of herself. She made up for her uncharitable attitude by welcoming Mr. Pemberton with extra warmth. He seemed inordinately taken aback, stammering a little in his response as he bowed over her hand.

Vanessa once again had to repent of her attitude, recognizing that anything out of the ordinary could only be confusing to the gentleman's simple mind. "Forgive me, Mr. Pemberton. I hope that I have not made you uncomfortable. I enjoy my rides so very much that I fear that my enthusiasm has made me appear somewhat forward," she said, smiling.

At once Mr. Pemberton's uncomfortable expression lightened. "Not at all, Miss Lester. I, too, enjoy being on horseback."

"Shall we go, then?" asked Vanessa, accepting her whip from her impassive butler.

Mr. Pemberton gallantly offered his arm to her and escorted her out of the front door. Mr. Pemberton's bridled gelding was held by a footman, while Vanessa's groom had charge of her mare. Mr. Pemberton did not wait for the groom to make a step for her, but himself tossed Vanessa into the saddle.

Vanessa straightened, her color heightened a little. She had been startled and disconcerted by Mr. Pemberton's assumption of authority. She had not expected such initiative from him. Nor had she expected the surge of comprehension along her nerve endings. The ease with which he had put her onto her mare had made her very cognizant of the strength of the man.

But as she looked down into Mr. Pemberton's amiable expression, she could detect nothing of her own awareness in his face.

There was a strange flicker in his eyes before he turned away. "We shall be away in a trice, Miss Lester," he said with a hearty chuckle, mounting his own horse. He gathered the reins, his wide grin still evident. Then a cloud of confusion seemed to descend upon his features as he looked around. "Will your groom not be accompanying us, ma'am?"

Vanessa realized that the gentleman must have just noticed that there were not three horses waiting. She glanced down at her groom's expressionless face. "I do not usually take my groom with me," she said quietly. "I hope that you do not object, sir?"

"No, of course not," said Mr. Pemberton hastily. But he seemed to be bothered by the omission.

Vanessa quietly spoke to her groom. The man nodded and trotted away. Vanessa turned toward her mounted companion. With a smile, she said, "Let us ride around to the stable. I have requested John, my groom, to accompany us after all. He has gone to saddle a mount for himself."

Mr. Pemberton expressed himself very ready to comply with this development and, indeed, appeared relieved. He explained his thoughts. "I am glad, Miss Lester. It would not do to give the gossips something to talk about, you know."

Vanessa stared at him. She could not speak, for the thought uppermost in her mind was that no one could possibly suspect Mr. Pemberton and herself of anything. The very idea was absurd. However, to indicate such to Mr. Pemberton would only wound him. The poor gentleman was too simple to realize that there was not the remotest possibility of such a thing. Finally, she managed, "Thank you for taking a care for my reputation, Mr. Pemberton."

Mr. Pemberton bowed from the saddle. "Not at all, Miss Lester. I am glad to be of service."

While Vanessa mulled over that undoubtedly sincere utterance, they walked the horses around to the stables. Her groom had saddled a small gelding for himself in record time and was just then mounting. He nodded to her and fell in behind Vanessa and Mr. Pemberton as they passed.

Vanessa took the lead, assuming that Mr. Pemberton would wish her to do so since they were on Halverton lands. As Vanessa had anticipated, she and Mr. Pemberton quickly exhausted such polite topics as the weather and the general gossip of the county. In truth, Vanessa carried most of that conversation herself since Mr. Pemberton's contributions were often confined to monosyllables. Out of desperation, Vanessa kept up a running commentary on what was going on with Halverton, what concerns she had, and what she anticipated. As they passed a certain field that had been harvested of its grain, she remarked that she must see about rotating another crop into it.

"Perhaps you should let it remain fallow until spring. If it is allowed to rest a season the ground might produce a higher yield when next it is worked," remarked Mr. Pemberton.

Vanessa turned an astonished expression to him. His suggestion was so sensible and knowledgeable that she could not but marvel at it. "What was that you said, Mr. Pemberton?"

Mr. Pemberton appeared both apprehensive and confused. "Have I said something I shouldn't?" he asked anxiously.

"No, of course not. Quite the contrary," said Vanessa. "I was just surprised that—" She broke off, appalled at what she had been about to say.

Mr. Pemberton shook his head, smiling in an understanding way that went straight to her heart. "You mustn't think that I am always a fool, Miss Lester. I know that I am not as quick as some others, but I do understand the land."

Vanessa allowed an answering smile to hover over her lips. "I am most happy to hear that, Mr. Pemberton." On impulse, she said, "Come, I will show you my latest project. You will tell me what you think."

She jumped her mare over the fence and started across the meadow. She heard Mr. Pemberton's surprised exclamation and she tossed a laughing glance over her shoulder. He sat his horse on the opposite side of the fence, staring after her. "You did say that you liked to ride, sir! Let us see if that great beast of yours is a match for my Ladyfly!" She saw Mr. Pemberton's expression alter into one of unusual liveliness.

"Very well, ma'am!" Mr. Pemberton backed his gelding and then set him at the fence. The gelding and its rider sailed over the fence, landing neatly. Mr. Pemberton grinned at her, holding in his sidestepping horse. "Now we shall see some sport, ma'am!"

Vanessa laughed, glad to have found at least this one area that she could share with her companion on an equal footing. "Indeed we shall, Mr. Pemberton!" She set spur to her mare, urging her into a run.

The couple raced across the meadow. Vanessa thought that she had the advantage, knowing that her mare was fleet and surefooted and herself to be an excellent horsewoman. She had judged Mr. Pemberton to be equally adept on horseback, but had estimated that his weight would handicap his larger mount. For several moments it appeared that she had been correct and that she had a fair chance of winning. The horses ran neck and neck. But then the gelding started edging ahead and finally took the lead. Mr. Pemberton swept by her at last, waving his arm with a flourish.

Vanessa pulled up her mare, drawing her down to a canter. She was breathless and laughing. The chill air had put roses into her cheeks and her eyes danced. As she came up to her companion, who had pulled up to wait for her, she exclaimed, "That was wonderful, Howard!"

Mr. Pemberton was also laughing. But as his eyes fell on her animated face, his grin faded a little. A blankness came into his expression. "We have left your groom behind," he said.

Vanessa glanced back, somewhat impatient of her companion's observation. "John will catch up with us, I daresay. He knows the field that I mean to show to you."

She turned her horse and again led the way, tossing a polite stilted comment to Mr. Pemberton as he followed her. It was such a disappointment to have seen the light of fun fade from his face, just as though a candle had flared bright before it guttered out.

Vanessa supposed that that was the way it would always be

with Mr. Pemberton. She would think that she had seen something in him, only to realize yet again that she had been wrong. Almost, she wished that she did not catch these glimpses of what he had once been. The Howard Pemberton she had known was gone forever and she should simply accept that fact.

Vanessa urged her mare into a slightly faster pace. The sooner this ride was over, she thought, the better it would be. There was too much about Mr. Pemberton that she could not readily deal with.

She and Mr. Pemberton rode in silence for some minutes. Then Vanessa pulled up and gestured toward the bottomland in front of them. "There it is. That is the field I wished to show to you."

"Much of it is underwater," said Mr. Pemberton, surprised.

"Yes," agreed Vanessa. She flashed a glance at her companion. "I have consulted with an engineer, who believes that the field may be properly drained. He proposes to break a way from the opposite end and create a series of ditches to carry away the water."

"Much like a farmer will use a spade to break a patch from the lane into ditches to drain the roads and their yards," said Mr. Pemberton thoughtfully.

"Precisely." Vanessa was glad that he had understood so readily. Apparently it was true what he had said of himself. Mr. Pemberton did understand the land. "I have decided to give the engineer permission to put his plans into execution. I expect to be able to put the field immediately into production, but I have not yet decided on the crops that I should plant. This field will always be somewhat wetter than I should like, which of course narrows my choices."

"The remaining water wouldn't matter to trees," offered Mr. Pemberton diffidently.

"Trees?" echoed Vanessa.

Mr. Pemberton cleared his throat. He appeared somewhat hesitant to voice his thoughts. "Perhaps I am speaking out of turn," he said.

"No, no. Do go on," said Vanessa, curious to hear what her companion had to say. It did not seem possible that a man such as Mr. Pemberton could actually have come up with a useful idea, but she was not going to discourage him from expressing himself. That would be an unnecessary cruelty. "Pray continue, sir."

"A new wood would be profitable over time," said Mr. Pemberton. "Good oak timbers for shipbuilding are becoming as valuable as gold, you know. And each year the cullings could be sold for posts and rails."

Vanessa looked at him thoughtfully. She had read more than once in the London papers of the growing need for ship timbers. England's fleet was destined to become the most formidable one on the high seas. Not once had it occurred to her that she could invest in her country's navy in quite this way. It had taken a gentleman of handicapped capabilities to open her eyes to the possibility.

Mr. Pemberton glanced away, obviously becoming uncomfortable under her steady regard. He gathered his reins. "I've said too much," he muttered.

Vanessa put out her hand to stay him. "I think not, Mr. Pemberton. It is a very worthwhile idea. In fact, I intend to pursue it," she said quietly. "I thank you for bringing such a simple solution to my problem."

Mr. Pemberton met her eyes, his face expressionless. His eyes appeared shuttered so that his feelings could not be discerned.

Vanessa smiled encouragingly at him. "I am not being at all condescending, Mr. Pemberton. I truly meant what I said. You have provided the answer to a rather ticklish problem. I do thank you."

Mr. Pemberton's face broke into the wide, amiable grin that she had come to recognize. "I am glad that I have been able to be of service to you, Miss Lester."

Vanessa turned her horse. "Shall we turn back now, sir?"

Mr. Pemberton cast a glance up at the sun. He nodded. "It is growing late in the morning, indeed. I am ready whenever you are, Miss Lester."

The groom had rejoined Vanessa and Mr. Pemberton by then and he trailed along behind them as they made their slow way back the way that they had come.

Vanessa and Mr. Pemberton occasionally addressed a remark to one another, but most of the ride was accomplished in a companionable silence since Vanessa no longer felt compelled to introduce and sustain a conversation.

She had discovered that Mr. Pemberton was simply a good riding companion.

It was odd how it had turned out, Vanessa thought idly. She had initially issued her invitation to Mr. Pemberton out of compassion. Then she had hoped that he would not remember it. Now she could not think of any other gentleman half as pleasant or as comfortable to be around than Mr. Pemberton. He enjoyed riding and he enjoyed her company. He did not require entertaining, nor did he strive to amuse. It was all very pleasant and quite different.

Vanessa and Mr. Pemberton met Mr. Nashe on the way back to Halverton. Mr. Nashe rode up to them, his countenance for once unmarked by its world-weary smile. He was obviously astonished to see Vanessa in such company.

He looked from one to the other as he greeted them. "Well met, Miss Lester. How are you, Pemberton? Robust as always, I presume," he said. He did not wait for Mr. Pemberton to reply before returning his glance to Vanessa. "Miss Lester, you have surprised me. If I had known that you desired a companion on your morning rides, I would instantly have offered my escort to you."

"Oh, I do not think that I require yet another squire, Mr. Nashe," said Vanessa with a laughing expression, indicating her companions.

"No, I suppose not," agreed Mr. Nashe, flicking a dismissive glance at Mr. Pemberton and the groom. "However, perhaps you might have wished to have a more voluble one."

"I doubt even you could have waxed eloquent about the farms and fields, Mr. Nashe," said Vanessa, still smiling but with a cool expression forming in her eyes.

"Is that what you have been doing? Inspecting crops?" asked Mr. Nashe in mock horror.

"And drainage," contributed Mr. Pemberton with his wide grin. "There is a field that Miss Lester has had an engineer to look over. It will be just the place for a new wood and—"

"Yes, yes, all highly interesting, I am sure," interrupted Mr. Nashe. He shook his head and his narrow mouth curled as he regarded the larger man. "I am surprised that you are able to express such an interest, Pemberton. Surely such matters are rather too weighty for you to grasp."

"I am quite able to understand the tenets of good management," said Mr. Pemberton quietly.

Vanessa interposed hastily, not willing to allow Mr. Pemberton to be made the butt of Mr. Nashe's quick quelling tongue. "So you see, my dear Mr. Nashe, that it would have been quite superfluous of you to have accompanied us," she said.

Mr. Nashe edged his horse closer to Vanessa's mare. Lowering his voice, he said in teasing complaint, "I do wish that you could bring yourself to address me by my given name, Vanessa. We are, after all, old acquaintances."

Mr. Pemberton's free hand clenched suddenly on his thigh. He unobtrusively heeled his horse, but yet held it in with an iron hand. The gelding, confused by conflicting signals, jibed and sidestepped. "Whoa, there. It seems that Colonel has gotten his second wind and wishes to run again," he said on a hearty laugh.

Vanessa turned toward Mr. Pemberton almost with relief. Mr. Nashe's attention was almost cloying after an hour of Mr. Pemberton's easy and undemanding companionship. "Yes, I can see that he is! I, too, could do with another run. Shall I race you, sir?"

"You may try it, Miss Lester. However, pray do not bet on the outcome," said Mr. Pemberton.

Vanessa laughed. "I am challenged, as you see, Mr. Nashe. Will you join us?"

Mr. Nashe's smile was very slight. He glanced in Mr. Pemberton's direction. "I think not today, Miss Lester. Perhaps another time."

Vanessa nodded, putting spur to her mare. "Very well, then! Good day, Mr. Nashe!" She lifted her hand in quick farewell as her horse leaped forward.

Mr. Pemberton's mount had already gained the advantage and so the outcome was all too quickly apparent. But Vanessa did not give in easily and she urged her mare to the outermost. Ladyfly managed to hold her own for some lengths, only dropping securely behind when the gelding gained his full stride.

By the time that Mr. Pemberton and Vanessa pulled up their horses, Mr. Nashe had been left far behind and was in fact out of sight behind a hillock. In the short distance came the groom, gallantly spurring his mount even though it was far out of its league.

"Your groom has been left behind again," observed Mr. Pemberton.

"And so has Mr. Nashe," said Vanessa.

"Yes," agreed Mr. Pemberton, and Vanessa thought that he seemed rather pleased. "Shall I call for you again tomorrow, Miss Lester?"

Vanessa looked over at him with surprise in her eyes. "Why, yes, Mr. Pemberton," she said slowly. She smiled suddenly. "I think that I would like that."

Mr. Pemberton reached out to catch her hand. He carried her gloved hand to his lips and placed a light salute on the tips of her fingers. "Au revoir, Miss Lester," he said with his wide grin.

"Until tomorrow," agreed Vanessa. She watched the large gentleman ride away. Her groom caught up with her and she turned her mare's head. "We are for home, John."

"Very good, miss," said the groom.

"Mr. Pemberton shall be riding with me again tomorrow morning," said Vanessa casually. "But it will not be necessary for you to accompany us, John."

The groom cast a swift glance at her profile. "O'course not, miss," he said. "Mr. Pemberton be as good an escort as anyone could wish for yers."

"Do you think so, indeed?" asked Vanessa, glancing curiously at her groom. "And what do you think of Mr. Nashe's offer to ride with me?"

The groom snorted. "Mr. Pemberton be a horseman, miss."

Vanessa nodded. "Quite so," she agreed dryly.

Chapter Nine

The week flew past. It became an established custom for Mr. Pemberton to call on Vanessa early each morning to go riding. Vanessa could not recall ever enjoying anything so much as Mr. Pemberton's quiet, undemanding companionship.

Vanessa began to fall into the habit of confiding in Mr. Pemberton. She did not actually expect him to offer her anything beyond an encouraging monosyllable or a sympathetic grunt. Nevertheless it was liberating to be able to unload all of her cares onto another's shoulders and yet know that whatever she might say would not be repeated.

Of that, Vanessa was perfectly certain. Mr. Pemberton was simpleminded, but he was not loose-lipped. As a consequence, Mr. Pemberton probably knew more about Vanessa and Halverton affairs than anyone else could possibly have guessed.

Of course, it was not a relationship solely based upon one-sided confidences. Vanessa and Mr. Pemberton shared a love for the land and often she discussed with him various estate matters, for she had accepted that he could speak quite intelligently on the subject. They also shared a passion for fast, cross-country riding. Invariably they chose to ride with a reckless abandon that would have horrified less stalwart individuals.

Whenever Vanessa returned to Halverton for breakfast, her color was heightened from the cold exercise and her eyes sparkled with the excitement of those rides. Within days it was noticed by the servants that Miss Vanessa seemed happier than before. Vanessa was unaware that her servants were beginning to talk and that fascinated speculation about herself and Mr. Pemberton had begun to circulate the halls of Halverton.

The whispers eventually reached Lady Cecily's ears and she was both astonished and pleased. Apparently she had been correct. Mr. Pemberton did indeed possess redeeming qualities to a girl as sports-minded as Vanessa.

Lady Cecily could not have been more satisfied. Apparently all was going well in at least two directions. Vanessa had captured the attentions of Mr. Pemberton and also of Reverend Haversaw, for the visits to the rectory had continued.

"But I do wish that Mr. Nashe might come up to scratch," murmured her ladyship to herself, slipping her glistening pearls lovingly through her fingers. "He would be the better catch by far." Rather complacently, she dropped the heavy strand and smoothed her hair in front of the mirror. "However, I shall not repine. It is going far more successfully than I ever dreamed. I shall be established in London next Season, I am certain."

Vanessa did not inform Lady Cecily that she had added to her ladyship's guest list until the very day of the dinner party. She had correctly gauged her mother's probable reaction and was prepared to weather the resulting storm.

"You have done what?" Lady Cecily's face had stiffened and her voice expressed frozen disbelief.

"I have invited Lieutenant Copperidge and his sergeant to dinner this evening," said Vanessa again, quite calmly. "I think that you will find the lieutenant to be an amiable guest, ma'am. He is obviously well-bred, and though I know nothing of him beyond what I have observed and the little that I have gleaned from our brief conversations, I seem to recall that he mentioned that his family is from Yorkshire and fairly well-connected. I suspect that he is a younger son, for otherwise it would not have been desirable for him to enter into military service."

"But an exciseman! What outrageous thing will you do next, Vanessa?" exclaimed Lady Cecily.

However, even as Lady Cecily expressed her displeasure, her expression was already changing. Outrage was giving way to thoughtful calculation. "A prominent Yorkshire family, I trust? I wonder whether I am acquainted with them? I must certainly invest a few minutes' conversation with your Lieutenant Copperidge, if only to be certain that you have not committed a complete *faux pas*. You must send round a note to him that he is to come a quarter hour early. As for his sergeant, the man shall naturally be more comfortable in the servants' hall. Fortunately, there will not need to be an adjustment required to round out the numbers since Reverend Haversaw has declined my invitation. Really, Vanessa, you are putting me to a great deal of trouble over this young man. I do hope that he proves worth my efforts."

"As do I, ma'am," said Vanessa with a small smile.

The evening augered well. Though Vanessa had initially objected to the dinner party, she now rather thought that it might serve to good purpose if it directed her mother's energies into channels other than blatant matchmaking.

Entertaining on a small scale could not be considered shocking when they were almost out of black gloves. Perhaps Lady Cecily's thoughts would not turn so much on a London Season when she became more thoroughly involved in producing her own amusements. Certainly the respite would be welcome to Vanessa, who had endured another short lecture on the disadvantages of her single state only the day before.

Nothing occurred to mar the agreeable outlook of the evening. Lady Cecily joined Vanessa downstairs in the drawing room and was gracious enough to bestow a compliment upon her daughter's gown. "You appear very becoming in that corbeau challis, my dear. I had forgotten that you possessed it."

"I had it made up just before Papa's final illness," said Vanessa. "He always liked me in the darkest of greens."

"Sir Charles was correct. The dress brings out the fiery highlights in your hair. I shall be surprised if you do not receive several compliments," said Lady Cecily. Her ladyship smoothed her own watered silk. "Naturally my own gown must excite envy. I doubt if many of my guests will have had the opportunity to visit a London modiste in the last several months."

"No, ma'am," agreed Vanessa with a smile. "I am certain

that your gown will be carefully scrutinized tonight and copied before the week is out."

"Do you think so, indeed? How perfectly alarming, to be sure," said Lady Cecily, highly pleased.

The door opened and the butler announced, "Lieutenant Copperidge, my lady."

The excise officer strode into the drawing room. Lady Cecily turned, her patrician features settling into arrogant lines. She stared down her nose at the uninvited guest. "Lieutenant Copperidge. You are prompt, sir."

Lt. Copperidge took her ladyship's hand and bowed. As he straightened, he said, "It is a habit peculiar to the military, my lady. Miss Lester, your servant."

"Thank you for coming, Lieutenant Copperidge," said Vanessa with a smile.

"Pray sit down, Lieutenant," said Lady Cecily, seating herself. She waited until her daughter and the excise officer had chosen their own places, then said, "My daughter tells me that you are from Yorkshire. I am acquainted with a few personages from that part of the country, most notably the Wycombes and Lady Nesbitt. Are you perhaps familiar with them?"

"I am not personally an intimate with either family. However, I believe that my aunt is a great friend of Lady Nesbitt's and my father was at school with a Wycombe," said Lt. Copperidge.

"Indeed!" Lady Cecily's cold demeanor thawed a trifle. She put a few more home questions that were designed to precisely pin down the Copperidge family background. Lt. Copperidge answered all that was asked of him with courtesy and a near-expressionless face. At the end of a quarter hour, Lady Cecily pronounced herself satisfied that she was indeed acquainted with at least two of Lt. Copperidge's relations.

"I am happy to say that your connections do you well, Lieutenant," said Lady Cecily. She rose and held out her hand. "I trust that you will enjoy the entertainment this evening."

"Thank you, my lady. I am certain that I shall," said Lt. Copperidge, rising at once in response to the unmistakable dismissal. "I know that I am arrived a few minutes early. If it will not discommode you, my lady, I should like to see that my sergeant in suitably engaged for the evening."

"Of course, Lieutenant. Do just as you wish," said Lady Cecily with a gracious nod.

Lt. Copperidge bowed and took his leave of Lady Cecily and her daughter. Before releasing Vanessa's hand, he said quietly, "I shall make my entrance with the other guests, I think. That will be the best course. Then I shall not draw undue speculation by showing myself to have arrived so early."

Vanessa nodded her understanding. "Very well. I shall ask Sims to show you into my study where you may be comfortable."

Vanessa walked with Lt. Copperidge to the door and gave him into the butler's care. When she had retraced her steps, she was unsurprised that her mother immediately launched her observations.

"There is an inordinate amount of pride in that young man, but perhaps that is more to his credit than otherwise. Certainly he comes of good family," said Lady Cecily. "I do not understand why you have chosen to befriend the lieutenant, Vanessa, but at least he will not embarrass me with an ill-bred manner."

"I trust not, indeed, ma'am," said Vanessa.

The door to the drawing room opened. Upon seeing the butler, Lady Cecily at once rose to her feet. "Ah, I see that Sims is ready for us. Let us adjourn to the top step, Vanessa, and make ready to greet our guests."

With the exception of a very few who had sent their excuses, Lady Cecily's guests began to arrive. The more prominent among those who were shown into the drawing room were Lord and Lady Nashe, making their first venture into society after their illness, accompanied by their son, Mr. Nashe. Squire Leeds and his wife, along with their eldest son, a youth of eighteen, and their marriable-age daughter, Mary, were present. Mr. Howard Pemberton escorted his aunt, the formidable Mrs. Dabney. Reverend Haversaw was conspicuous by his absence, having sent his regrets. The Claridge ladies expressed loud disappointment that the rector had not come. The rest of the party was made up of the humbler families of the county gentry.

A murmur of disbelief was heard when Lt. Copperidge was announced. Vanessa ignored it as she went forward to greet the exciseman with warm courtesy. Lt. Copperidge's hard gaze swept around the staring gathering, before settling upon Vanessa's face. "I am as a lamb among the wolves," he murmured as he took her outstretched hand.

Vanessa chuckled. "I do not think that you will be easily eaten, Lieutenant," she said.

He smiled slightly. "No, I am made of rather tough meat. I shall survive the stares and the cuts. One becomes innured."

"I trust that you will not be treated so discourteously under my roof, sir," said Vanessa. "Come, I shall present you to my mother and a few others. No doubt your natural amiability and charm shall soon melt the most frigid disapproval."

Lt. Copperidge laughed outright, for he was a man who understood himself better than most. He was all too aware that his stiffness of manner was something of a detriment to him in social situations such as these. However, he did not realize that with his spontaneous outburst of laughter his stern features had relaxed in an amazingly attractive way. Those who observed the transformation were at once struck by it and saw a part of the exciseman that had hitherto been hidden away. It gave them reason to suspend judgment and revise their opinions of the young lieutenant. Perhaps it was not so very odd of Lady Cecily to have invited such a low personage, after all.

Vanessa presented Lt. Copperidge as she had promised, leaving him at last with the squire, whom she knew could be counted on to enter into courteous conversation with the excise officer. She then moved through the gathering, bestowing a smile and a few words to each individual.

When Vanessa stopped to speak with Lord and Lady Nashe, she expressed her happiness that they had been able to attend. "My mother was quite certain that the invitation was a futile gesture until she received your gracious acceptance," said Vanessa. "I am glad that your recovery has been so complete, my lord, Lady Nashe."

"Oh, do sit down a moment beside me, Miss Lester," said

Lady Nashe, patting the cushion invitingly. "It is always a rare treat to speak to a member of the younger set, is it not, my lord?"

"Indeed, my dear. Pray spare us a moment, Miss Lester," said Lord Nashe, also gesturing for Vanessa to join them.

Vanessa was faintly surprised by the warmth of their response. She felt it would be impolite to refuse their invitation and so she sank down beside Lady Nashe. With a smile, she said, "Thank you, my lady. I am always happy to further relations with good neighbors."

Vanessa had always considered the Nashes to be a rather reserved pair. Now they smiled benignly on her and proceeded to make much of her polite gambit.

"Kind of you to say so, Miss Lester. It is just the sort of thing you would say, of course," said Lord Nashe. "We could scarcely disappoint the Halverton ladies when Lady Cecily herself called upon us several days ago to inquire how we went on and to personally issue her invitation."

"So kind of Lady Cecily," sighed Lady Nashe. "We enjoyed such a comfortable cose over tea, you know."

"I am happy to hear it," said Vanessa politely, almost blinking in her disbelief. The thought of Lady Cecily taking on the guise of a friendly neighbor was astounding.

"Aye, and her ladyship certainly spoke most highly of you, dear Miss Lester," said Lord Nashe jovially.

"Did she do so, indeed?" Vanessa eyed the Nashes in fascination. More and more she was hearing about the actions of a woman who was not at all like her mother.

"Oh, yes. Lady Cecily told us in particular of your admirable dedication to Halverton and the estate interests. Her ladyship quite commended your determination not to finance a London Season before settling all the necessary business that was created by Sir Charles's untimely death," said Lady Nashe, beaming at Vanessa.

"Your dedication to duty and your good sense are exceptional, Miss Lester. It is unusual to find such a conservative young lady. Sir Charles would have been proud that you have carried on his own tradition of fiscal soundness. I wish that my own family had had such a level head at the helm a generation or two ago," said Lord Nashe with the flash of a smile.

Vanessa perceived that Lord Nashe had made a little joke and she smiled in response. It was well known that the Nashe estates were mortgaged to the hilt. The rumor was that the heir, Mark Nashe, was an expensive man of fashion and was an additional drain on the estate. It would be wonderful indeed if there had not been envy for a neighbor who was not set in similarly bad circumstances, but she had detected nothing of that in Lord and Lady Nashe. On the contrary, they seemed extraordinarily pleased for her and for Halverton. "You flatter me, my lord, but I thank you nevertheless for the compliment. It is due as much to my agent's dedication as mine that Halverton is in such good point," she said.

"You are surely too modest, Miss Lester. An agent is useful, certainly. But one must keep one's eyes upon them, mustn't one? My son has remarked more than once about your dedication to overseeing the environs of Halverton for yourself," said Lord Nashe.

"Yes, indeed! On any number of occasions Mark has expressed his admiration for you," said Lady Nashe. She reached over to briefly squeeze Vanessa's hand. "You must come to visit us often, Miss Lester. We should so enjoy your company."

Lord Nashe added his agreement to this sentiment. Vanessa graciously assented that she would most certainly accompany her mother soon to pay a call to Nashe Hall. She detached herself by remarking that she had just recalled something of importance that she wished to remind the butler about and made her escape.

As she left the Nashes, she chanced to catch Mr. Pemberton's eyes. She was startled to see what seemed to be a gleam of amusement in his gaze. On impulse, Vanessa crossed over to him. "Good evening, Mr. Pemberton. I trust that you are enjoying yourself?" she asked. "Is there anything that I may do for you?"

Mr. Pemberton bestowed his wide, innocent grin upon her. "I am very well, thank you, ma'am. My aunt, Mrs. Dabney, has given it as her opinion that it is a very elegant turnout."

"And what do you think, Mr. Pemberton?" asked Vanessa, smiling.

A startled expression flitted over his handsome features. "I? Why, I don't know what I should say, Miss Lester."

"Of course you do," said Vanessa gently. "I believe that you know everyone here this evening. Surely you have formed some opinion of the company that you find yourself in, Mr. Pemberton."

Mr. Pemberton began to look a little hunted. "I shouldn't think that you would be interested in anything that I might think."

"Of course I am. I am always interested," said Vanessa encouragingly. "You were the one who told me what I should do with my field, were you not?"

"That was different," said Mr. Pemberton simply. "I am no hand at drawing room chatter."

"No, you are certainly not!" A small thin woman had come up in time to hear Mr. Pemberton's confession. She was attired in a neat round gown of pale lutestring. A silk turban graced her head and a set of antique gold and diamonds flashed at her ears and throat. Her dark eyes were shrewd. She smiled up at Vanessa, tapping the younger woman on the elbow with her painted fan. "My nephew is a great ox, Miss Lester. You must not expect much of him in the way of conversation."

"Aunt Cassie," said Mr. Pemberton with almost palpable relief.

Vanessa also smiled, but there was a coolness in her expression. "Good evening, Mrs. Dabney. I know that you will think me impertinent when I disagree with you. Mr. Pemberton is really quite informed about certain things and I have enjoyed his conversation very much."

Mr. Pemberton looked astounded. His aunt's expression was almost equally taken aback. But Mrs. Dabney swiftly recovered. She smiled again, and there was real amusement in her eyes. "You are kind, Miss Lester. I appreciate your attempts to draw out the best in my nephew. I shall only caution you not to expect too much, for it causes him to become anxious."

Vanessa glanced swiftly up at Mr. Pemberton's face. She saw that he was laboring under some emotion that she could not identify and realized the truth of his aunt's statement. She was instantly contrite for trying to elicit a response that he was either unable or unwilling to make to her question.

"I am sorry, Mr. Pemberton. I did not intend to place you into an untenable position. I have not been a very good hostess, I fear. I shall not tease you again, I promise." With a smile and a nod, Vanessa moved on. However, the shadowed expression in Mr. Pemberton's eyes as he gazed after her remained with her.

Lady Cecily had also been circulating among her guests. But her manners were rather haughty and she did not generate the same friendly conversation that had characterized her daughter's progress. However, it was her ladyship who arranged the pairing off of dinner partners.

The butler announced the hour and the party sorted themselves out by social preeminence. Mr. Nashe approached Vanessa and bowed to her. With a flickering smile, he said, "I have not yet had the opportunity to exchange more than a polite greeting with you, Miss Lester. I am fortunate, indeed, to have been chosen to be your dinner partner. May I escort you in?"

Vanessa graciously inclined her head. Placing her fingers lightly upon his extended arm, she said, "Thank you, Mr. Nashe." She had misgivings about the seating arrangement, but there was nothing that she could do to change it and so she accepted with good grace the escort whom her mother had chosen for her.

The gentlemen led their partners into the dining room and seated them at the long table. Vanessa found herself situated between Mr. Nashe and Squire Leeds. The squire was more interested in the various entrees and vegetable dishes that were presented than he was in polite conversation and so Vanessa found herself confined almost exclusively to Mr. Nashe's company.

Rather to her surprise, Vanessa found herself enjoying Mr. Nashe's easy address. His sophisticated manners and his ability to tell an amusing anecdote just suited her mood. Even Mr. Nashe's launching of a lavish flirtation was not to be disdained. It was a welcome diversion from the faint twinge of guilt that she was still feeling over the debacle with Mr. Pemberton.

Vanessa did not forget Mr. Pemberton. Indeed, when she caught his gaze over her wineglass as she glanced across the table, she smiled at him. Mr. Pemberton appeared rather more somber than was his wont. At least, he did not return her smile. But Vanessa attributed that to his inability to properly join in with the genial exchanges going on around him.

Vanessa pitied the poor unhappy gentleman, but he was all but forgotten as she turned away to respond to something that Mr. Nashe had said.

For the first time in many months, Vanessa was rediscovering the pleasures of a convivial gathering. She had to concede to herself that Lady Cecily had been right, after all. It had been too long since Halverton had offered its hospitality. She had lost touch with most of her neighbors and she had forgotten how nice it could be to be admired as a woman.

All in all, it began to be a very pleasant evening.

Chapter Ten

After Lady Cecily's singularly successful dinner party, Mr. Nashe apparently felt that Vanessa's smiles and the mild flirtation they had enjoyed had given him carte blanche where she was concerned. Mr. Nashe began to be seen quite often at Halverton. He was a gentleman of indolent habits, however, and generally did not leave his rooms until luncheon. But nearly every afternoon he rode over from Nashe Hall to call on Vanessa and to pay charming address to Lady Cecily. In addition, he formed the habit of escorting the ladies to church on Sundays, taking his place beside them in their pew rather than in his own family pew.

Lord and Lady Nashe, who had come completely out of seclusion, did not appear to be in the slightest upset by this development. Instead, they exchanged the most amiable of commonplaces with the Halverton ladies after the services.

Reverend Haversaw observed Mr. Nashe's seemingly favored status with regret. He held certain private opinions regarding the scion of Nashe Hall and he was mildly surprised that Miss Lester, whom he considered to be a young woman of rare intelligence and discernment, could encourage the attentions of this particular gentleman.

But he was not a jealous man. He was comfortable in his own worth and at the same time had a humility of spirit that recognized he could not aspire to Mr. Nashe's exquisitely turned out person.

However, Reverend Haversaw was also a frequent visitor at Halverton and was always assured of Lady Cecily's benevolent hospitality. On occasion, the rector brought with him his three children to see Vanessa. She always received them warmly and was very patient to listen to all of their eager prattle.

Lady Cecily graciously welcomed the three younger Haversaws at these times, but she immediately packed them off to the stables or elsewhere in the custody of servants. "They will enjoy themselves so much more without our dampening their spirits," she always remarked.

Vanessa and Reverend Haversaw murmured agreement, though their glances often met in a sharing of mutual amusement. They were well aware that Lady Cecily preferred to appreciate children at a distance.

However, her ladyship never failed to inquire after the reverend's family and she encouraged him to talk about them. Somehow the conversation was always turned so that Vanessa was drawn deep into descriptions of entertaining childish antics or sayings. Lady Cecily listened with an unchanging expression of interest, only her drifting gaze betraying her boredom.

Lady Cecily had taken to calling on her more prominent neighbors with surprising frequency. Though her ladyship could not bring herself to like Mrs. Dabney, every week saw her order out the carriage to carry her to Pemberton Place. She invariably returned from these visits in a thoroughly bad temper and with ruffled pride.

After one of these visits, Lady Cecily vented her feelings with several scathing remarks upon Mrs. Dabney's manners and taste in attire.

"Why do you go so often when you and Mrs. Dabney clash so?" asked Vanessa curiously.

Lady Cecily started and stared at her daughter. Lifting her brows, she said, "I cannot very well slight the woman when she is mistress of Pemberton Place. Besides, my dear, it would be strange indeed of me not to be seen to be on friendly terms with Mrs. Dabney when you have established such a comfortable footing with Mr. Pemberton. It is common knowledge that you often ride together."

"You do not mind my morning rides with Mr. Pemberton, surely?" asked Vanessa.

"Certainly not! It is perfectly respectable to go riding with such a close neighbor," said Lady Cecily.

Recalling Lady Cecily's allusion to gossip over her visits to the rectory, Vanessa said, "Are you not afraid that people might talk? After all, you mentioned something of the sort when I began to call frequently at the rectory."

"My dear! Mr. Pemberton?" Lady Cecily gave a snort of laughter. "The very idea is ludicrous. None of our acquaintances would ever consider that gentleman to be a threat to one's reputation."

Though Vanessa could not deny the truth of this statement, she was nevertheless annoyed by Lady Cecily's undisguised amusement. Vanessa had come to have a fondness for Mr. Pemberton, borne out of compassion and pity. It annoyed her very much when the gentleman was slighted because of his lack of quick intellect, as he too often was in their close society where everyone knew everyone else.

Certainly there was respect for Mr. Pemberton's position and he was extremely well-liked due to his unvarying good nature. Nevertheless, it was not unusual for someone to make a laughing allusion directly to the gentleman himself concerning his slower thought processes. Mr. Pemberton never seemed to mind and he always laughed along with the jokester once he understood what was meant. But Vanessa was appalled by such indifferent cruelty and she had become swift to champion Mr. Pemberton whenever she could.

"I rather like Mr. Pemberton. He is always amiable and ready to oblige one," she said, very coolly.

Lady Cecily's brows rose. After the slightest pause, she said, "Quite true. Mr. Pemberton may be counted upon for his exquisite manners, at least. Will you be accompanying me to Nashe Hall today?"

"I think not. I had planned to spend the afternoon balancing figures," said Vanessa quickly.

"A pity, for you shall undoubtedly be missed. The Nashes seem to have taken quite a liking to you," said Lady Cecily, gathering her gloves.

"We seem to live in their pocket these days," said Vanessa dryly.

Lady Cecily did not deign to answer, but swept out of the room.

Her ladyship's visits to Nashe Hall were frequent. More than once Vanessa had been compelled out of simple courtesy to accompany Lady Cecily, but she did not particularly enjoy the visits. It seemed to her that Lady Nashe was too ingratiating, always eager to endorse any opinion held by Lady Cecily, no matter how supercilious. As for Lord Nashe, his lordship made it a point to lavish heavy compliments upon Vanessa herself before making very close inquiries into her management of Halverton.

Vanessa could see her mother's heavy hand at work in creating a closer tie with Nashe Hall. Lord and Lady Nashe appeared delighted by Lady Cecily's friendship and had only approving things to say about their son's increasing focus upon Miss Lester. Vanessa herself was beginning to feel besieged by Mr. Nashe. It was becoming a bit of a chore to hold him at arm's length since she was hampered by her mother's obvious favor toward the gentleman.

Vanessa could not imagine why Mr. Nashe had suddenly decided to enter a determined pursuit of her. They did not at all compliment one another, either in physical characteristics or in tastes. She was the taller by several inches, though it was not as readily apparent when Mr. Nashe was sitting down or on horseback. Vanessa preferred quiet elegance in her surroundings, whereas Mr. Nashe had commented once that he had seen very little in any of the county's houses that he could admire.

But more important than anything else, Vanessa was wed heart and soul to the land. She loved the change of seasons and the different tasks that each brought with it. Mr. Nashe was contemptuous of what he termed country living. He much preferred the excitement and amusements to be found in London and talked incessantly of his return to the capital.

Vanessa wondered rather more often than she liked why he simply did not go. Lord and Lady Nashe were obviously completely recovered. They had attended several neighborhood functions and had even begun to entertain on a small scale themselves. There was no tie that Vanessa could see that remained to hold Mr. Nashe in the county, unless it was his courtship of herself. That was a rather daunting thought and she did her best to disabuse Mr. Nashe of the notion that she was at all interested in a warmer relationship between them. Though she had learned to derive some enjoyment from Mr. Nashe's company, that was certainly not the basis upon which to build a courtship.

Vanessa much preferred Lt. Copperidge's astringent company over Mr. Nashe's fulsome compliments, sighing complaints, and haughty starts. Surprisingly enough, beyond a caustic comment or two, Lady Cecily had not objected to her daughter's continuing a friendship that could only be considered barely respectable. However, the excise officer had managed to carve himself a place in the county's social strata and Lady Cecily could scarcely protest Lt. Copperidge's occasional visits to Halverton to pay his compliments to Vanessa when he had been introduced to the neighborhood at her ladyship's own dinner party. Vanessa rather thought that discovering Lt. Copperidge to be a bachelor had also worked in his favor, for Lady Cecily preserved a certain cordiality for the excise officer despite his undoubtedly lower social position.

The exciseman was obsessed with his duty, but at least his was an honest, open preoccupation. Vanessa knew well enough where she stood with Lt. Copperidge. It was not so much admiration of her as his appreciation for her friendship that continued to draw him into her circle of admirers. Even if they were in the middle of the dance floor, he would begin to ask leading questions about one or another of Vanessa's neighbors.

Vanessa quietly, laughingly, pointed out that they were in the midst of company. "Such serious discussion seems out of place in these pleasant surroundings," she said gently.

Lt. Copperidge apologized instantly. He was silent for a few measures as they continued to dance. "The fact is, Miss Lester, I cannot stop the speculations and questions that come into my mind," he confessed. His hand clenched suddenly, painfully around her fingers. "I must break up this ring of smugglers. I must!"

Vanessa wriggled her fingers and was relieved when he

eased the pressure. "And you will do so, I have no doubt. There can be no one more dedicated to the cause than yourself," she said.

Lt. Copperidge's grim expression eased. "You are salve to my burning sense of frustration, Miss Lester. But it is at times like these that I wonder whether mere dedication is enough."

Vanessa smiled at the excise officer, privately certain that he had hit on a truth. Free trade with the continent was too ingrained in the people to be easily set aside. "Perhaps it is not. But I feel certain that if that is the case you will eventually know it and recognize that you have done all that can possibly be done."

The excise officer shook his head. "No," he denied decisively. "There is always more that one can do, if one only digs a little deeper. I shall not rest until I discover the information that I require."

Vanessa smiled and said no more. There was no point in doing so. She was rather relieved when the landler ended and her partner escorted her back to her chair. She fanned herself, surveying the company who had attended the squire's ball and supper. She had stood up with nearly all of the gentlemen twice. Soon it would be time to go in to supper.

Vanessa hoped that one of her father's old friends would gallantly claim her hand for supper before one of her recognized admirers did so. Lt. Copperidge was as much a bore in his way as was Mr. Nashe. It was a pity indeed that her two most eligible admirers made her yawn.

Perhaps not too surprisingly, Vanessa enjoyed most her dawn rides with Mr. Pemberton. She had no need to fend off unwelcome compliments or make attempts to soothe an unquenchable burning ambition. Though Mr. Pemberton was nowhere near as articulate as the other gentlemen of her acquaintance, he entered into the same delight that she felt in the harmony of rider and horse. Moreover, he was just such an intrepid rider as herself, taking jumps and fences without intimidation.

With Mr. Pemberton, Vanessa could fall easily into observations about the countryside or tell him specifics about whatever knotty problem had arisen with the functioning of the

estate. She had no need to guard herself against flirtatious sub-
tleties or to play the rallying confidante.

Vanessa had no real expectation that Mr. Pemberton would
hold his own in these discourses. Indeed, he appeared as
though he only understood half of what she was saying. But he
was a good listener and he was obviously content to allow her
to say whatever was on her mind, without sitting in judgment.
He was a safe sounding board, holding up his end of the conversations with occasional grunts or little noises of encouragement.

Vanessa had so fallen into the habit of confiding in him that
she even went so far as to tell him about Lady Cecily's
adamant desire to see her wed and about her ladyship's determined encouragement of Mr. Nashe's suit. "You will no doubt
tell me that I am foolish for minding so much," she said,
laughing.

"No, I will not!" said Mr. Pemberton, with rather more force
than was usual in one of his amiable character.

Vanessa stared across at her companion in utmost astonishment. At the sight of his lowered brows and tensed jaw, suspicion crowded into her mind. Surely Mr. Pemberton had not
understood all the implications of what she had said. "I beg
your pardon?" she said sharply.

Mr. Pemberton turned his head. His expression had
smoothed to one of mild surprise. "I am sorry, Miss Lester. I
was thinking of something that my aunt wanted of me. What
was it you said?"

"Nothing of importance," said Vanessa, still eyeing him but
with a measure of uncertainty.

It had seemed to her more and more frequently that there
was more to Mr. Pemberton than what first met the eye. Of
course, she had long ago discovered that he had an amazing
aptitude for agricultural management. But there had been hints
of something else, too.

Over the weeks since they had begun riding together, there
had been a sprinkling of rather shrewd comments to issue out
of the gentleman's mouth. It was as though his unconscious
mind was somehow caught off guard. Then he would say

something particularly obtuse and sink back into bovine stupidity.

Vanessa, always disappointed, would realize once again that she still harbored hopes of finding her old childhood friend tucked away inside the large agreeable gentleman. What saddened her most was that she knew that the boy she had known must still exist, but that he had become a prisoner and there was no key to unlock the gate.

"What was it that Mrs. Dabney wanted of you?" she asked gently.

Mr. Pemberton blinked in confusion. "My aunt?" A few seconds elapsed, then his face cleared. "Oh, did she tell you, too, Miss Lester? My aunt wants to have a party at Pemberton. I am to be a good host." Glumly he looked out over his horse's flicking ears.

"Will it be so very bad?" asked Vanessa.

Mr. Pemberton's gaze slid toward her. "I am not a great hand at polite conversation," he confessed hesitantly.

Vanessa's lips quivered, even as her heart was wrung with compassion. Misery sat so obvious on his countenance that he appeared positively comical, but she knew it was no laughing matter. "I understand perfectly," she said.

"Do you, Miss Lester? You do not think that I am being a great gowk over nothing?" he asked anxiously.

"No, I do not," said Vanessa firmly, inwardly fuming at what she perceived as Mrs. Dabney's callousness. It was natural for Mrs. Dabney to want to return the hospitality that she and Mr. Pemberton had enjoyed in recent weeks, but to expect her nephew to hold up his end as host was surely asking too much.

"It is a great piece of nonsense. You will not enjoy a party of that sort," said Vanessa.

Mr. Pemberton heaved a huge sigh of relief. "You do understand! But what can I do, Miss Lester? My aunt says that we must have a party."

"You must put your foot down," said Vanessa, and then realized from his astonished expression that her suggestion was useless to him. Mr. Pemberton could no more stand up to his formidable aunt than a leaf could to the wind, she thought. She shook her head. "No, I see that is not the answer. I shall think of something."

Mr. Pemberton was apparently satisfied with her assurance, for he smiled and fell into silence as they continued down the bridle path.

Vanessa studied her companion carefully. There must be some sort of gathering that Mr. Pemberton would feel comfortable in presiding over. She began naming off his good points to herself. Mr. Pemberton had all the born instincts of a gentleman and a landowner. He was an accomplished sportsman. He danced marvelously well. His nature was unfailingly cheerful. It was just so unfortunate that he was also dull-witted.

"I shall be glad when the first good frost takes hold," remarked Mr. Pemberton. "I shall be able to take my guns out."

"That's it!" exclaimed Vanessa.

Mr. Pemberton whipped his head around, wearing a wary expression.

Vanessa took it merely to be borne of startlement. "You must hold a hunt," she said. "You can do that, can't you?"

He stared at her for a long moment, then he gave a shout of laughter. His eyes gleamed with unusual awareness. "Yes, Miss Lester. I can do that."

"Then that is what you must do. Invite the ladies as well as the gentlemen, so that your aunt may entertain. And you may play host to the gentlemen who wish to take out their guns. That sort of conversation will not prove so awkward for you," said Vanessa.

Mr. Pemberton seemed to have been turned speechless. He regarded her with a rather curious expression, as though he was gathering his thoughts. Then he smiled. It was the wide, cheerful grin that was characteristic of him. "I will do just as you say, Miss Lester. I will hold a hunt. I like to hunt. And my aunt will be happy, too."

"I, also, like to hunt. I hope that you will allow me to ride neck or nothing, sir," said Vanessa with a quick smile.

Mr. Pemberton reached out his hand and briefly clasped hers. "You may do just as you wish, my dearest of friends," he said quietly.

Vanessa was quite taken aback. Quick color surged into her face as she stared in astonishment at her companion. With any other gentleman, she would have known precisely how to have taken such an intimate address. But Mr. Pemberton was very different from all the other gentlemen she had ever known. For the first time in her life, Vanessa felt thrown off-balance. Was it possible that Mr. Pemberton had developed a tendre for her? Her emotions were oddly conflicting, but uppermost was the absolute conviction that she could not encourage him.

Then Mr. Pemberton laughed again, quite unself-consciously. His wide familiar grin lighted up his handsome countenance. "Neck or nothing it is, Miss Lester! I should like to see Ladyfly take the shine out of all the rest. We shall see some sport, shan't we?"

He looked so eager and unloverlike that Vanessa was reassured. She laughed also. "Yes, we shall indeed!"

Chapter Eleven

The invitation to a hunt issued from Pemberton Hall occasioned surprise. The assumption had been that Mr. Pemberton would always be the amiable guest, never the host. However, it swiftly came to be agreed in the neighborhood that Mr. Pemberton, despite his unfortunate mental deficit, was yet a gentleman born and therefore had naturally realized the obligation of returning the various hospitalities that he and his aunt had enjoyed.

Two days after the invitation had gone out, Vanessa was transacting business in the village. She was amused to discover that the hunt was an item of curious discussion wherever she went.

But her amusement was quickly quenched when a trio of ladies entered the dress shop after her and she overheard the tenor of their remarks.

"Depend upon it, if Mr. Pemberton did not think of it himself, Mrs. Dabney certainly did. That lady does not let the grass grow under her feet, I'll warrant," said one dame.

"Oh, indeed! Mrs. Dabney is exceptionally high-bred. Despite having an idiot for a nephew, she will not let the conventions slide past," said another.

"I think it rather telling that we are not bid to a literary or musicale," said a third. This sally garnered several titters.

As Vanessa had talked quietly with the proprietress of the shop, she listened with a sense of outrage. It was cruel to hold poor Mr. Pemberton up to derision. The only greater cruelty would be to say such things to his face. When she had finished her request, she turned toward the ladies. She greeted them all by name, for they were all well known to her.

Once the civilities had been observed, one lady asked, "What do you think of this hunt, Miss Lester?"

It had become known that the mistress of Halverton was frequently to be seen in Mr. Pemberton's company of a morning. Of course, as one good lady had pointed out, Miss Lester was nearly as frequently in Mr. Nashe's escort. Vanessa's visits to the rectory had not gone unnoticed, either. Speculation of some sort of match being in the offing was bruited about, though Mr. Pemberton was scarcely thought of as a true contender. Miss Lester's kindness toward that gentleman was almost certainly just an expression of her nobility of character.

"For my part, I shall enjoy a rousing hunt. I think it is a wonderful notion and so I shall tell Mr. Pemberton when next I see him," Vanessa said with a smile. "It will certainly gratify him that his invitation has found favor with all of us."

The other ladies murmured skeptical agreement, unwilling to meet the challenge in Miss Lester's eyes. They knew her strongly held views of Christian charity and though most espoused the same tenets in comfortable conversation, it was another thing altogether to put it into practice as had Miss Lester. Some in the county felt that Miss Lester had gone too far out of her way to extend compassion and friendship to a gentleman who was obviously incapable of appreciating it.

As one of those dames later observed to Mrs. Leeds, "I suppose Miss Lester believes it to be her duty to encourage that poor man. But my thought is that one cannot expect much out of poor Mr. Pemberton. Nor out of this extraordinary invitation!"

"Oh, do you not think so?" asked Mrs. Leeds, mildly surprised. "I had rather thought it would be a nice entertainment, particularly for the gentlemen. They so much prefer sporting affairs over the dance floor, do they not?"

"That may well be. However, I doubt that this particular hunt will appeal to them," said the dame with a scornful laugh. "Miss Lester seems to believe that it will be a well-managed affair, but I am not so sanguine. Indeed, I cannot think of anyone who regards it with anything better than misgiving."

"It is true that Mr. Pemberton is not particularly clever, but surely that will not matter overmuch," said Mrs. Leeds, her pleasant countenance troubled.

The dame snorted. "My dear Mrs. Leeds, Mr. Pemberton will not have the least notion how to go on. Unless Mrs. Dabney takes the arrangements firmly in hand, I daresay we may expect an entirely insipid affair."

Mrs. Leeds subsequently passed on this daunting report to her spouse. "It seems to be the general opinion, dear sir. I am uncertain whether we should attend at all, though naturally I should be reluctant to affront Mrs. Dabney. But then, I do know how very much you dislike a paltry affair."

The squire guffawed. "My good wife, you must not give credence to such naysaying. Why, I have no doubt at all that this hunt will be just the thing to shake us all out of our doldrums."

"Then you believe it will be the sort of hunt that Miss Lester expects?" asked Mrs. Leeds, surprised.

"Indeed, I daresay it will be something like," said Squire Leeds, rubbing his hands together in anticipation. "I have seen Pemberton up on his hunter. He shall undoubtedly lead the field."

"Pray, how can you say so?" asked Mrs. Leeds, growing astonished. "The poor gentleman can scarcely rub two consecutive thoughts inside his head."

Squire Leeds snorted. "That is all it takes, my dear, plus a steady pair of hands and a good seat. No, unless I miss my guess altogether, Pemberton will lead us all a very merry chase."

A new unforeseen concern rose in Mrs. Leeds's breast. "Squire, if it is to be as you say, I very much doubt that there will be the proper protocol observed. Mr. Pemberton, though an amiable soul, has not the necessary qualities required for a master of the hunt. I should not wish our son to be out on a chaotic field. Ronald is too wild a rider to keep his head."

"Come, my dear, you must not be anxious on Ronald's account. The boy is growing up. He will not lose his head over a fox or two. I shall keep an eye on him, besides, while we are coursing over the fields," said Squire Leeds comfortably. With that, he went off to inform his son of the treat in store.

Mrs. Leeds looked after him, her expression perturbed. It was all very well for the squire to announce that he would watch after their son, but she knew very well that the squire himself would be at the front of the field. He would like as not forget all about keeping a close eye on Ronald. She had half a mind to dig out her own habit.

Her daughter entered the room, saying, "Mama, I have just seen Papa. He says we are to go to the hunt. Is it true?"

Instantly Mrs. Leeds made up her mind. "Certainly, Mary. I cannot think why we should not. Furthermore, I believe that I shall myself join the hunt."

Mary's eyes opened very wide. She said in astonishment, "You, Mama?"

"Miss Lester is not the only lady with a good seat, Mary. I was once counted a bruising rider. I shall enjoy a good hunt," said Mrs. Leeds staunchly.

Mary at once made an excuse to leave the room and sped in search of her father and brother. The news that her mother was going to participate in the hunt was too momentous to keep to herself.

Several other households around the county were affected to one degree or another. Most of the sporting gentlemen expressed delight over the first hunt of the season. Their ladies, too, were mostly willing to accept the invitation. Balls and dinners had palled as entertainment. The beginning of the hunting season was welcomed with open arms.

The fact that the first hunt of the season was to be held at Pemberton Hall gave it all the more spice, for none knew quite what to expect. Since none but the older generation could recall being guests of Pemberton hospitality, the event was looked forward to with lively curiosity.

The day of the Pemberton hunt, as it came to be referred to, dawned bright and clear. The wind was in the south quarter, which meant that there was the possibility of rain. But no one regarded that possibility with real anxiety except perhaps the ladies who had accepted the invitation with nothing more strenuous in mind than a leisurely stroll in the gardens and taking tea while hardier souls were coursing over the countryside.

Lady Cecily did not hunt. She disliked everything about

horses except that they were useful to pull her own carriage. Since Lady Cecily would not be out in the field, she would be ensconced with her hostess, Mrs. Dabney, and other ladies of sedentary habits. Her ladyship did not anticipate a fine entertainment.

"The society will undoubtedly be mundane and rather common," she had declared disdainfully as she prepared to climb up into the carriage. "I shall undoubtedly be bored to tears."

"I am sorry that you feel that way, Mother. Perhaps you would prefer to remain at home?" asked Vanessa, not pausing as she pulled on her riding gloves. She was attired in a smart black habit, ruched lavishly with lace at throat and cuffs. Her head was graced with a hat and veil. She stood erect and slender, a touch of wind bringing color into her cheeks. Her eyes gleamed as she made her query, for she rather thought that she knew her mother's reaction. Lady Cecily would not miss an opportunity to escort her into society.

It was just as Vanessa had surmised. "I believe that I know my obligations, Vanessa. This invitation is the only one likely to come forth from Pemberton Hall. It would be an unforgivable social slight if I declined," said Lady Cecily. "I do not transgress the polite courtesies, as well you know. Mrs. Dabney will find me all affability."

"Of course, ma'am," said Vanessa, hiding a smile.

Lady Cecily disappeared inside the carriage. The door with its crested panel was shut securely by an attending footman. He signaled to the driver, but before the horses could be given the office Lady Cecily put down the window. "Pray do not dawdle, Vanessa. You know how much I detest tardiness of any sort."

"Yes, ma'am. John is bringing up Ladyfly now," said Vanessa.

Lady Cecily did not acknowledge Vanessa's reassurance, but snapped shut the window. The footman signaled the driver again and the horses were whipped up. The carriage started away down the drive.

With the aid of her groom, Vanessa mounted. Settling herself, she nodded dismissal to her groom. "I shall not need you further today, John," she said.

"Well I know it, miss," retorted the groom.

Vanessa laughed as she turned her mare and cantered after the carriage.

It was only a short distance to Pemberton Hall. At the manor the guests were welcomed by Mr. Pemberton's aunt, Mrs. Dabney. Wraps that had been donned to guard against the cold were removed and given into the waiting hands of the footmen. The ladies who did not hunt were urged by Mrs. Dabney to partake at once of refreshments while she enumerated to them the several gentler entertainments, such as playing cards, visiting the library or conservatory, walking in the gardens or ordering out carriages for a pleasure drive, that they might indulge their hours.

Those ladies dressed in flowing habits and who had ridden their own hunters over were privileged to a special word from Pemberton's hostess. Mrs. Dabney engaged every lady for a few moments to make certain that each had either brought a groom and if they did not, she assured them that she would have one assigned to them.

Mrs. Dabney and Mrs. Leeds spoke at some length, agreeing in the end that a trustworthy groom would follow young Master Ronald's progress at a discrete distance. "I shall rest so much easier in my mind," confided Mrs. Leeds. "The squire told me that I am too anxious. But Ronald can be so reckless of his own safety."

"I can readily understand," said Mrs. Dabney, her glance touching briefly upon her nephew's tall figure. She reassured Mrs. Leeds once more before pressing on to her next object, which chanced to be the mistress of Halverton.

Mrs. Dabney smiled at Vanessa. "I know you well by reputation, Miss Lester. I doubt very much that you have brought your groom with you, have you, my dear?"

Vanessa shook her head. Her eyes twinkled as she ruefully confessed, "I fear not, ma'am. I am an intrepid rider to hounds. There has never been the least need for a groom to shadow my course!"

"Naturally it is not at all what I approved of," said Lady Cecily, gently waving her fan. "However, my daughter will not heed wiser counsel, as I think you will find, Mrs. Dabney." In a patronizing tone, she added, "But certainly you have my permission to make the attempt."

Mrs. Dabney glanced at Lady Cecily. "You are gracious, my lady."

Lady Cecily inclined her head very slightly, acknowledging what she took to be a compliment.

Mrs. Dabney smiled slightly. Returning her attention to Vanessa, she said, "However, I have never been one to force my views on another. Therefore I shall allow you to do just as you like, Miss Lester."

"Thank you, ma'am," said Vanessa. She heard the sharp snap as Lady Cecily shut her fan. Vanessa knew that her mother was annoyed by Mrs. Dabney's neat sidestepping of a potential conflict. Mrs. Dabney had preserved an air of generosity, while Lady Cecily had been made to appear rather uncharitable.

A burst of laughter came from the gentlemen who had grouped loosely in one corner of the room around their host. Vanessa decided that she would not allow Lady Cecily's disgruntlement to dampen her own enjoyment.

Mr. Nashe sauntered over to greet Lady Cecily and Vanessa. Her ladyship received him with cordiality. After a few moments, Lady Cecily excused herself on the pretext of speaking to her acquaintances, leaving her daughter with Mr. Nashe.

Vanessa was amused by her mother's stratagem. There was not the least chance of Mr. Nashe making an offer to her, nor of her ever accepting one from him. She therefore was able to speak to him without the least reservation. "It is quite a gathering this morning," she said.

Mr. Nashe looked around the crowded drawing room. There was a thin smile on his face. "Yes, indeed. It appears that half the county is here. Curiosity is a curious thing, is it not? Even my father insisted upon attending, though naturally he will not hunt."

"Lord Nashe looks much improved," remarked Vanessa, looking over at the elderly gentleman seated in a wing chair in front of the blazing fire. Several other gentlemen were standing close about Lord Nashe, but their attention was focused more nearly on their host, Mr. Pemberton, who was greeting Reverend Haversaw.

"My father is always revived when finding himself at the center of things," said Mr. Nashe with a small laugh. "I see that you hunt today, Miss Lester. I am honored that I shall be sharing the field with such a beauteous companion."

"You flatter me, sir," said Vanessa, smiling. "I do not see Lady Nashe. I hope that she is well?"

"My mother preferred to remain at Nashe Hall. She is making lists of preparations for my sister Cressida's visit," said Mr. Nashe.

Vanessa's face lighted up. "Oh, are Cressy and Lord Akers coming down for the hunting season? How marvelous! I shall so enjoy seeing them again."

"You were once friends with Cressida, were you not? It is odd that I had forgotten," said Mr. Nashe, looking at her.

"Cressy and Eleanor were both among my dearest of friends," agreed Vanessa. "When do Lord and Lady Akers arrive?"

"In a sennight, I believe," said Mr. Nashe in a somewhat bored fashion. "You must call on my mother so that she may give you all the details."

"I shall be certain to do so," said Vanessa. Another burst of laughter came from the manly group around the fire, catching her attention.

After the initial greeting by their hostess, the gentlemen had been left to their own devices. They had at once fallen into talk of the likely sport to be had that day and each new arrival began the same round of queries and opinions. Mr. Pemberton was asked several times of the likelihood of flushing game for the hounds. Mr. Pemberton assured all that his bailiff had located several foxholes and that there would be a capital run.

Now that the last of the latecomers had arrived, the preliminaries were over and the gentlemen pronounced themselves eager to be off. Mr. Pemberton agreed that the hour was drawing on and he started a general remove to the stables.

The ladies and a handful of elderly gentlemen who were remaining behind came to the door to see the hunters off. The large group prepared to mount amid a flurry of grooms and milling, barking hounds. With smiles and waves and bally-hoos, the riders clattered out of the yard.

Vanessa thought that she would never tire of the excitement generated by a hunt. The red-coated riders exchanged sallies and laughter from the backs of their sleek hunters of bay and gray and white and black. The liver-spotted hounds bounded alongside with barks and shrill yips, while the gardeners' boys ran behind the melee to shout encouragement.

Vanessa gathered the reins a little more firmly into her gloved hands, already enjoying the rhythm of the excellent mare beneath her. She breathed deeply of the chilly air. The swift passage through autumn-tinted splendor was invigorating.

Mr. Pemberton came alongside her. "A fine morning, is it not, Miss Lester?" he inquired with a grin.

"Indeed it is, Mr. Pemberton," said Vanessa, liking the sight of his gleaming eyes and open expression. "I know that I shall enjoy myself very much. No doubt it will be a wonderful hunt."

"I have you to thank for it, Miss Lester. I do not believe that I would have thought of it otherwise," said Mr. Pemberton. He glanced around them at the other riders. "It is a good way to bring all of my neighbors together."

"I hope that Mrs. Dabney is satisfied," said Vanessa.

"My aunt?" Mr. Pemberton turned his head to her. There was a momentary blankness in his expression, which swiftly vanished. "Oh, yes, my aunt! Of course, she is delighted. She likes nothing better than entertaining friends."

"It must have seemed strange to Mrs. Dabney at first, coming into this county. It is probably far different than what she is used to," remarked Vanessa, reflecting idly on that lady's unmistakable air of sophistication.

Mr. Pemberton threw a surprised and somewhat wary glance at her. "Why, what should cause you to say that, Miss Lester?"

"I meant merely that Mrs. Dabney appears to be used to a far grander society than what we offer here," said Vanessa. She flashed a smile. "Your aunt must think all of us terribly countrified."

"Nonsense," said Mr. Pemberton staunchly. "My aunt is all amiability. She likes everyone."

"I think that there may be one or two exceptions," murmured Vanessa.

Mr. Pemberton chuckled. When she directed an inquiring look at him, he smiled a little sheepishly. "I am not all wool, Miss Lester. My aunt and Lady Cecily remind me of two cats, circling one another with raised fur. I do not think that there is much love lost between them. They may speak civilities, but their expressions tell another story."

"You are quite right," said Vanessa. She looked curiously at her companion. Mr. Pemberton had made an acute observation. Surely that was somewhat out of character for someone who had been dismissed by the majority of his peers as a half-wit. But then, it was said that one's faculties sharpened in one area when a handicap was present in another. Perhaps Mr. Pemberton was able to discern some things that others might miss.

"You are more astute than some give you credit, Mr. Pemberton," said Vanessa. She was hailed by Mrs. Leeds and she set heel to her mount to join that lady. As she left her host, she thought that she glimpsed a startled expression on the gentleman's face.

The fox was quickly flushed and the hounds gave chase, baying their excitement. Hounds and hunters alike charged over the uneven ground, jumping all obstacles in their paths as they followed the wily fox's twisting progress.

The field was just as wild and as exhilarating as any of the most exacting riders could have wished. Mr. Pemberton was often in the lead, pointing the way with his intrepid style of riding for those who followed. There were several tumbles taken that served to shake up the fallen, but none were badly enough hurt to give up the sport. Mr. Pemberton himself seemed impervious to danger as he urged on the field.

At one point Mr. Nashe came alongside Vanessa, but his eyes were on their host. "By God, the man can ride!" he exclaimed.

But even the best rider is subject to accident. Vanessa watched Mr. Pemberton's mount lift over a stone fence and clear the ditch behind it as well. The horse landed well, but suddenly the lip of the bank crumbled under the horse's back hooves. The gelding slipped and went down.

Mr. Pemberton was thrown hard over his horse's head. He lay stunned for a second or two as his horse scrambled up and trotted a few yards away.

Most of the field swept on past, only calling out encouragement to their host. But Vanessa reined in to retrieve the horse. She caught up the dragging reins and brought it back. By that time Mr. Pemberton was back on his feet. He brushed himself off, laughing at the anxious queries put by those few of his guests who had stopped.

When Vanessa handed the reins to Mr. Pemberton, he thanked her. Grinning up at her, he said ruefully, "I have made a rare spectacle of myself. My aunt shall roast me finely for it."

"I am certain that Mrs. Dabney will express only a natural concern," said Vanessa.

Mr. Pemberton laughed at that and shook his head. "You do not know my aunt." Immediately he stepped back up into the saddle.

Vanessa saw him wince slightly. She suspected that he had bruised his shoulder when he had landed on it. But Mr. Pemberton gave no other indication of hurt. Instead he clapped spurs to his mount and once more plunged to the front of the field.

It was a long, satisfying day. The shadows drew long and dark over the ground when the hunters turned back to Pemberton Place. Mrs. Dabney and the rest of her guests were waiting. Amid much animated talk, all sought refreshment in the dining hall and the evening concluded with much hilarity and enjoyment.

As the company was breaking up, Reverend Haversaw requested that Vanessa wait upon him the following day if it was convenient to her. Vanessa agreed, thinking that he wished to speak to her about the pony. Shortly thereafter, Lady Cecily and Vanessa returned to Halverton.

Chapter Twelve

The following morning, Vanessa drove herself in the gig to the rectory. Reverend Haversaw greeted her with a slight reserve that puzzled her. But she put it out of her mind as she was greeted by the three Haversaw children.

When the reverend judged that enough of their guest's time had been taken up by childish confidences, he gently shooed the children away with the promise that he and Miss Lester would certainly follow them outside so that they could show off their equestrian prowess. As they made their way out through the gardens, Vanessa listened in as much admiration as amusement as the reverend patiently acknowledged the lively observations that were tossed over his youngsters' shoulders.

Vanessa commented on his gentle management. "You have a gift for listening and encouraging, Reverend. I envy you that."

"We each have our own unique talents and gifts given us of God, Miss Lester," said Reverend Haversaw, smiling. "I am not extraordinary in any degree. You, too, are gifted. I have observed it many times as you encouraged and taught the children to ride."

"I enjoyed it. The children are very sweet," said Vanessa.

A smile hovered over Reverend Haversaw's mouth. "I trust, then, that they have always been on their most saintly behavior."

Vanessa laughed, her eyes alight with humor. "For the most part," she agreed.

They continued down the garden walk. Reverend Haversaw was an avid gardener and through the changing season had often shown Vanessa the altering blooms in his prized beds. Most of the flowers were going dormant, but there was still a splash of color. He escorted her to a stone bench where they could both see the children cantering on the pony in the meadow and enjoy what was left of the garden before it slept for the winter. When she was seated, he remarked, "It is a pleasant time of the year. I have always enjoyed the turning of the seasons."

"Yes," agreed Vanessa. "When I was out riding this morning, I could only wonder at the turning of the leaves. It seemed to happen almost magically overnight."

Reverend Haversaw sat down beside her. His expression sobered until he looked almost grave. "Miss Lester, for some weeks now I have wished to speak with you on a most particular subject. I hope that the time may be deemed appropriate to reveal to you what has been much in my thoughts of late."

"Of course, Reverend," said Vanessa. She was surprised and faintly alarmed by her companion's suddenly serious mien. "It is not Timothy, I trust?"

"It is like you to think first of my son. Your character has proven over and over to be entirely selfless," said Reverend Haversaw warmly. He caught up one of her hands and placed on it a brief salute.

Vanessa was astonished. In all of the years that she had known Reverend Haversaw he had never addressed an overly familiar word to her or made a personal overture of any sort. Now he had done both. With a sudden sense of foreboding, she wondered what the good reverend was working himself up to, for it was obvious that something of import exercised his mind. "Reverend Haversaw, I fear that I do not follow you," she said.

Reverend Haversaw released her hand immediately, himself surprised that he had exercised such a liberty. He shook his head, looking off toward his neat flower beds. "I am no hand at this, certainly."

"Reverend—" began Vanessa.

He turned back and this time captured both of her hands. "Miss Lester, I am a simple man. I have seen a bit more of life than have you and I have three precious children. All of these things must surely weigh against me in the eyes of any lady. Nevertheless, I hope that my sincere affection and my respect for you may speak in my favor." He took a deep breath. "Miss Lester, will you do me the honor of becoming my wife?"

Vanessa was utterly dismayed. She felt nearly speechless. "Reverend, I—" She shook her head helplessly.

He seemed to realize her discomfiture. Releasing her hands, he rose and took a hasty step away from the bench. "I have been too precipitate. Even, perhaps, overly bold. Forgive me, Miss Lester. It was not my intention to distress you. I had only hoped—"

"You need say no more, sir," said Vanessa gently. She rose, her hands tightly clasped before her. "Though I am most reluctant to wound you, sir, honesty compels me to reject your suit."

Reverend Haversaw managed a smile. "I am sorry. I realize now that I should not have spoken."

Vanessa placed her hand lightly upon his sleeve. "Reverend, though I cannot give you the answer that you have asked of me, nevertheless I hope that you will believe me when I say that I honor no man higher. You have been a wonderful friend and your children are a delight to me. But I . . ."

When she seemed to find difficulty in finishing her statement, the reverend gave a melancholy smile. "I do understand, Miss Lester. I knew it and yet I had still hoped. You do not have that regard for me that a woman should have toward the man whom she intends to wed."

Vanessa was highly embarrassed, both for herself and for him. It was the most difficult interview that she had ever experienced. Quietly, she said, "Yes, that is it exactly."

Reverend Haversaw bowed. "I honor your integrity, Miss Lester. We shall not speak of this again. Let us continue as we were, as good friends."

"I should like that, sir," said Vanessa, managing a smile. She wondered whether such a thing was actually possible, for certainly neither of them could ever quite forget what had transpired between them. Their relationship must forever be changed, she thought.

Reverend Haversaw suggested that they return to the drawing room for tea. Vanessa assented. She allowed him to escort her inside, thinking that she would make her escape as soon as good manners allowed.

Reverend Haversaw called his children to join them as a special treat. Over biscuits and cakes the three small children chattered about their innocent deeds. Vanessa actually enjoyed tea because of the children's prattle. The embarrassment and awkwardness between the reverend and herself was quietly dissipated. Vanessa respected Reverend Haversaw's wisdom in providing a way to overcome the awkward situation.

However, some stiffness descended again when it came time for Vanessa to leave. As was his usual custom, Reverend Haversaw walked out with her to the front gate and handed her up into the gig.

"Pray convey my respects and regrets to Lady Cecily. I do not think that I shall see her again this week," said Reverend Haversaw quietly.

Vanessa met the reverend's somber brown eyes. It had been his habit of late to call at Halverton at least once a week for tea. She understood now that this pleasant practice would now end. It was a pity, for she had always enjoyed the reverend's visits. She very much regretted his decision, even as she agreed with its wisdom. "Yes. I shall be certain to do so, sir," she said with equal dignity.

Reverend Haversaw stepped back. "Good day, Miss Lester."

Vanessa gathered the reins and gave her team the office to go. She glanced back once as she turned the corner into the lane, and Reverend Haversaw lifted his hand in farewell.

Vanessa was in an unusually agitated frame of mind when she arrived back at Halverton. The reverend's offer for her hand was the first she had ever received. His declaration had taken her completely by surprise. During the drive, she had come to the conclusion that she had been incredibly naive not to have seen the signs of his increasing devotion.

It had pained her considerably that she had had to turn down the reverend's offer, for Reverend Haversaw was truly one of those rare kind souls one never wished to hurt. And she had hurt him, Vanessa thought. She felt awful. The whole matter had been a terrible experience for them both. If she had been more sophisticated, more intuitive, she might have been able to do more to head off the good reverend's declaration. Certainly if she had been able to hint him away, it would have saved them both from pain and embarrassment and the loss of that former warm friendship that they had enjoyed.

But what puzzled Vanessa most about the whole affair was how the reverend could ever have taken the notion into his head at all. She had never indicated by word or gesture that she wished for a closer relationship with him. She had never encouraged him. Why, then, had he begun to think of offering his suit?

Certainly Reverend Haversaw had not fallen in love with her. He had said that he admired and respected her. That was quite a different thing, as Reverend Haversaw had well known. He had at once understood the reason for her reservations.

Without conceit, Vanessa knew herself to be thought of as one of the wealthiest and most prominent young ladies in the county. It was almost inconceivable that a gentleman in Reverend Haversaw's position could aspire to her hand. He had himself cataloged what might be called his personal detriments. In addition, the reverend was so self-effacing and humble it was difficult to believe that he had come to the decision to ask for her hand on his own.

It was then that the truth hit Vanessa like a bolt of lightning. Reverend Haversaw surely would not have taken his dignity and his courage into his hands that afternoon without first having received strong encouragement that his suit had a chance of prospering. Vanessa had not herself offered that encouragement, but there was one individual who might very well have done so.

Vanessa went at once in search of Lady Cecily. She found her mother in her ladyship's private sitting room. Upon knocking and gaining permission to enter, Vanessa waited only until Lady Cecily's maid had withdrawn from the room before she voiced her suspicions.

"Mother, have you at any time encouraged Reverend Haversaw to dangle after me?" she asked quietly.

Lady Cecily glanced speculatively at her daughter. There

was a tension about Vanessa's person that immediately alerted her. "Of course I have not encouraged the reverend to *dangle* after you, Vanessa. What a vulgar term, to be sure."

"Mother, I wish for you to tell me the truth," said Vanessa. Her voice vibrated with steel and there was a hard expression in her eyes.

Lady Cecily recognized the signs. She realized that she would not be able to fob off the question. Almost petulantly, she said, "Oh, very well. If you are asking whether I have casually pointed out to Reverend Haversaw your many admirable qualities, then, yes, I have done that. That is certainly no more than any mother might do."

"Mother, how could you encourage Reverend Haversaw in such a fashion? Yes, and even put the notion into his head that I might be amenable to his suit! It was utterly inexcusable," said Vanessa heatedly.

"I presume that Reverend Haversaw has made his interest known, then?" asked Lady Cecily, ignoring her daughter's disrespectful tone. "Well! That is more than I ever expected, to be sure!"

"He did more than that, ma'am. Reverend Haversaw made me an offer," snapped Vanessa, taking an agitated turn about the room.

There was a short silence.

"I trust that you did not disappoint Reverend Haversaw," said Lady Cecily.

Vanessa rounded on her mother. Her eyes glinted with suppressed anger. "Disappoint him, Mother? The interview was attended by all of the awkwardness and embarrassment natural to the circumstances. The poor man was humiliated, as was I, to be thrust all unwitting into a situation that should never have come to be. I have greater respect for Reverend Haversaw than ever I did before. It was scarcely due to my efforts that our friendship remains intact despite such a debacle."

"Vanessa!" Lady Cecily sat bolt upright in her chair, clutching the armrests. "Am I to infer that you have actually turned down Reverend Haversaw's most obliging offer?"

"Of course I did! What, did you believe that your sly scheming would result otherwise? Come, ma'am! Reverend

Haversaw is one of the kindest, gentlest, most worthy gentlemen of my acquaintance, but I do not wish to marry him!" exclaimed Vanessa.

"You must marry someone. Why should it not be a gentleman of such sterling character?" snapped Lady Cecily. She saw the implacability settle over her daughter's mouth and she made an effort to soften her tone. "I do not wish you to be unhappy, Vanessa. I am of the opinion that Reverend Haversaw would do very well for you. Pray do not be overly rash. Reflect upon the reverend's flattering offer. He is a man settled in his ways, of a stable character, and he enjoys a good living. Of course, it is not so high a social position as I might wish for you, but assuring your happiness must count for much."

Vanessa felt that she had stomached all that she could. She threw up her hand. "Peace, Mother! I'll not hear another word spoken about it. I have turned down Reverend Haversaw as gently as I was able, but with absolute finality. He will not speak of it again, and nor shall I."

"Naturally you must not broach the subject again. That would be unbecomingly forward. However, Reverend Haversaw may be encouraged to come to the point again if only you would—"

"Listen to me closely, Mother. I have no intention of being thrust into marriage. You may as well set aside all of your schemings to see it otherwise," said Vanessa. "If I discover that you have approached Reverend Haversaw upon this subject again, or anyone else, I shall at once inform the gentleman that you are acting out of a misguided fantasy. I fancy he would be wary of anything that you said to him after that."

"You are a great fool," said Lady Cecily with cold fury.

"No, ma'am, that position you have reserved for yourself," snapped Vanessa. "I tell you, I shall not tolerate such impertinent tinkering with my life. I am well able to manage my own affairs, which I trust that you will recall in future."

"Why, you insufferable little twit," gasped Lady Cecily, almost rendered speechless by outrage.

A glimmer of humor shot into Vanessa's eyes. "I am scarcely little, as you must agree, Mother," she said dryly. She made an effort to retrieve her loss of temper and spoke in a more moderate tone. "I warn you, ma'am, such manipulations as you have exhibited regarding Reverend Haversaw must end. They will only come to naught and our relationship, such as it is, will suffer. Pray do not compel me to address this issue again." She strode rapidly to the door, opened it, and left the sitting room.

Lady Cecily rose from her chair. She made a swift turn about the drawing room, her skirts swishing. Her maid entered quietly to inquire whether her ladyship required anything. "No! I wish only to be left alone!"

Lady Cecily did not even notice her maid's exit. She sat down at her desk, still seething. Her expression was cold and her eyes had narrowed to pinpoints of temper. Restlessly, she drummed her nails on the satiny wood surface of the desk.

She had already rejected her daughter's remonstrance. What could Vanessa do, after all? Lady Cecily doubted very much that Vanessa would actually go to the length of informing her admirers that they were the focus of matchmaking plots. That recourse would be attended by a certain embarrassment and was one that Lady Cecily could not imagine undertaking for herself. Surely Vanessa would not be so lost to her own consequence that she would willfully court such embarrassment.

She must get the obstinate girl wedded.

Never in her fondest dreams had Lady Cecily expected Reverend Haversaw to actually spring forward with an offer. He had seemed to be a rather flimsy hope. But now that the reverend had done so, and had been rejected, Lady Cecily was more determined than ever to do whatever she could to bring another gentleman up to scratch.

Mark Nashe and Howard Pemberton were the only other true eligibles in the neighborhood. One or the other must be made to make Vanessa an offer.

Lady Cecily refused to entertain the possibility that Vanessa could again reject a suit. It was not to be contemplated. Her daughter would be wed. She would see to that. All that was required was the exercise of determination and wit.

Chapter Thirteen

The relationship between Vanessa and Lady Cecily was noticeably strained. All in the Halverton household speculated over the meaning of it, but few came close to guessing the real reason. Only Tremaine knew the true story. He had gently pried it from Vanessa herself. Tremaine had shaken his head over Lady Cecily's foolishness. Her ladyship's scheming had cost her daughter a precious friendship and Vanessa would not soon forget it.

"The thing of it is, Howard, is that I was too complacent. I did not realize that Lady Cecily would go to such lengths as to encourage a gentleman when there was no basis for it," said Vanessa.

"Her ladyship has undoubtedly laid other groundwork," warned Tremaine.

Vanessa nodded. "Oh, undoubtedly. But I am wise now and I hope that I may see the signs before the circumstances come to a head as they did with Reverend Haversaw. You may well believe that I shall take whatever measures are required to nip them in the bud."

"At least there is respite for you in Lady Akers's arrival," said Tremaine.

"Yes, indeed! It is wonderful having Lady Akers here. It is almost as though we have never been parted," said Vanessa, smiling.

"This evening's dinner party in Lord and Lady Akers's honor will undoubtedly prove entertaining," said Tremaine.

"So I hope. And planning for such a large party must surely have given my mother's thoughts a different turn," said Vanessa.

Tremaine agreed, but with reservations. Lady Cecily was not easily sidetracked. He had shown Vanessa her ladyship's guest list, which had included every unwed gentleman in the county and every male houseguest known to be at that moment staying with any of their neighbors.

Vanessa had glanced up from it and met her secretary's wise eyes. "It seems to me that Lady Cecily's list is too short, Howard," she had said quietly. "Pray add those personages that come most readily to your mind."

Thus it was that the company of guests that evening had swelled in number so that the dining room was filled to capacity. There were as many unattached ladies as gentlemen since Tremaine had been careful to include a note in the invitations that all of their neighbors' houseguests were also welcome.

Many of the new faces had recently come down from London for the hunting season just as the guests of honor, Lord and Lady Akers, had done. The gathering had therefore been lent a peculiarly metropolitan glitter that did it no disservice in anyone's eyes, least of all in Lady Cecily's. Her ladyship had felt cold outrage that her private dinner party had been transformed by means unknown. However, now Lady Cecily basked in complacent certainty that the evening had become a gala event.

Even a young earnest excise officer was not immune to the heady atmosphere. It was rare that Lt. Copperidge had been granted the opportunity to be a part of such a party and he had relaxed considerably. He nodded thanks to the butler for refilling his wineglass.

Smiling at a witticism that had caused a burst of laughter, Lt. Copperidge picked up his glass. At the first sip, he stiffened. His thoughts slammed into a furious track. He drank again, only to be certain of what he was tasting. Dull color surged into his lean cheeks. With absolute certainty he knew that a contemptuous hand had directed this outrage.

Lt. Copperidge jumped to his feet, overturning his chair. He snatched the bottle from the butler, slopping wine onto the white linen tablecloth.

"Sir!" exclaimed Sims, outraged.

All heads turned and conversation faltered. Lt. Copperidge

paid no heed. He stepped close to the lighted candelabra and turned the bottle to the light.

"Is there anything wrong, Lieutenant?" asked Vanessa quietly, attempting to take control of the unexpected interruption.

The lieutenant looked up. There was an expression of vivid anger on his face. "Yes, Miss Lester, there is most definitely something wrong! This is a French wine, outlawed by the trade embargo between Britain and France!"

Vanessa threw a swift glance toward her butler. The man's expression was aghast. As well it should be, she thought grimly. "I am sorry for the shock, Lieutenant. I was not aware that we possessed any such at Halverton. You may rest assured that we do not make a practice of free trading. It is undoubtedly one laid down a generation ago, perhaps by my grandfather."

The excise officer's expression registered disbelief. "Too brown by half, ma'am! I do not accuse you personally, but there are those present who no doubt seek to make a maygame of me. But I know my position and my duty. I shall not bow to such ridicule!"

"Really, Lieutenant! This passes far enough. It is but a bottle of wine. Pray make your apologies and sit down!" exclaimed Lady Cecily imperiously.

"That I shall not, my lady!" Lt. Copperidge glanced slowly around the dinner table at the faces that were all turned in his direction. Most were familiar to him from his sojourn in the county, but there were several strangers present, as well. It would not be beyond any one of them to play such a trick on an honest excise officer, he thought bitterly.

Not one face showed friendliness or sympathy toward him, unless one counted Howard Pemberton's frowning confusion as benign. Even Miss Lester, whom he had come to regard in a certain friendly light, registered a faintly distant expression.

"You make a mountain out of a molehill, young man," said an older gentleman with a touch of contempt.

Lt. Copperidge rounded on the man, glad for a target upon which to vent his lonely frustration. "Are you indeed so blasé, sir? Perhaps I shall search your cellars once I have finished with Halverton."

"*What* did you say, Lieutenant Copperidge?" Lady Cecily's voice snapped like a whip. "I assure you, you will do no such thing at Halverton!"

The exclamations came thick and fast. "An outrage, that's what it is!"

"On the contrary, it is too amusing. We have never had such a scene played out in London."

"I shall have your stripes for this impertinence, sirruh!"

"Hah! The crowing of a banty rooster!"

"I do not understand why the man was ever allowed into our circles! Really, I do not!"

The dinner party was in an uproar. Several gentlemen leaped to their feet. One offered to give the excise officer a good caning. Lt. Copperidge stood at bay, his posture very straight. There was a thin smile on his face that spoke volumes. His cause was just and right and he would proudly bear the consequences of performing his duty.

Lord Akers leaned past his wife, who sat perfectly immobile in her chair with an expression of horrified astonishment. "My dear Miss Lester, if something is not done and soon, your guests will rend that young gentleman limb from limb," he said quietly.

"Yes, I know." Vanessa sought out the butler's frozen face. He gave an imperceptible shake of his head. She interpreted it as an apology. But much good that did to settle the dust, she thought.

Vanessa laid aside her napkin and stood up. She picked up her knife and tapped it insistently against her glass for quiet. A few heard the ringing and turned toward her, their voices dying away.

When Vanessa had at last gained everyone's attention, she said, "There is no need for this commotion. Lieutenant Copperidge, pray step into my study with me and we shall discuss this matter more fully."

"There is nothing to discuss, Miss Lester," said Lt. Copperidge. He was acutely aware that he had created a hideous stir, something that was simply not done, and he did not know how to extricate himself gracefully. However, he was too proud to back down from the stand that he had taken. "Halverton is obviously consorting with smugglers. I shall order a search to be made of the premises and any contraband found shall be seized."

Murmurs again started to arise, but Vanessa once more tapped her glass. "I do appreciate your sentiments, but I ask that discretion prevail," she said, glancing around at her neighbors. Her words were received by some with visible reluctance.

Squire Leeds addressed the excise officer. "These are wild accusations, boy," he said warningly.

"Nevertheless I stand by them, sir," said Lt. Copperidge grimly.

"I think it best that you leave at once, young man," said Lady Cecily. "You have disgraced yourself and brought humiliation down upon my home. I shall not tolerate another moment of this insult."

"As you will, my lady," said Lt. Copperidge, giving a jerky bow. He strode out of the hushed dining room, all gazes following him. The bottle of French wine was still clutched in his hand, but no one chose to challenge his possession. The door swung shut behind him.

All eyes turned collectively to Vanessa, who still stood. She looked around. A slight smile touched her lips. "I must apologize. I hope that you will not allow this contretemps to spoil the remainder of our dinner." She signaled the butler and the footmen to begin serving again and sat down.

Lady Akers reached out and squeezed her hand. "Oh, Vanessa, I am so sorry," she whispered.

Vanessa shook her head, still smiling. "We shall muddle through, Cressy," she said, hoping that it was true.

The guests made a show of resuming their meal. But no one could think of anything else except what had happened and it became the general topic of a spirited discussion.

At the head of the table, Lady Cecily sat in cold fury. The dinner party that she had contemplated with such pride was in a shambles. Her guests were muttering and exclaiming over Lt. Copperidge's outrageous, odious behavior. She overheard the squire murmur into her butler's ear a recommendation that any more such bottles of wine should be immediately lost.

Several of the ladies began to express their opinion that the hour was growing late. Some of the gentlemen were quick to pick up on it and agreed that it was fast approaching time to take their leave of Halverton.

Vanessa tried valiantly to stem the rising tide of disengagement. She conversed with her partners on either side of her with determined cheerfulness. At that point it mattered little what others might think about the accusations that had been laid at Halverton's door. More important, no one must go away with a bad taste for Halverton hospitality lingering in their mouth. That was just the sort of ill feeling that could blossom into the worst sort of poisonous gossip.

Mr. Pemberton rose to his feet. Raising his wineglass, he said, "A toast! A toast to Lieutenant Copperidge!"

A stunned silence greeted him. Mr. Pemberton gazed about him, unaffected alike by censure and disbelief. "The fellow discovered the best wine in the house," he said with his wide grin.

"Aye, and he has run off with it, too," said one gentleman sourly. A guffaw greeted this sally.

Mr. Pemberton's grin faded a little. Falteringly, he asked, "But isn't there any more?"

There was another stunned silence, then a spluttering laugh.

"I'll wager that there is, indeed! Let us break out the rest before he thinks to come back for it!" exclaimed the sour gentleman, his countenance transforming.

"Well said, Pemberton!" exclaimed Squire Leeds. He also got to his feet, wineglass in hand. "To Lieutenant Copperidge. May we thank him for sniffing out the best!"

"Hear, hear!"

"Bring up the rest, old fellow!"

"Aye! We know now what Halverton has hidden away!"

The butler looked to Vanessa for direction. She nodded, a smile flickering over her face.

The rest of the evening was one of convivial merriment. The guests were determined to save Halverton from the disgrace of being forced to give up what had been pronounced contraband and the wine flowed copiously. When at length the ladies withdrew from the dining room and retreated to the drawing room, it was with the awareness that their spouses would be long in joining them. The gentlemen had all expressed their determination to drink up all of the incriminating evidence.

When at last the dinner party could be said to be over, the greater number of gentlemen had to be helped into, or even carried to, their carriages.

The front door was closed at last and the ladies of Halverton were alone. Lady Cecily gathered her skirt and put her hand on the balustrade. "Never in my life have I presided over such a drunken set," she said distastefully.

Vanessa agreed, but thoughtfully. "It ended rather well, however. I do believe that if it had not been for Mr. Pemberton's unwitting intercession, we would have seen all of our guests leave before dessert. That would have been disastrous."

"Yes." Lady Cecily reflected for a moment. "I never thought I would have occasion to be grateful to Mr. Pemberton. I shall make a point of being kind to him when next I see him."

"And Mrs. Dabney?" asked Vanessa quizzingly.

"I shall be polite," said Lady Cecily majestically. She swept upstairs.

Vanessa was about to follow when the butler requested a short word with her. Vanessa stepped over to him. "Yes, Sims?"

"I am sorry, miss. I wasn't thinking proper or otherwise I would have made certain that exciseman was served from another bottle," he said apologetically.

"It is of no matter now. I doubt that there is anything left in the cellars for Lieutenant Copperidge to find," said Vanessa dryly.

The butler's expression registered shock. "You'll never let the excise troops to search Halverton, miss!"

"The best way to curb suspicion is to invite your opponent into your house," said Vanessa. "We shall lay all of our cards on the table, Sims. At least, those cards that we wish Lieutenant Copperidge to see. I trust that you take my meaning?"

"Yes, miss," said Sims slowly. He looked at her with enlarged respect. "Lieutenant Copperidge shall find nothing, miss. I promise you that."

"Thank you, Sims. That is all I ask." Vanessa started toward the stairs, then paused. "By the by, Sims, *is* there anything left of my father's best selections after this evening's inroads?"

The butler allowed himself a prim smile. "There came a point when the gentlemen would not have been able to tell excellent French wine from the rawest blue ruin, miss. Nor did they seem to care overmuch."

Vanessa chuckled as she went up to bed. She allowed her maid to undress and ready her for bed. When she slipped under the covers, her most prominent thought was that she was exceedingly glad that the evening had ended.

Next morning, Lt. Copperidge presented himself at Halverton to offer an apology to Lady Cecily and Miss Lester. He did not excuse his behavior in any way, but instead stood quite still while Lady Cecily read him a stern lecture on proper deportment. Only the rigidness of his jaw betrayed how tightly his emotions were being held in check.

Recalling abruptly that Lt. Copperidge was one of her daughter's admirers, Lady Cecily stopped short in her discourse. "But I have said enough! Lieutenant Copperidge, I accept your apology in the spirit in which it was given. I trust that in future I shall have no cause to be angry with you."

"No, my lady," said Lt. Copperidge, somewhat woodenly.

Vanessa judged it time to rescue the lieutenant from Lady Cecily's overpowering presence. "Lieutenant Copperidge, if you will be so good as to accompany me to my study, I have a matter that I wish to discuss with you."

Lt. Copperidge bowed. He took his leave of Lady Cecily and then politely gestured for Vanessa to precede him out of the drawing room. She led him past the stairs to one of the doors that led onto the hall.

When Vanessa entered the study, she turned to the excise officer. "Lieutenant, you mentioned that you wished to search Halverton. I am giving to you my permission to do so. I ask only that your troops show proper respect for my house."

Lt. Copperidge shook his head. In his view her offer was an oblique insult. Somewhat stiffly, he said, "While I appreciate your expression of cooperation, Miss Lester, it is not necessary. I shall not inaugurate a search of Halverton at this time."

Vanessa raised her brows. "Pray, what has altered your decision, sir?"

The excise officer permitted himself a thin smile, but it did not quite reach his eyes. "I suspect that such a search would prove to be futile, ma'am."

Vanessa contemplated him for a long moment. "As you will, Lieutenant," she said quietly.

He bowed.

Vanessa walked to the door and opened it. "Thank you for coming this morning, Lieutenant Copperidge. The gesture was sincerely appreciated."

Lt. Copperidge left the study. His boots beat a rapid retreat on the marble tiles of the entry hall. A few seconds later, Vanessa heard the front door open and shut again. She left the study and returned to the drawing room, where she knew that Lady Cecily would be awaiting her. She looked at her mother with the glimmer of a smile. "Lieutenant Copperidge will not be searching Halverton after all, ma'am."

"I am exceedingly happy to hear it," said Lady Cecily. "You have handled it very well, Vanessa, better than I expected."

"It was not I, but Lieutenant Copperidge. He declined the opportunity to search Halverton," said Vanessa, frowning slightly. "It has made me wonder a little at his reasoning."

"His reasons are of no moment to me," said Lady Cecily. "I perceive only that Lieutenant Copperidge, despite his disgraceful display yesterday evening, has some faint notion of what is due to our position. Undoubtedly the lieutenant's aberration in proper behavior comes from being a younger son. I am reluctant to pass judgment, of course, but I feel that he has grave omissions in his social breeding."

"I think your opinion too harsh, ma'am," said Vanessa.

"Pray, what other explanation could there be? I know that you took an early and completely unreasonable liking to that young man, Vanessa, but pray do not carry it too far," said Lady Cecily. "Even you cannot completely excuse Lieutenant Copperidge's behavior."

"No, I do not excuse him, ma'am. Merely, I believe that

Lieutenant Copperidge's zeal and earnest desire to accomplish his duty led him into an indiscretion that he now regrets," said Vanessa.

"No doubt that is true enough," said Lady Cecily. "He will certainly regret it even more when he discovers that he no longer finds a place on any hostess's guest list."

Vanessa looked gravely at her mother. "And yours, too, ma'am?"

"Well, you cannot expect me to have him at Halverton now!" said Lady Cecily. "Really, Vanessa, it is the outside of enough when I consider that I allowed you to bring an excise officer in on us to begin with."

"I do understand. I only regret that it has ended in this unfortunate way," said Vanessa, thinking about the lieutenant's leavetaking. There had been something final about it. The excise officer had drawn an unmistakable line between them. She had lost another friend, but this time it had not come about through any machinations of Lady Cecily's.

"Perhaps it is just as well," said Lady Cecily. "I never really considered Lieutenant Copperidge to be quite worthy of you, Vanessa."

Vanessa looked over at her mother, her fine brows raised. "Was Lieutenant Copperidge ever a possibility, ma'am?"

Lady Cecily studiously avoided her daughter's quizzical glance. "Why, as to that, only you could have made the final judgment. But let us not be forever boring on about that excise officer. I wished to discuss with you the Nashes' ball and supper. I did not wish you to appear again in that mauve crepe and so I took the liberty of ordering a new gown to be made up for you. It was delivered while you were closeted with Lieutenant Copperidge and I had it taken up to your room. You will be delighted with it, I am certain."

Vanessa stared. "A new gown?" Suspicions instantly popped into her mind. "Mother, I have told you before that I shall observe the very letter of our mourning. My crepe will do very well until then."

"Perhaps you should suspend judgment until you have tried on the gown," said Lady Cecily with an icy smile. "Then if you dislike it, you may send it back."

"Be assured that I will do just that, ma'am," said Vanessa.
She turned on her heel and left the room with but one thought
on her mind. She would indeed look at this gown that Lady
Cecily had commissioned.

Chapter Fourteen

The gala ball and dinner at Nashe Hall was attended by every person of note in the county. Vanessa went with her mother, wearing the new gown that Lady Cecily had commissioned. Vanessa had been prepared to return the dress, but when she saw it she decided that Lady Cecily was not far off after all in what was suitable for the waning days of her mourning. The gown was an amaranth silk, cut on becoming lines. The soft purple shade was the first color that Vanessa had worn in months and it garnered for her several compliments.

The company quickly filled the ballroom and adjoining supper and card rooms. Despite the formal nature of the affair, there was an indefinable air of familiarity about the atmosphere. Vanessa knew every face, even those who had just come down from London only a week or two previously to join a house party. However, there was one glaring absence and it was commented upon frequently.

Directly after the hunt, Mr. Pemberton had announced that he was leaving the neighborhood with the express intention to visit his parents. One local wit expressed the hope that Mr. Pemberton would be able to make his way safely across England without becoming lost.

That week Vanessa had missed her morning rides with Mr. Pemberton. It did not seem quite the same without him. She had even asked her taciturn groom to ride in attendance, thinking that his presence would alleviate the vague loneliness that she felt. But it had not sufficed.

Odd how Mr. Pemberton's company had grown to feel so natural and comfortable. Undoubtedly the ease between them

stemmed from the mutual love that they both had for the land
and for equestrian exercise. Certainly there had been no great
intellectual depth to their conversations, thought Vanessa, as
she smiled politely at her dance partner's venture into humor.
But neither had there been this tedious game of flirtation. As
the movement of the dance allowed her to turn away from her
partner, Vanessa smothered a yawn.

Lady Cecily watched her daughter twirl about on the dance
floor. She tapped her fan into her palm. Beyond a polite greeting, Mr. Nashe had not once approached Vanessa that evening.
Vanessa had not lacked for partners, of course. Nearly every
gentleman in the room had asked to lead her out in a set. However, Lady Cecily was after bigger fish than a plain mister
from London or the compliments of a married lord with a rov-
ing eye.

The truth of the matter was that Lady Cecily was growing
impatient. The efforts that she had made to get her daughter
wed had not progressed as she had hoped. She had done everything necessary to effect a quick denouement. She had established an acceptable social footing with all of the
better-connected families in the county. She and Vanessa had
entertained and been entertained. She had even drawn a lowly
excise officer into her circle of acquaintances based solely on
the circumstance that Vanessa had taken a peculiar fancy to
the gentleman's company. And only see what had come of
that!

There had been flattering notice taken of Vanessa by Mark
Nashe and Mr. Pemberton. The excise officer, Lt. Copperidge,
had seemed to be something of a dark horse but nevertheless
an outside hope. But none of these gentlemen appeared to be
at all in a hurry to declare themselves.

Unfortunately, her scheming had completely misfired with
the reverend. Lady Cecily still viewed the patent loss of Reverend Haversaw as one of Vanessa's admirers with bad grace.

Yet perhaps Vanessa's rejection of the reverend's offer was
for the best, reflected Lady Cecily. Lord and Lady Nashe had
bestowed their smiling approval on Vanessa of late. That must
surely influence Mr. Nashe.

Lady Cecily judged that her careful seeds had finally begun

to sprout. She had casually broadcast to the Nashes how well the estate had been managed over the years; that Halverton was unencumbered; and that Vanessa was sole heir to all of Halverton and would take all with her to a husband. Lady Cecily had carefully watered these seeds, expecting them to appeal to proud but somewhat penurious nobility.

How well Lady Cecily knew the type. Her father had been the perfect example and he had virtually sold his daughter for financial relief. Now Lady Cecily was using the same sweetened hook with her own daughter as bait. If Lady Cecily ever felt the least twinge of conscience, she instantly dismissed it with the reasoning that Vanessa could do worse than accepting an offer from Mr. Nashe. For all intents and purposes, Mr. Nashe was the most eligible bachelor that the county could boast.

Over the past few months, Lady Cecily had observed with mingled impatience and hope the growing attentions that Mr. Nashe lavished on Vanessa. She sensed that Mr. Nashe was on the brink of making an offer. However, Mr. Nashe had continued to be elusive. It was most frustrating.

Lady Cecily suddenly saw Mark Nashe cross the ballroom to claim her daughter's hand; then he led Vanessa into the refreshment room. Lady Cecily's eyes narrowed as she regarded the couple's departure. Perhaps Mr. Nashe was going to come to the point at last. It would be wonderful indeed if an understanding could be reached this very evening, she thought.

Lady Cecily was not far off in her assumptions. Mr. Nashe did have that very idea in mind, as Vanessa quickly discovered. She had been glad of the suggestion to leave the hot ballroom for refreshment. Vanessa accepted a lemon ice from Mr. Nashe with a smile and a gracious word.

Mr. Nashe inclined his head. He glanced around them at the small throng that was also crowding the refreshment table. "It is too crowded here for you to properly enjoy the ice," he remarked. He held out his hand. "Come; there is a small alcove just off the ballroom where we can observe the dancers. You may be comfortably seated and we may talk without competing over this chatter."

"I own, that sounds most welcome," said Vanessa, accepting his escort.

Mr. Nashe led her out of the refreshment room and to the promised destination. He seated Vanessa, then appropriated the other end of the settee. "This is much better," he said, resting an arm along the back of the settee. "If my father notices our informal tête-à-tête, pray pretend that you have not seen his disapproving face."

Vanessa chuckled. "Is Lord Nashe such a stickler, then?"

"Invariably. However, I daresay that my sister and Lord Akers will enliven the evening to a degree that his lordship is so unaccustomed that he will scarcely notice my neglect of our other guests," said Mr. Nashe, smiling.

"It is lovely having Lady Akers here. We have enjoyed several long talks this past week," said Vanessa.

"No doubt," said Mr. Nashe politely.

Vanessa glanced at her companion. His lack of enthusiasm for his sister's return was palpable. "Do you not care for Lady Akers's visit, sir?" she asked.

Mr. Nashe flashed a smile. "It is always worthwhile to see one's relations again, of course. But it is not my sister that I wished to discuss with you, Miss Lester." He took her free hand between his own. Looking into her face, he said, "Miss Lester, I realize that I have chosen an unconventional place to declare myself. However, I feel that we have become such good friends that you must excuse it. Miss Lester, will you do me the honor of entertaining my suit for your hand?"

Vanessa felt awkward. One hand was holding her ice; the other was grasped in a firm hold. "You have surprised me enormously, Mr. Nashe," she said quietly. "I scarcely know what to say."

"You may begin by addressing me by my given name, Mark," said Mr. Nashe, smiling again.

Vanessa gently attempted to free her hand. He would not let her go. She shook her head. "Mr. Nashe—"

"Mark," he insisted.

"Very well. Mark, I am fully conscious of the honor that you have done me. However, I fear that I cannot give you the answer that you desire," said Vanessa. She tried again to loose her hand and this time he let her go. She set down the ice on a small round table beside the settee, avoiding his eyes. She was half-afraid of his reaction, not knowing what the depth of his disappointment might be. It was really too bad that she must turn down another gentleman so soon.

"I do not despair, however," said Mr. Nashe.

Vanessa glanced around at him in surprise. His expression was the same as always, faintly amused and world-weary. "Do you not?" she asked curiously.

Mr. Nashe laughed. "Not at all, Miss Lester. I may call you Vanessa, I hope? For you see, I am well aware that I have caught you off balance. Why, you had to think about where to put that ice amidst the surprise of my declaration. That was very ill-planned on my part, I must confess. The next time that I offer for you, I shall do so in a less awkward circumstance."

Vanessa was dismayed. Surely he had understood that her refusal was final. "Forgive me, sir, but I do not believe that my answer shall ever alter," she said quietly.

Mr. Nashe stood up and held out his hand to her. "One never knows, Vanessa. Shall I escort you back to your chair?"

"Yes, please," said Vanessa with some relief. She did not quite know how to counter Mr. Nashe's sudden leap in familiarity with her. She supposed that since she had availed herself of his permission to use his first name, he had presumed that the same permission had been granted to him. It was awkward now to tell him that he was mistaken in his reasoning. She needed time in which to reflect upon this surprising turn of events. Never had she considered that Mr. Nashe would ever offer for her. The very thought was ludicrous, for they simply did not suit.

After Mr. Nashe had returned Vanessa to her chair, he stayed a few moments to talk on idle topics before he sauntered away. Vanessa saw that her mother was trying to catch her eye and she immediately pretended that she had found a piece of torn lace on her gown. Vanessa rose and walked quickly toward the mending room, where sewing maids waited to make quick repairs, but then she ducked quickly out into the garden.

The air was cold and she shivered a little. Her sleeves were short, but fortunately she had brought a lovely Norwich shawl with her gown and she drew it over her shoulders and bare arms.

Vanessa stepped slowly down the wide marble steps. She found an out-of-the-way bench and sat down on it. It was cold, yes, but there was the advantage of being able to order her thoughts before her mother asked about Mr. Nashe's maneuver of taking her off for a semiprivate tête-à-tête. Vanessa was absolutely certain that Lady Cecily was going to react badly to the information that Mr. Nashe had solicited her hand and had been turned down. Vanessa wanted to be able to weather the storm with her own composure intact.

She looked up at the brilliant night sky. There was almost a full moon and the garden was very well lit, but the corner in which she had ensconced herself was in deep shadow from the hedges. Vanessa could hear the music of the orchestra and the laughter and din of conversation.

Almost absently she took note of the crack of a broken branch behind the hedge. Then she heard quick steps and a low query.

"Yes, it is me! Do not speak again, only listen. It will be to-morrow night at the same place. Is there any word of the Frenchman?"

There was a muffled question and a sharp reply.

Vanessa had stiffened. She listened with appalled comprehension. This was talk of a clandestine rendezvous a day hence, of a Frenchman. There were no French among the house parties in the county. That meant that this allusion was to a spy. And that voice. It sounded tantalizingly familiar. She strained, trying to place that voice.

The meeting was swiftly over. Vanessa listened to the vanishing footsteps, absolutely riveted to the stone bench. The cold had seeped into her limbs and she was shivering in earnest, but she did not notice it.

It occurred to her that whoever had been speaking might come upon her. She glanced around with quick anxiety. It would not do to be caught where it was obvious that she had been able to eavesdrop. But equally dangerous would be running into one of the conspirators as she returned to the house.

Vanessa sat for a moment longer, caught by indecision. She suddenly realized it would be best just to be away from the hedge even if she did meet someone on the way. At least then she could only be suspected of eavesdropping.

Vanessa stood up and swiftly made her way back up the marble steps. She was tense, at every moment waiting to be hailed. But she saw no one, nor was there any to call out to her.

Vanessa reentered the ballroom. She looked around quickly, but no one appeared to pay the least interest to her entrance. Vanessa stood still for a moment, uncertain of what she should do. Her first instinct was to confide in someone what she had overheard. It had been so disturbing. There was something about that one voice, some quality about it, that made her certain that she had heard it before.

Vanessa's gaze lighted on Lt. Copperidge's tall figure. The excise officer was standing a little apart from the rest of the company. His behavior at Halverton's party had earned him censure. It would not have been surprising if Lt. Copperidge had been socially ostracized, but a few in the neighborhood had spoken up for him. The squire and Reverend Haversaw had both said that the young officer had been merely overzealous in his duties. Lady Cecily had let drop that she had accepted the excise officer's apology, and since her ladyship had chosen to excuse Lt. Copperidge, others followed her lead.

Vanessa made up her mind. Despite her misgivings, it was patently her patriotic duty to divulge the little that she had heard to the excise officer.

"Lieutenant Copperidge!"

He turned. When Lt. Copperidge saw who it was that had hailed him, he bowed. "Miss Lester."

His manner was reserved, but Vanessa cared little enough for that. She glanced around briefly to be certain that there was no one within direct earshot. "Lieutenant, I have just chanced to overhear the most extraordinary thing."

At once Lt. Copperidge's gaze sharpened. "Have you, indeed?" He took her elbow and turned her toward the window embrasure. "Let us move a little more to the side, Miss Lester. I do not wish us to be interrupted."

When they stood beside the heavily draped window, he let go of her elbow. "Now, Miss Lester, what was it that you overheard?"

Vanessa told him in succinct words. She looked at him, frowning. "That was all, but it greatly disturbed me. I caught at once the significance of the allusion to the French. What do you think that it means, Lieutenant?"

Lt. Copperidge's face was quite expressionless but for his eyes. His gray gaze burned with a hot light. "I believe that you have stumbled upon a clue to the identity of some of those who could be involved in smuggling, at best. At worst, there is a traitor among us."

Vanessa said falteringly, "I—I thought that the one man's voice sounded familiar. I know that I have heard it somewhere before."

"Do you recall whose it was, Miss Lester?" asked Lt. Copperidge sharply.

She shook her head. "Unfortunately, no. They were speaking so quietly, you see. I would not have paid any attention at all except that I heard that one phrase and then I simply had to listen."

"Of course. Thank you, Miss Lester. I am indebted to you," said Lt. Copperidge. "I shall act upon your information at once. Perhaps I shall be able to bring this smuggling to an end once and for all. Pray excuse me, for I must take leave of Lord and Lady Nashe." He bowed and strode away.

As Vanessa watched the excise officer across the crowded ballroom, her uneasiness increased. There was suppressed excitement in Lt. Copperidge's very walk. He was wasting no time in acting upon what she had told him. There had been such a hot look in his eyes. In short, he had carried away the information that she had relayed to him with blood in his eye.

Vanessa was buffeted by second thoughts. If Lt. Copperidge was willing to act against the conspirators simply on the basis of a repeated word or two from an imperfectly heard conversation, might he not be so eager that he would order his troops to shoot? She didn't care so much about the smugglers as a whole. But what if the voice she had overheard belonged to one of her neighbors or acquaintances or the brother of one of her friends? If someone was hurt, the blood would be on her hands.

Vanessa was so wrapped up in her unease that she forgot to watch out for her mother. While Vanessa was still reflecting over the possible consequences of her decision, Lady Cecily came up to her.

"Well, Vanessa? What did Mark Nashe have to say to you?" asked Lady Cecily sharply.

Vanessa was taken off balance. Swift color rose in her face. "Oh, Mr. Nashe? It was a brief conversation."

"Did he make you an offer?" demanded Lady Cecily.

Vanessa sighed. She nodded. "Unfortunately, yes. I have rejected his suit."

Lady Cecily stared at her daughter. Her features were quite expressionless except for the hardness of her eyes. "We will talk of this matter again, Vanessa. I will make our good-byes to Lady Nashe. You will join me at the door." Lady Cecily swept around on her heel.

Vanessa grimaced to herself. It was not precisely the perfect end to an evening, she thought. She really had no desire to leave with her mother, who was obviously in a towering rage. But it would be best to humor Lady Cecily and accompany her ladyship home to Halverton. Vanessa would far rather have this matter thrashed out in private.

As soon as the Halverton carriage started away from Nashe Hall, Lady Cecily lashed out at her daughter. "What an unutterable fool you are! I could scarcely believe my ears. You have rejected Mark Nashe! You fool!"

"You may believe what you will, Mother. However, I stand by my decision. Mr. Nashe and I simply do not suit," said Vanessa.

"Nonsense! It is a fine match! I could wish for nothing better for you," exclaimed Lady Cecily.

"Actually, you could wish for nothing better for yourself. Oh, yes! I am quite aware of your ambitions, ma'am. But I'll not marry simply to oblige you," said Vanessa, rather wearily.

Lady Cecily was not deterred in her condemnation. The remainder of the drive back to Halverton was filled with bitter recriminations. Vanessa was never more glad in her life than to step down from the carriage and enter the manor house.

She turned to her mother. "I am going to my study. There are a few matters that I wish to finish before I retire, so I will say good night here, ma'am."

"We are not finished with this conversation, Vanessa!"

Vanessa coolly regarded her mother. "On the contrary, ma'am. It is quite finished where I am concerned. You have made your opinion abundantly clear to me. I trust that I have made my own equally clear. There is nothing more to be said. Good night." She turned away and walked rapidly down the hall.

"Vanessa, I demand that you attend to me!"

Vanessa did not respond. When she reached her study and went in, she shut the door and turned the key in the lock.

Chapter Fifteen

Over the next few days, Vanessa avoided her mother as much as possible. It was uncharacteristic of her, but it certainly was better than enduring another confrontation each time she happened to find herself in her mother's company. She discovered that social activities provided a neat buffer. Vanessa had never thought that she would be grateful for the round of entertainments to which they were committed.

Lady Cecily's displeasure was an ongoing, unavoidable annoyance. Vanessa managed that well enough, but her decision to confide in Lt. Copperidge continued to plague her. She thought over and over about the possible consequences.

As the time of the rendezvous approached, Vanessa felt the urge to confide in someone else and solicit their advice. Her secretary, Howard Tremaine, was the most logical choice. He had grown old in service to her family and he had once dealt with the free traders. But she knew that he would be more anxious on her account than for any question of morality.

Vanessa ran through the short list of those that she trusted. There was the squire. Reverend Haversaw. Mr. Pemberton.

Vanessa shook her head in bewilderment. She did not know why she had even thought of Mr. Pemberton. He was certain to be of no help to her. She supposed it was simply due to the comfortable habit that she had fallen into of talking to him of whatever was on her mind. In this instance, however, poor Mr. Pemberton's easy geniality would be completely wasted.

Vanessa rejected each of the other gentlemen on other grounds. The squire would no doubt recommend that she put the entire incident out of her head. Reverend Haversaw would

look gravely at her and inquire whether she felt that she had
done her duty to the best of her ability.

There was no question of that, Vanessa thought. She moved
restlessly about her study to the window. She gazed out on the
green that sloped down to the woods that marked Halverton's
environs. She had early given her word to Lt. Copperidge that
she would pass on any information that she might come into
possession of that had any bearing on French spying. No, she
had done right. It was not necessary to consult with anyone
else for their reassurance on that fact.

Vanessa turned away from the window. Whatever happened
now was in Lt. Copperidge's hands. Even if it meant the possibility of death for one of her neighbors or a member of her
own household. It was not a pleasant thought.

Vanessa held to her decision until the evening of the rendezvous. Then she could stand it no longer. Her conscience
would not let her rest. She joined her mother for dinner. After-
ward, Lady Cecily retired to her own quarters as Vanessa had
hoped that she would.

Quietly Vanessa sent orders for her mare to be saddled and
she went upstairs to change into her habit.

It was a cold, clear night. The new moon floated in the sky,
its light limning the shadows. It was a perfect night for riding.
Vanessa urged her mount on, any enjoyment she might have
felt tempered by the knowledge that she had taken a dangerous
venture into her hands.

It was mad, really. It was mad to ride to warn a group of
smugglers of a trap. A trap set by the excisemen with the information that she had herself supplied. But the more she had
thought about it, the more she had become convinced that the
low decisive voice she had overheard was known to her.
Something inside her would not let a friend or acquaintance
suffer the consequences of their ill-advised foray into smuggling.

Her mount stumbled into a hole and Vanessa pulled her up.
Vanessa was glad that she had the surefooted mare. Any other
horse would already have gone down.

It was all of five miles to the rendezvous point. Vanessa had covered most of the distance when she heard the flurry of shots. Her heart suddenly in her mouth, she urged the mare into a faster pace.

Suddenly a horse leaped out in front of her. Vanessa turned the startled mare, just managing to keep her seat.

A hand grasped her bridle and a pistol was thrust toward her.

"Not a sound, my friend," said a harsh voice. The other rider backed both horses under cover of the brush, making certain that the pistol was riveted on Vanessa.

The two horses were held very quietly. Vanessa could hear the thrashing of horses and the curses of men, which then faded away. She turned her head to find that her companion was slumped forward over his horses' withers. The pistol dangled from his hand.

"You are wounded," she exclaimed.

The man raised his head. In the moonlight Vanessa saw that he was masked. "A woman?" he murmured. "What black fortune rides me this eve?"

"Perhaps if you were not in such a dangerous trade, your fortune would be more to your liking," said Vanessa tartly.

"Me trade? What mean ye, lass?" asked the man.

"Pray do not bother to disguise your speech at this juncture, sir. I know you to be more than a low ruffian," said Vanessa.

The man chuckled quietly. "I fear that you are bound to be disappointed, ma'am. I am as much a ruffian as the next man."

"Hush," said Vanessa, listening. The search seemed to be returning and she had no doubt that before too many more minutes had elapsed the excise troops would be upon them. "They are returning. We must leave here now."

"True; it does not seem to be a healthy location," said the smuggler.

"Come. I shall take you to a safe spot," said Vanessa, gathering her reins.

The smuggler's hand was still on her horse's bridle. "Can I trust you with my life, ma'am?" he asked, half-mocking.

"It is your choice, sir. Leave me here, dead or alive, and the excise shall certainly find me as a clue to your direction. Or come away with me and trust that I do not lead you into a trap," said Vanessa quietly.

The smuggler released her bridle. He pocketed the pistol. "Lead on, mistress. I am wholly in your hands."

Vanessa did not answer, but at once turned her mare. With the ease of long familiarity, rider and horse faded quickly into the woods. The smuggler followed closely behind.

For several minutes they rode silent, their mounts trodding carefully. Their passage was marked by a scarce rustling of bushes that grazed their thighs and their horses. The search could no longer be heard.

"We are nearly there," said Vanessa softly.

"The abbey, is it?" murmured the smuggler.

Vanessa did not reply, but she shot a sharp glance at her companion. The abbey had been nearly forgotten by most people. No strangers to the county would even know of its existence. More than ever she was convinced that the smuggler was one of her neighbors.

They emerged from the woods into a moonlit meadow studded with silhouetted daisies. She turned her horse sharply left and went through a narrow archway in a shattered wall. The smuggler followed her. The archway opened into what had once been the nave of the abbey. Two centuries before, the abbey had been destroyed in England's bloody civil war. Once prosperous and peaceful, now its ruins lay forgotten and shrouded by the woods.

The roofless court of the abbey was deep-turfed, thick with slim trees and bounded by ragged walls hung deep with ivy. Fluted pillars of stone, ruined and scarred and hacked, rose on four sides. At the end rose another, taller archway with its rounded stone window still intact. The window had once held stained glass, but now thick ivy grown over it framed the night sky. Above the archway floated silver-limned clouds. The moon bathed the ancient, once beautiful abbey with a haunting light.

The smuggler pulled up his mount, looking around. "You have brought me to a quiet place, indeed. I expect the spirits of kindly monks to come forward at any instant to inquire our needs."

"Pray do not be foolish. There are no ghosts here but those of one's own making," said Vanessa, dismounting. She looked up at her companion. "Can you manage?"

"Of course," he said. He swung his leg over the horse's head and slid from the horse, giving a grunt as his boots made impact with the ground. He put his hand up to his shoulder. "It has been jarred a good bit, I fear."

"Sit down there, against that stone," said Vanessa. "I shall see to your wound."

The smuggler hesitated, then nodded. He eased himself down to the thick turf where she had indicated. Vanessa knelt beside him and pulled free the edges of his coat. He sucked in his breath, but said not a word. She looked critically at the seeping wound in his shoulder. "I shall have to remove your coat so that I can bandage it," she said matter-of-factly.

"I begin to wonder what you will require of me next," said the smuggler.

Vanessa glanced into his masked face. "Come now, surely you have not lost your nerve. You must remove your coat."

"Yes, ma'am," said the smuggler meekly. He endeavored to shrug out of the coat and with Vanessa's help managed to do it. He lay back then, spent by the exertion. His mouth was held in a firm line against the pain that had been endured.

Vanessa made as thorough as examination as she could in the moonlight, wishing all the while for a lantern. She saw that the wound was clean. There had been no fracturing of the bone and the bullet appeared to have passed cleanly through. "You are fortunate, sir. The bullet did not lodge itself," she said.

"I am fortunate to have fallen into your fair hands, I think," commented the smuggler in a low tone.

"I shall have to bind it. The bleeding has not yet stopped," said Vanessa, ignoring him. His words had struck almost a flirtatious note. It seemed incongruous that she should be receiving such in these circumstances. She stepped into the deep shadow of the arched wall and turned away so that she could tear a portion off of her petticoat. The rip of the linen seemed loud in the stillness of the old abbey. She tore another strip as long as the first but wider.

Vanessa returned to her companion and knelt beside him. She made a pad and then began binding it about his shoulder.

There was a breath of male laughter in her ear. "You are a darling." His voice was low and threaded with amusement.

Vanessa glanced up for a fleeting second at the masked face above her. Her hands never faltered in knotting the rough bandaging of his shoulder. "I am annoyed, so none of your free gallantries, if you please! You have caused me to be an unwilling accomplice in a crime against the Crown and I have sacrificed my best petticoat besides."

"I should hang," he said contritely.

"Yes, so you should," said Vanessa with asperity. "But instead you shall live to remember this night's work. I hope that it serves to turn you from your wicked ways."

"I shall remember the one who saved my life," he said softly.

Vanessa snorted at that. Whomever the smuggler was, he had a silver tongue in his head. She felt sure that she knew him, but his disguised face and the low timbre of his voice frustrated her efforts at recognition. She gave a last tug and sat back on her heels. "There, I think that it is tight enough now."

"Thank you, my lady." He tested his shoulder cautiously. "Yes, it will do."

Suddenly the smuggler lifted his head. His whole posture, which had been relaxed, became one of listening. "I must be off to a safer lair. The hunters are casting closer."

Vanessa also heard the faint queries and shouted commands. Dismay struck her. The old abbey had been safe enough for such a short time. But it could be discovered at any moment. There could even be someone with the excisemen who had heard of it and they could actually be approaching it at that very moment. She rose gracefully to her feet, the hem of her riding skirt falling to her ankles. "Can you stand?"

"I am not so paltry a creature that a bloodling will poleax me," he retorted, picking up his coat and pushing himself up. He got to his feet. The smuggler swayed suddenly. Vanessa caught his arm to steady him. He put his hand upon her shoulder for a moment and she felt his weight as he regained his balance and breath. "I am worse off than I believed."

"You are fine," said Vanessa encouragingly. Her straining ears had caught again the sounds of the excisemen as the troop coursed the wood. The noises sounded clearer. "Now you must be off."

"So eager to be rid of me?" mourned the smuggler.

"Of course I am. What should I want with a wounded free-booter?" said Vanessa, a smile hovering at her lips.

"You are a hard wench, indeed," he said. He stepped away from her and took up the reins of his horse. Vanessa caught the horse's bridle to steady it while the smuggler mounted. With some clumsiness and difficulty, he got up into the saddle. Vanessa released the bridle and stepped to one side out of the way of the horse. The smuggler looked down at her. "Farewell, my lady. I shall not forget your mercy nor your bravery."

Vanessa laid her palm against the horse's shoulder, looking up at him. His eyes gleamed down at her through the slits of the dark mask. "You will be all right? You will find sanctuary?"

For answer, the smuggler suddenly bent down and with his good arm lifted her up against him. Vanessa's lips parted on a surprised gasp. Then his lips found hers. It was a thorough, totally consuming kiss.

Vanessa was breathless when he let her slip to the ground. She stood staring up at his form silhouetted black against the night sky. Without a word, he turned his mount. He slapped rein and the horse leaped forward. Within seconds the horseman was gone, disappeared into the mist.

Vanessa could well have believed that the entire episode had been a figment of her imagination, except that she could still feel the pressure of his lips against hers. She marveled at herself, for she could find no objection in her to the free-booter's outrageous liberty.

The night air carried a curse to her ears with disconcerting clearness, recalling her with startling speed to her surroundings. It would be prudent to get well away from this place.

Vanessa used a dead log to mount her mare. When she was seated, she gathered her reins and started for home at a cautious walk. She took care to make as little noise in her passage through the wood as possible. When she was free of the wood and had put good distance between herself and the still-searching excisemen, she nudged the mare into quicker motion. Halverton was now scarcely a stone's throw away.

When Vanessa reached the stables, it was to find her groom waiting for her. He had a shielded lantern at his feet. When she dismounted, he at once led the mare inside. Vanessa picked up the lantern and followed.

Hanging the lantern on its nail on one post, she turned toward her groom. He had already stripped the mare and was wiping the steaming flanks dry with wads of straw. "I am grateful that you waited for me, John," she said quietly.

"And wot else would I be doing when ye take it into yer head to ride off wi'out telling anyone where ye be going?" grumbled the groom.

Vanessa recognized that he had been concerned for her. She moved to lay her hand on his shoulder and squeezed the hard-muscled shoulder affectionately. "Thank you, John."

He had turned his head at her approach. His eyes dropped to her skirt and his expression froze. Vanessa glanced down at herself. The light was faint, but it showed the darker area where blood had stained her skirt.

"It is not mine," said Vanessa quietly.

The groom's eyes rose swiftly to meet hers. There was a short pregnant silence, then the groom nodded. "Ye'll be wanting to give that to Rose, the second housemaid, for cleaning, I'm thinking," he said deliberately, turning back to the mare.

Vanessa narrowed her gaze on him. His hands moved rhythmically over the mare's sides and he gave no indication that he was interested in anything else but caring for the horse. Vanessa knew that his suggestion had not been an idle one. The groom had asked no questions, nor had he evidenced more than that one instant of alarm. It was obvious that the man at least suspected what she had been about.

"Good night, John."

Vanessa pulled her cloak close around her and let herself out of the stables. Swiftly she crossed the yard to the side door of the manor. She would indeed do well to give her blood-stained garment into the second housemaid's care. There must be no questions raised by any member of her household over the details of this night's work.

When she reached the side door and pushed the latch, the door swung open independent of her hand. Her butler stood in the passageway, a candle raised above his white head. Vanessa entered quickly and the butler closed the door. "Thank you, Sims. I suppose that all are abed?"

"Safely abed, miss," said the butler, stressing his brief words. He set down the candle and took her damp cloak from her. "I shall see that it is properly aired, miss." Picking up the candle again, he went before her to the small stairs at the back of the house. "Go softly, miss."

"I shall need Rose the second housemaid to take my riding habit," said Vanessa, pausing on the first step.

The butler did not bat an eye. "Of course, miss. I shall awaken her at once and send her up to you. Your own maid is waiting up for your return."

"Thank you, Sims," said Vanessa, digesting that. She climbed the stairs, the tail of her habit draped over her arm. It would be a ticklish matter to persuade her maid to allow a mere second housemaid to take the riding habit. The dresser considered the care of her mistress' wardrobe as being entirely her own special responsibility.

As good fortune would have it, however, the dresser had been suffering from a progressively worsening head cold. When Vanessa entered the bedroom, it was to the sound of a miserable sneeze. "Mattie?" She advanced closer to the fire and was able to discern her maid's puffy eyes and reddened nose. "You should be in bed, Mattie, not waiting up for me!"

"Far be it for me to shirk my duty, miss," said the dresser, sniffing dolefully.

"I will allow you to help me out of this habit, but you are not to do anything else. I insist that you go directly to bed," said Vanessa firmly.

The dresser feebly protested, but in truth she felt so wretched that she wanted nothing more than to be able to comply with her mistress' wishes. She undid the habit and helped her mistress out of it. When she would have carried it away, she was told simply to leave it draped over a chair.

Vanessa finished tying a robe close about her trim waist. "The habit can wait, Mattie. Now go to bed. I intend to slip under the covers myself in a few moments, after I have read a little of my Bible."

"Yes, miss," said the dresser obediently. She saw nothing odd in Vanessa's stated intention because her mistress always ended the day with reading Scripture. As for the habit, there would be no real harm done in leaving it for the morrow. The dresser shuffled off to her own small chamber that was adjacent to Vanessa's and closed the door.

There came a scratching at the bedroom door from the hall. Vanessa went swiftly over to the door and opened it. The second housemaid slipped inside. The woman was in her nightgown and she had thrown a voluminous wool shawl over her shoulders. "Ye wished to see me, miss?" she whispered.

"Yes. Thank you for coming so promptly," said Vanessa in an equally soft voice. She picked up the riding habit and handed it over. "I wished to have my habit cleaned. There is an awkward stain on the front of the skirt. I would be grateful if you would see to it personally."

The second housemaid eyed her shrewdly. "Aye, miss. I'll be doing that. Mr. Sims did say that you asked for me particular. I'll not be letting you down, miss."

"Thank you," said Vanessa.

The second housemaid slipped back out of the bedroom. Vanessa closed the door again. Then she went slowly over to her bed. The covers had been pulled back invitingly. Beside the bed was a stand holding a small branch of flickering candles and her Bible. Vanessa got into bed, made herself comfortable and opened her Bible. It was a night for the Psalms, she thought.

Chapter Sixteen

The following day Vanessa dealt with her dresser's questions concerning the habit by saying that she had not wanted to burden her maid with the soiled garment when she was feeling so poorly. She had therefore delegated the responsibility this once to someone else.

Beyond grumbling that the habit was not as well-pressed as she would have liked, the dresser accepted the explanation. However, with all the familiarity of an old retainer she did scold her mistress over the torn petticoat. "As many years as I have served you, miss, never have you come home with your petticoat in rags," she said.

Vanessa threw up her hand. Her eyes gleaming in amusement, she said, "Let be, Mattie, I pray! I promise not to be so careless again."

"So I should hope, miss," sniffed the dresser, bustling away.

Vanessa went downstairs, glad to escape without further questions. It was one of the advantages of having loyal retainers, she reflected. Neither her groom nor Sims had asked anything about her nocturnal ride. Of course, they at least had shown that they had a fairly shrewd notion of her purpose.

As she crossed the wide hall to enter the dining room, Vanessa hoped that no word of the particulars of last evening's ride became known. The resulting speculations could prove awkward. However, she felt that she could trust those who had been drawn into her little escapade. None of the three members of her household who knew anything would let drop even a hint to anyone else. She had emerged unscathed from her abrupt foray into free-trader business.

When Vanessa entered the dining room, she greeted her

mother with a smile. "I trust that I have not kept you waiting," she said as she was seated by a footman.

"I would inform you of it if it were so," said Lady Cecily indifferently. "You may begin serving, Sims."

While at luncheon, Lady Cecily and Vanessa were informed that Lt. Copperidge and his troop were outside in the hall. "The lieutenant desires speech with your ladyship and Miss Lester," said Sims woodenly.

Vanessa looked quickly at the butler, a question in her eyes. He inclined his head almost imperceptibly. Vanessa drew in her breath slowly. She had been too complacent, after all, in thinking that there would not be repercussions from the night before.

Lady Cecily's thin brows rose in an expression of mingled surprise and hauteur. "I am not in the habit of answering a summons by persons standing in my own entry hall," said her ladyship pointedly.

"No, my lady," said the butler woodenly.

"Pray convey my regrets to Lieutenant Copperidge. It is not a convenient time," said Lady Cecily.

The butler bowed and started to turn away. Vanessa stopped him. "Sims, what sort of humor is Lieutenant Copperidge in?" she asked.

"A most insistent and forceful one, miss," said Sims, patent disapproval displayed in his posture.

"Apparently something untoward has taken place, Mother. Perhaps there has been some alarm along the coast that Lieutenant Copperidge has come to warn us about. Surely it would be prudent to give audience to whatever he might have to say to us," said Vanessa.

Lady Cecily drummed her fingers on the tabletop. She seemed to make up her mind. "Very well! Let it be as you wish, Vanessa. If we do not see him, the man will only return later, perhaps at even a more inconvenient time. Sims, you may inform Lieutenant Copperidge that he may wait upon Miss Lester and me here."

"Very good, my lady," said the butler. He held himself very stiff as he exited, obviously disliking his errand.

Vanessa poured herself another cup of tea. She was glad to

see that her hand did not shake. She supposed that she should not have been surprised that the excisemen would pay a call that day. The shooting had taken place near Halverton, after all. Lt. Copperidge would want to know whether anyone of the household had seen or heard anything.

The butler showed in the lieutenant and a small guard. The grim-faced excisemen appeared threatening in their neat uniforms. Lt. Copperidge bowed to Lady Cecily and to Vanessa. He addressed himself to Lady Cecily, but his intent gaze rested on Vanessa's face. "Forgive this intrusion, my lady. I am here in discharge of my duty."

Lady Cecily gave a cold nod. "Of course, Lieutenant. It is understood. What is it you wished to convey to us?"

"I am searching for a wounded man, my lady, a criminal against the laws of the Crown. A coterie of smugglers was flushed last night." Lt. Copperidge gave a thin-edged smile. "No doubt the shots could be heard even here at Halverton."

"Yes, I believe that I do recall some sort of noise," said Lady Cecily.

"We wounded one of the leaders, but he managed to slip away. I do not believe that he could have done so without aid. Have you any knowledge of this man?" asked Lt. Copperidge.

"Certainly not. I am not in the habit of consorting with such low characters," said Lady Cecily.

"And you, Miss Lester?" The lieutenant's eyes had scarcely wavered from Vanessa's face.

Vanessa shook her head. "I am sorry, Lieutenant. I know of no one at Halverton who has suffered a wound of any kind," she said quietly. She was amazed at her own outward composure when her heart was fairly hammering in her chest. She was not in the habit of dissembling and it came awkwardly to her.

Lt. Copperidge apparently sensed something of her disquiet. He was not satisfied with her answer. "Information then, Miss Lester. Have you any information that I might find useful? I warn you, ma'am, against withholding any such information."

"Exactly what are you implying, Lieutenant Copperidge?" demanded Lady Cecily, roused to cold affront. "I assure you that my daughter does not possess any such information as you seek."

Lt. Copperidge allowed his gaze to transfer to her ladyship. He sketched a perfunctory bow. "Perhaps my words were ill-chosen. I am aware that Miss Lester goes riding frequently about the countryside. I am merely attempting to ascertain whether Miss Lester might have noticed something unusual, some unusual feature, in her rides without precisely realizing its significance."

"Pooh; nonsense," said Lady Cecily with asperity. "What should she have seen to the purpose? There is absolutely nothing to see, for this is the dreariest, most monotonous landscape imaginable."

For the first time since she had heard that the excisemen had come, Vanessa felt her tension ease. She chuckled. "I do not think that Lieutenant Copperidge is referring to the scenery, ma'am." She turned her gaze to the exciseman. "I am sorry, Lieutenant Copperidge. Her ladyship is correct. I really cannot help you, sir."

"Cannot or will not, Miss Lester?" asked Lt. Copperidge quietly.

Once again Lady Cecily came unwittingly to Vanessa's aid. "Really, Lieutenant! This is effrontery, indeed. This interview is swiftly degenerating into harassment. I am fast coming to the opinion that I shall be forced to drop a word in your superior officer's ear."

"That will not be necessary, my lady," said Lt. Copperidge stiffly. His lean face was a hard chiseled plane. "I shall naturally accept your statements that there is no wounded man hidden away on Halverton premises and that you both deny all knowledge of any such person."

"Unequivocally," said Lady Cecily coldly. "Good day, Lieutenant!"

The lieutenant made an abbreviated bow, his mouth drawn into a taut line. His posture was stiff, his expression remote and cold. He barked a short order to his men to withdraw and himself exited. The troop followed swiftly on his heels. The door was closed behind the excisemen by the butler, who showed a certain measure of satisfaction.

Sims turned to inquire whether he would be needed for anything else.

"No, nothing. Thank you, Sims," said Vanessa. The butler bowed and left the breakfast room, presumably to make certain that the excisemen were able to find their way to the front door.

Vanessa felt pity for the lieutenant. His was a harsh, thankless job. She herself had knowingly placed stumbling blocks into his way. She had rarely had such a low opinion of herself. She had bungled this affair to a degree that she would not have believed possible. She was usually so certain of her course. It was unlike her to have gone back on a decision and then followed it up by uttering falsehoods.

"I have never been more insulted in my life," said Lady Cecily. "The nerve of that young man in accusing us of harboring a criminal ruffian. I am profoundly disappointed in Lieutenant Copperidge, Vanessa. I had thought him to be fairly well-bred, but he has consistently displayed a lack of sensitivity that I find appalling."

"Lieutenant Copperidge was merely following the tenets of his duty, ma'am," said Vanessa.

"Was he indeed! It is a strange duty that calls for the persecution of two ladies," said Lady Cecily. "Vanessa, I must insist that you utterly cut your unfortunate friendship with that young man."

Vanessa gave a dry chuckle. "I do not believe that there will by any difficulty in that, ma'am." Her reflections had already brought her to the inevitability of that happening. She had seen the implacable expression in the lieutenant's face. This circumstance, coming on top of the debacle over the French wine, had made any true friendship between them impossible. In the lieutenant's eyes, she had become someone not to be trusted.

"Thank you, Vanessa," said Lady Cecily. She was surprised but pleased by her daughter's seeming tractability. It put her into a more benevolent mood. She rose from her chair. "Now I must go upstairs and begin my correspondence. You will, I know, have some sort of estate business that must be attended to, so I shall not see you again until later this afternoon."

"Yes, Mother," said Vanessa, smiling a little.

Lady Cecily paused before exiting through the door. In a far gentler tone than her daughter had ever recalled her ladyship using, Lady Cecily said, "Lieutenant Copperidge was not for you, Vanessa. Pray do not think that I am angry with you over him."

A startled expression came into Vanessa's face. When Lady Cecily saw it, she gave the slightest of smiles and left the breakfast room.

Vanessa shook her head in astonishment. How very extraordinary. Her mother had actually extended something of an olive branch toward her. And all because Lt. Copperidge had so greatly affronted Lady Cecily that she could no longer accept him in the guise of a suitor for Vanessa, despite her ladyship's ambition to see her wed as soon as possible.

Vanessa wondered suddenly what her mother would think about the gentleman smuggler. She rather thought that Lady Cecily would merely raise her brows and inquire whether he was good *ton*. Lady Cecily would care little about the ethics of smuggling. Her ladyship was supremely above such paltry moral issues.

Vanessa reflected that she was in a very uncomfortable position. She had given aid to the wounded man, knowing that he was being sought as a criminal, and she had allowed her mother to speak for her to the excisemen, which in essence had constituted a falsehood on her part. Her conscience was troubled on that account. At the same time, she knew that she would have done the same thing all over again if given the choice.

When she had seen Lt. Copperidge's expression as she relayed what she had overheard about the smugglers' rendezvous, she had realized that the exciseman meant to shoot to kill. In the end, she had not been able to sit idly by while it happened. She had thought there was a good chance that some of the smugglers might be known to her or at least to others at Halverton. Obviously she had been correct. There were indeed some at Halverton who had connections with the smugglers. Her groom, John, and Rose, the second housemaid, and Sims. There were probably others, as well. She could not have easily reconciled it with her conscience if she had been instrumental in causing a massacre.

As for the wounded smuggler whose identity teased at her memory, she did not think that she could have done differently there, either. The man had needed help and she had chanced to have been in a position to offer it. Vanessa hoped that the unknown gentleman was hidden well enough to escape detection by the excisemen. It would be unfortunate indeed if he should be found after she had gone to such trouble on his behalf.

Vanessa allowed a smile to curve her lips. She might attempt to dismiss the incident lightly, but she could not quite disguise from herself her true feelings. It was ironic in the extreme that she had been swept off her feet by an unknown, lawbreaking, but charming scoundrel.

Vanessa felt a burning desire to know the identity of her freebooter. She had instinctively recognized him for a gentleman by his speech and his manner toward her, but that might prove meaningless in the clear light of day. He might be completely ineligible, as either a suitor or an acquaintance. His allure might very well lay solely in the extraordinary circumstances of their meeting.

But as Vanessa recalled the smuggler's kiss, she did not believe that it was so simple. She had never been kissed quite like that before. She had received her share of admirers' salutes, pressed onto her hand and, once, to her cheek. None had moved her in quite the same way as had the smuggler's. For the first time in her life, her heart fluttered at the thought of being held in a particular man's arms.

Vanessa knew that she had to discover who he was, if for no other reason than her own peace of mind. She could not go about weaving fantastic daydreams because of one snatched kiss. That was completely nonsensical and utterly unworthy of Sir Charles's levelheaded daughter.

Vanessa toyed with the idea of appealing to her butler for a clue to the smuggler's identity. Lt. Copperidge had said that he thought it had been one of the leaders who had been wounded and surely that would mean that someone would know who he was. However, Vanessa reluctantly let go of the idea. It would not be right to place Sims in such a position. He would be forced to make the choice between his loyalty to her and those who trusted in his silence. Such a choice could possibly even place the old butler in danger. She could not do that to Sims.

The only alternative left to her was to make more of an appearance at the round of entertainments that had begun with the several house parties. Presuming that her smuggler was in truth a gentleman born, he could very well be a guest in the neighborhood.

Upon long reflection, Vanessa had rejected the notion that the smuggler was one of her neighbors. She could not imagine any one of those gentlemen exhibiting the smuggler's reckless determination. But the freebooter could very well be a close family friend who had been told about the abbey and who had plunged into a vicarious adventure, not fully realizing the possible consequences.

Despite the disadvantages of the smuggler's deliberately low-pitched voice and his mask, Vanessa was fairly confident that she would be able to recognize him if she ever came face to face with him. There could not possibly be two gentlemen in the world who could make her heart race as he had done. No, even in a crowded anteroom she was certain that she would be able to pick him out if not by his face then by his voice.

Vanessa wasted no time in putting her flimsy plan into effect. At the earliest opportunity she informed Lady Cecily that since they were now officially coming out of black gloves, she was perfectly amenable to accepting the several invitations that had come to Halverton. "I have thought, too, that it would be pleasant to commission another gown or two," said Vanessa, adding hastily, "in suitable colors, of course."

Lady Cecily was astonished. For an instant it shot into her mind to question Vanessa's extraordinary turn of front, but she swiftly dismissed it. She did not care what had brought about her daughter's capitulation. It was enough that Vanessa was more compliant.

Lady Cecily at once exploited her daughter's unusual tractability, returning acceptances to every invitation and sending an imperative summons to the local dressmaker. She did not want to grant Vanessa even so much as an hour to change her mind.

On the eve of the Nashe dress ball, Lady Cecily had the satisfaction of observing her daughter gowned in a stunning blue silk. It was the first color that Vanessa had consented to wear for months. Her ladyship was all affability when they arrived at Nashe Hall and were shown inside.

The ballroom was already crowded when Lady Cecily and Miss Lester were announced. Lady Nashe surged forward to greet them, giving her hand to each in turn. After the necessary civilities were exchanged, Lady Nashe managed to signal her son to her side. Lady Nashe made certain that Miss Lester's first partner of the evening was the scion of the house. It was a stratagem that earned Lady Cecily's unqualified approval.

Mr. Nashe was a very credible dancer. Though he preferred to highlight his skills with the waltz above the country dances, he chose to acquire Miss Lester's hand for one of the latter sets. He was only too well aware that Miss Lester towered a good six inches above him, and he felt the difference in height would be less remarked in the country dance.

Vanessa smiled and held up her end of the spritely conversation, responding to the gentleman's sallies and observations with her usual cool wit. But her attention was not focused on Mr. Nashe. Her gaze roamed over the faces of the scores of gentlemen in attendance.

A small number of them were unknown to her. Undoubtedly these gentlemen were houseguests come down since Lord and Lady Akers had arrived. She wondered if one of them could possibly be the smuggler she had met and aided. She scrutinized each one, looking for some characteristic familiar to her that might point to the identity of her outrageous gentleman smuggler. Most particularly she looked for someone who handled his left arm a little awkwardly. The smuggler's wound had not been a serious one, but no doubt it was still painful.

Mr. Nashe eventually realized that his partner's attention was wandering. In a break in the dance, he said quizzingly, "Surely I am not boring you, Vanessa."

"Of course not," said Vanessa. She glanced at him quickly. "I am sorry, Mr. Nashe, if I have seemed rude. I was merely taking note of the several new faces here tonight. I suppose that most are acquaintances of Lord and Lady Akers and have come down for the hunting season?"

Mr. Nashe shrugged slightly. "Most have done so, yes. It makes this little affair more interesting, certainly."

"Yes," agreed Vanessa.

The country dance wound down. Mr. Nashe escorted Vanessa to a chair before inquiring whether he could claim her hand later for another set. "I do not wish you to suspect me of neglecting you," he said with his thin smile.

"No, indeed," said Vanessa. "That will be most pleasant, Mr. Nashe."

"You must excuse me for now, however, Miss Lester," said Mr. Nashe, his gaze going lazily to a small coterie of gentlemen. "My duties compel me to leave your side, for I have just now recognized some old acquaintances of mine from London."

Vanessa graciously acceded. She watched curiously as Mr. Nashe made his way over to the gentlemen. Since the advent of the house parties and the influx of guests, many of whom had come down from London, there had been rumors circulating about Mr. Nashe. Apparently he had built a reputation for himself as a gamester of sorts. It was now said that the ill health of Lord and Lady Nashe was not the only reason that Mr. Nashe was rusticating. He had also left behind a few financial embarrassments, such as outstanding tradesmen's bills.

There was a brief discussion, then Mr. Nashe gestured toward the door into the cardroom. The gentlemen all exited the ballroom, presumably to sit down to a game of cards.

Chapter Seventeen

Almost the moment that Mr. Nashe's slight figure disappeared, Vanessa forgot about him. She continued to survey the crowd as she accepted greetings from other guests. More than once she was solicited to dance, invitations which she gladly accepted. She did not want to appear too obvious in her search.

Vanessa had seen Lt. Copperidge among the guests, mingling with his correct manners. The exciseman seemed also to be inordinately interested in different personages, allowing his eyes to roam idly over the crowd. Once his keen gaze chanced to meet Vanessa's and he made a small bow of acknowledgment.

Vanessa nodded in recognition of his courtesy, but she was not surprised when the lieutenant did not seek her out as he might once have done. She felt a twinge of regret. For all of his stiff manner and unyielding belief in his own infallibility, she had liked the exciseman. But just as she had anticipated, Lt. Copperidge's duty, as he interpreted it, now precluded their former friendship.

Vanessa was not the only one who took note of Lt. Copperidge's omission. When Lady Cressida Akers came over to greet Vanessa, she said, "The lieutenant appears very stern this evening. Have you had a falling out with the gentleman, Vanessa?"

Vanessa smiled at her old friend. "In a manner of speaking, I suppose that we have. Lieutenant Copperidge suspects Halverton of being hand-in-glove with the smuggling interests. A veritable hotbed of intrigue, in fact."

"And are you?" asked Lady Akers with interest.

Vanessa laughed and shook her head. "No, I do not think so. Though I am certain that there are a few in the household who have kin involved, I certainly cannot claim such notoriety for Halverton."

"Oh, I see just what it is! Lieutenant Copperidge went to Halverton breathing fire and voicing suspicion that you might be harboring a wounded smuggler," said Lady Akers.

Vanessa looked at her with amazement. "Never tell me that he came here to Nashe Hall, too."

At Lady Akers's nod, Vanessa said, "Poor Lord and Lady Nashe. It is a wonder that Lieutenant Copperidge was even allowed into the ball. Why, no one could possibly suspect them. They have been virtual recluses for months."

"Yes, that is precisely what Mark told the lieutenant. Believe me, Vanessa, I have never seen my brother in such a taking," said Lady Akers. "Mark was so enraged that I feared he would offer a violence to Lieutenant Copperidge. Indeed, if Geoffrey had not caught him by the shoulder I am still not certain that he would have come to his senses in time."

A slight frown marked Vanessa's brows. She could not imagine the elegant, rather foppish Mr. Nashe seized by impetuous anger. "Somehow I have never connected your brother with the more brutish emotions."

"No, indeed! I was utterly amazed, I can tell you. However, I do recall that as a boy Mark had a rather unpleasant habit of flicking his kid gloves at Eleanor's face and mine, just enough to sting our cheeks. But he never seemed to enjoy the rougher play that dearest Benjamin and Howard Pemberton were wont to indulge themselves. Fisticuffs and fencing and shooting and hunting! Do you remember? Those two were never still and they teased us girls unmercifully," said Lady Akers.

Vanessa laughed. "Indeed I do remember. We liked them nonetheless. I suppose it is a commentary upon our own adventuresome natures."

Lady Akers also laughed. "I suspect that you may be right. You and I and Eleanor were not milksop maids. Oh, here comes Howard Pemberton now." She smiled and waved in the direction of the approaching gentleman. "He is coming to claim a dance of you, I suspect."

"Perhaps he has you in mind instead," suggested Vanessa.

Lady Akers shook her head, still smiling. "Oh no, he could not possibly. I am a married woman and he is far too afraid of my husband to do anything so bold as to ask for the honor of my hand."

"Whatever has given you that idea?" asked Vanessa.

"Why, he confided it to me himself. Oh, Vanessa! I started to tease him a little, just as one does with an old childhood friend, and he simply looked at me in the greatest alarm and confusion. My heart was positively wrung with pity. He has turned into such a handsome fellow, but he is nothing like he was as a boy," said Lady Akers.

"Yes, I know," said Vanessa quietly.

Lady Akers flashed a bright smile up at Mr. Pemberton as he reached them. She offered her hand to him. "Good evening, Mr. Pemberton. I trust that you are enjoying the evening's entertainment?"

"Capital! Capital good fun," said Mr. Pemberton, bowing over Lady Akers's hand. He released her fingers and turned to her companion. "Miss Lester, well met! I am delighted to pursue my acquaintance with you. I hope you will honor me with this set?" His smile was wide and guileless, just as was the expression in his eyes.

Vanessa and Lady Akers exchanged glances. Lady Akers made a grimace of regret. Vanessa turned resolutely to Mr. Pemberton. "I am honored, sir," she said, bestowing her hand in his larger one.

Mr. Pemberton led her onto the dance floor. It was not until she heard the first notes strike up that Vanessa realized that she had granted a waltz to Mr. Pemberton. It was an honor for a gentleman to secure a waltz from a lady and was a signal that he had earned her approval. If a lady chose to honor the same gentleman with more than three waltzes in an evening, it was a certainty that they were to be engaged.

Vanessa shrugged aside the social implications of the waltz. Surely no one would place serious construction upon the fact that she was partnered by Mr. Pemberton. Over the past few months several ladies had discovered that Mr. Pemberton had few equals on the dance floor. For that reason he had become a prime favorite at any function that included dancing. Vanessa felt that she had no need to be anxious that anyone would construe something out of the fact that she had allowed Mr. Pemberton to lead her out. She would simply enjoy her dance with the gentleman and return to her chair.

Though she had often danced with Mr. Pemberton, his grace never failed to amaze her. He was surprisingly light on his feet for such a large man. Just as he rode his horses with instinctive grace, he brought the same natural ability to dancing. Vanessa always enjoyed being squired by her childhood friend, even though his conversation could never equal that of other gentlemen of her acquaintance.

This evening she noticed a peculiar clumsiness in the way that he held his arm about her waist and she quizzed him on it. "What, have you become stiff with me, Mr. Pemberton?"

He stared down at her with a blank look for so long that Vanessa was on the verge of begging his pardon for her oblique comment. But then his face cleared as though by magic. "Oh, you are referring to my lack of expertise."

He took on a confiding expression. "The thing of it is, Miss Lester, that tumble I took on the field bruised my shoulder to an unlooked-for degree." He laughed heartily. "You will no doubt call me a Bartholomew baby for still feeling the effects of such a paltry accident."

"I would not be so uncivil, sir," replied Vanessa, smiling up at him.

The most astonishing suspicion had flashed through her mind, but it was so absurd that she instantly dismissed it. Mr. Pemberton simply could not be one of the smugglers. The poor man was incapable of something so devious and dangerous. Besides, it was quite true that Mr. Pemberton had taken a hard tumble from his horse over a deceptive jump. Though he had brushed himself off and disclaimed any hurt in answer to solicitous inquiries by several other witnesses, she had seen him wince upon remounting. It would not be unusual for a bruise to deepen into stiffness some days later. Undoubtedly that was what had happened.

Vanessa scanned the ballroom once again from her vantage point on the dance floor.

"Whom do you search for, Miss Lester?"

The question startled her. Vanessa looked up quickly into her partner's face. She had not expected to be observed so closely by Mr. Pemberton. He was regarding her with a smile in his eyes, almost as though he had guessed what she was thinking. But that was nonsense, of course. It was only her own guilty conscience that lent discernment to Mr. Pemberton's expression.

"Why, no one, Mr. Pemberton. I was merely noting that it is a bit of a squeeze this evening," said Vanessa. "There are so many unfamiliar faces with the several house parties in the neighborhood."

"Yes." There was almost a grim note in Mr. Pemberton's voice.

Again Vanessa glanced upward, her brows contracting this time. It had almost sounded as though Mr. Pemberton had some thoughts on the matter. She started to question him. But then Mr. Pemberton trod on the hem of her gown. Vanessa felt and heard the distinct sound of ripping lace.

Instantly Mr. Pemberton broke into awkward apologies, lamenting his clumsiness and making such a noise that others overheard. In between reassuring Mr. Pemberton that it was a common accident and pushing down irritation that he had been so unusually clumsy, Vanessa completely forgot what she had been thinking about.

With an abject expression, Mr. Pemberton escorted Vanessa to a small anteroom where a team of maids waited to repair just such damage to the ladies' gowns. Vanessa was relieved when she was at last rid of him, for his moanings and unending apologies had become an embarrassment. She was also very much annoyed. She liked as little as anyone else being made a public gazingstock.

When her hem was repaired and she was able to return to the ballroom, she decided to avoid Mr. Pemberton for the remainder of the evening. She would make some excuse if he should want to lead her out again.

However, Mr. Pemberton seemed to share her inclination. He did not approach her again, which was unusual for him. Vanessa was mildly surprised until she realized what must have happened. The poor man had been so cast down by his inadvertent clumsiness that he was actually afraid of what she might say to him.

"As though I would scold him," she murmured to herself, her gaze resting on his tall figure. The thought that Mr. Pemberton might be in a quake over any ill-chosen words of hers softened her heart toward him, and if he had decided to come over to her again she would have received him graciously.

Vanessa's hand was claimed for the next set and she embarked upon a series of partners. An hour passed very pleasantly. When next Vanessa gave thought to Mr. Pemberton, it was to discover that he had left the ball.

It was not until after the ball was over and Vanessa had returned to Halverton that it occurred to her that Mr. Pemberton had never before exhibited any clumsiness on the dance floor.

Vanessa thought about that while her maid finished combing out her hair in preparation for bed. Finally Vanessa shrugged to herself. The poor man was simply a hazard. One never knew when he might bumble, whether in word or deed. It was just part and parcel of poor Mr. Pemberton.

Her last thought before sleep overtook her was that she must reassure Mr. Pemberton that she had not taken affront at his clumsiness. She would tell him so when they met to go riding together in the morning.

However, Vanessa did not find Mr. Pemberton waiting for her at their usual meeting place. After idling there for several minutes, disappointed, Vanessa went on for her ride on her own.

Perhaps Mr. Pemberton's shoulder had become inflamed or had stiffened so much that he had chosen to forgo the exercise that morning. Vanessa's compassion was roused by the thought. But it was swiftly superseded by another. If that was truly the case, it would have been a courtesy on Mr. Pemberton's part to send around a note to Halverton before she had left. But Vanessa supposed that Mr. Pemberton could not be expected to remember all the proper protocol.

She dismissed the gentleman from her mind and set herself to thoroughly enjoy her solitary ride. It had been some time since she had been alone on horseback. It was rather pleasant for a change.

Vanessa returned to Halverton refreshed. She was quite able to forgive Mr. Pemberton for his neglect. She was met with the intelligence that Mr. Nashe had come to call on her and was even then waiting in the drawing room.

Vanessa was surprised. It was early for Mr. Nashe to drive over. He usually confined his visits to the afternoons. Perhaps there was something wrong at Nashe Hall, an accident or sudden illness, and he had come over to inform them.

"I shall come at once," said Vanessa.

She entered the drawing room impetuously, still clutching her whip. She did not close the door behind her. "Mr. Nashe! This is an unlooked-for visit," she said, holding out her hand to him.

"Yes, it is early for me, is it not?" he asked, smiling. He nodded at her attire. "I have caught you just returning from your ride, I perceive. Forgive me that I have been so inconsiderate."

"Not at all, sir. But tell me, is there something wrong at Nashe Hall?" asked Vanessa, sitting down and gesturing for him to be seated as well. "Lord or Lady Nashe have not met with an accident or fallen ill again, surely?"

"Wrong at Nashe Hall?" repeated Mr. Nashe, somewhat blankly. Then his expression cleared and he smiled. "Oh, I see! Naturally my visit at such an early hour must have excited some concern and curiosity on your part. No, Miss Lester, everyone is perfectly well. I am come on quite a different errand entirely."

"You relieve my mind, sir," said Vanessa. She gestured at herself. "I trust that you will forgive me for receiving you in all my dirt. I was so anxious to discover the reason for your visit that I did not go up to change."

"Pray think nothing more of it, Vanessa. Indeed, I am flattered that I was able to excite such anticipation," said Mr. Nashe. "It admirably sets the stage for the purpose of my visit. I have come to beg your pardon for the gauche manner in which I declared myself the other evening. It was poorly executed."

Vanessa was vaguely embarrassed. "That is quite all right, Mr. Nashe. Pray do not regard it."

"I believe that we settled between us that you would call me by my given name," said Mr. Nashe, smiling. He took up one of her hands. "Vanessa, that night I was at my most unsophisticated. This morning I am entirely myself. I offer to you my humble adoration. You are not unaware of my feelings, I believe, for I have attempted in a thousand different ways to impress you with my devotion. Vanessa, I am asking you to honor me with your hand."

Vanessa felt ready to sink. Once again she had been placed in just the position that she most wanted to avoid. Especially now, when all of her being yearned to discover the identity of a certain charming freebooter. "Mr. Nashe—Mark, pray do not think ill of me. I am sorry, but in all conscience I cannot accept your most flattering offer."

Mr. Nashe's face became suddenly tinged with dull color. "Will you not, Miss Lester?"

Vanessa freed her hand from his grasp. "I am sorry, Mr. Nashe."

"I have laid before you my honor, my person, and all that I am in worldly goods. I have abased myself to you, even," said Mr. Nashe. His head had come up at a proud angle and his expression had grown haughty. "But yet you still reject me, Miss Lester?"

"I am sorry, Mr. Nashe," said Vanessa, rather helplessly. "I do not wish to hurt your feelings."

Mr. Nashe rose from the settee. He stared down at Vanessa with narrowed eyes. "I fear that this interview was a mistake," he said. "I will leave you now, Miss Lester." He did not bow, but immediately turned on his heel and exited the drawing room.

Vanessa waited a few minutes until she could be certain that Mr. Nashe had left the premises. She did not wish to come face to face with the gentleman in the entry hall while he collected his hat and coat. When she heard the front door close, she emerged from the drawing room.

Lady Cecily was coming down the stairwell. "Vanessa, I

have been told that Mr. Nashe has come to call. I will naturally join you in visiting with him."

Vanessa hesitated, reluctant to reveal to her mother what had just transpired. However, there was no point in concealing it. Lady Cecily would hear in any event, either through servants who might have overheard the conversation or through the Nashes themselves.

"Mr. Nashe has just this moment left," said Vanessa quietly. "Pray come into the drawing room, Mother. I shall tell you about our conversation."

Lady Cecily narrowed her eyes, but she said nothing more until she had followed Vanessa into the drawing room. When Vanessa had closed the door, she said sharply, "Well, Vanessa?"

"Mr. Nashe again made an offer for my hand. I have once more rejected his suit," said Vanessa baldly.

Lady Cecily's face whitened and her nostrils pinched. Quite deliberately, she picked up a figurine and threw it. It shattered against the wainscoting, but the noise it made could not be heard over her rising and vicious diatribe. Her ladyship verbally ripped her daughter to shreds.

Within moments, Vanessa was shaking equally from shock and anger. She raised her own voice, exclaiming, "Enough! I shall not hear another word, do you understand?"

"You dare to order me?" shouted Lady Cecily.

Vanessa's eyes glittered like steel. Anger coursed hot through her veins. "Yes, my lady, I do! And I hold the reins, pray recall! I would rather take a vow of celibacy than stand for another moment of this abuse. You will do well not to push me any further, ma'am, and so I warn you!" Jerking open the door, Vanessa swiftly exited the drawing room.

For the rest of that day, Vanessa remained upset. She felt that the beloved walls of Halverton were closing in on her until she could not breathe. How odd that the place that she called home could come to feel almost like a prison. She spent most of her hours in the saddle, trying to exorcise the depression and anger that had attacked her.

When dusk fell and she returned to Halverton, she requested that dinner be served to her in her rooms. She sent a message also to the hostess of the soiree that she was supposed to attend that evening, begging off because of a headache.

Lady Cecily was startled and alarmed by her daughter's actions. She was not so much concerned about Vanessa as she was about the fact that her daughter was closeting herself away from social contact. It was not a trend that Lady Cecily wished to see permanently established. Vanessa must circulate if she was to snare a husband.

At that point, Lady Cecily would have settled for any *parti*, eligible or otherwise, who solicited her daughter's hand. Things had come to a pretty pass, indeed. Vanessa had actually thrown away her best chance.

Lady Cecily did not think that Mark Nashe would return again. The gentleman had been rejected twice. His pride surely would not allow him to risk it for a third time.

Lady Cecily began running through her mind what gentlemen were currently being entertained at the various house parties and she felt a faint hope. Perhaps she might yet get Vanessa betrothed. At least, she might if Vanessa did not persist in these terrible tactics.

Lady Cecily saw that there was but one course open to her if she was to circumvent Vanessa's surprisingly strong show. Her ladyship tightened her lips and went off to apologize to her daughter. It was absurd. It was ludicrous. It went completely against the grain. However, Lady Cecily was not one to shirk an unpleasant necessity if it meant gaining the upper hand.

Vanessa was surprised but wary of her mother's apology. She knew Lady Cecily very well. Her ladyship was too arrogant to willingly acknowledge a wrong. No, Lady Cecily had simply acted with her usual cold, calculating selfishness. But Vanessa was willing to accept the olive branch, no matter how rotten, for it meant a temporary cessation of hostilities.

Lady Cecily was satisfied that her action seemed to have the desired result. Her daughter came out of what her ladyship referred to as Vanessa's sulks and continued to appear socially.

If Lady Cecily had but known it, Vanessa was just as anxious to remain circulating. She still had not discovered her smuggler. It was beginning to perturb her. She had been certain that she would recognize the gentleman if she came face to face with him.

Vanessa would have liked to have confided her dilemma to someone. A problem was always easier to bear or to solve when one had the support of others. However, Vanessa knew that no one could possibly understand the depth of her need to discover the identity of the smuggler. Not even Lady Akers, who had been one of her best friends for many years, could be expected to enter completely into her feelings.

On Sunday, Vanessa attended church as usual. When she discovered that Mr. Pemberton had not, she became mildly alarmed. She had not seen Mr. Pemberton all week, nor had he ever sent an explanation for his continued absence from their morning rides. Now Mr. Pemberton was absent from services, which had never before happened.

As Vanessa took leave of the reverend, she said, "I do not see Mr. Pemberton here this morning, Reverend Haversaw. Has he perhaps gone out of the county again?"

"Why, no, Miss Lester. Quite the contrary, unfortunately. It is my understanding that Mr. Pemberton has been laid low by a terrible bout of the influenza," said Reverend Haversaw.

Vanessa was at once astonished and concerned. "I had not heard. I trust that he recuperates swiftly. One's mind positively boggles at the thought of Mr. Pemberton laid down with any sort of complaint."

Reverend Haversaw chuckled. "That is precisely what I told Mrs. Dabney when I called on her yesterday to inquire about Mr. Pemberton. She agreed, and confided to me that Mr. Pemberton is not at all a good patient. He frets over being tied to his couch. No doubt that same energy will cause Mr. Pemberton to bounce back to his customary health in short order."

"I do hope so," said Vanessa. She took her leave then and got into her carriage. Lady Cecily had not attended church that morning, pronouncing herself too fatigued to make the effort and so Vanessa had the carriage to herself.

On the short ride home to Halverton, Vanessa decided that she would make a condolence call at Pemberton Place. There could be no possible objection to her doing so, for it was the neighborly thing to do.

There might be some who would look askance, for Mr. Pemberton was a bachelor and she was herself unwed. One did not call alone upon gentlemen at their domiciles. But Mrs. Dabney was in residence. That must satisfy the conventions for even the highest sticklers. And even if it did not, she would still go. Mr. Pemberton was a very dear friend.

Chapter Eighteen

Vanessa took her groom with her when she went over to Pemberton Place to pay her condolence call. His presence was not a last-minute sop to the conventions. She cared little about what others said. But the groom carried the basket of fruit and jelly tarts which Lady Cecily had insisted that Vanessa take to Mr. Pemberton.

Vanessa was still puzzling over that stroke of generosity from her mother. She gave little credence her mother's explanation, for in her own memory Lady Cecily had never exhibited such thoughtfulness.

Lady Cecily had said that she knew her neighborly duty, and though she would not call herself because she was so susceptible to influenza, she was deputizing Vanessa to act in her stead.

Vanessa knew it was not so much fear of catching the influenza that worked on Lady Cecily as it was an intense dislike of Mrs. Dabney. Lady Cecily had not enjoyed her previous encounters with the redoubtable lady. Mrs. Dabney was not to be cowed by an earl's youngest daughter, not when her own proud lineage was impeccable.

"You will say all that is proper to Mrs. Dabney, of course," Lady Cecily had said.

"Of course," agreed Vanessa, pulling on her gloves.

"I would not send you in my stead except that you are such good friends with Mr. Pemberton. It will be a comfort to him to be told that you delivered the basket with your own hands. No doubt there will be very few others who will make the effort of showing such a kindness," said Lady Cecily.

Vanessa nodded, her lips thinning a trifle. "It is difficult for me to understand how so many people can look down on or avoid those who are less fortunate than they are; but they will do so."

"It is a pity that Mr. Pemberton is such a slow-top," said Lady Cecily, agreeing with what she felt was the crux of her daughter's observation.

Vanessa knew full well why Lady Cecily regretted Mr. Pemberton's lack of wits. Her ladyship would have liked to have encouraged him as a possible suitor for her. "He is not an idiot, ma'am, merely slow-witted," Vanessa said quietly.

Lady Cecily looked at her speculatively. "You come swiftly enough to the gentleman's defense, Vanessa. Perhaps it would not be a bad thing to push for a match between you and Mr. Pemberton."

Vanessa's eyes flashed. "I do not think that it would profit you to enter into any such scheme."

Lady Cecily threw up her hand, mindful of the last time her daughter had become angered. "Very well! I shall say no more. Convey my compliments to Mrs. Dabney and inquire after Mr. Pemberton. You will tell me when you return whether he is making progress."

"It is odd that Mr. Pemberton has fallen ill at all," said Vanessa. "He told me once that he was never ill."

"Nonsense. Everyone is ill at one time or another," said Lady Cecily.

"I am not. I thank God daily in my prayers for the blessing of health," said Vanessa quietly.

Lady Cecily's mouth curled with a superior air. "Yes, I know that you and Reverend Haversaw share the same simple conviction that God is interested in even the smallest details of our lives. That is the sort of belief that I might have expected from uneducated peasants, but certainly not from you or a gentleman of such scholarly habits as the good reverend. It is a pity that you did not accept his offer, Vanessa. You would have been very comfortable with the reverend."

"I will not argue with you over either of these topics, ma'am," said Vanessa firmly, taking up her whip and the basket. "We each exercise the right to make the choices that seem best to us."

"I wish that at least one of your choices had been to my benefit," said Lady Cecily somewhat bitterly.

Vanessa was still reflecting over this latest clash with her mother as she was ushered into the drawing room at Pemberton Place. Mrs. Dabney received her kindly and expressed her appreciation for the basket of fruit and jellies, giving it discreetly into the hands of her butler before ushering Vanessa to a chair.

"It is good of you to come, my dear. Poor Howard will be so pleased that you have showed him such condescension," she said.

"Nonsense. What else should I do when I hear that a neighbor has been struck down with illness?" asked Vanessa, smiling.

Mrs. Dabney glanced over at her visitor as she poured tea. "You would be amazed at how many people forget the small courtesies, Miss Lester. However, I am glad to see that you and Lady Cecily are not among their number." She handed the cup and saucer to Vanessa, smiling slightly. "You may convey my regrets to her ladyship that she felt unable to accompany you. But naturally I understand Lady Cecily's anxiety that there may yet be infectious air here at Pemberton."

"My mother declares herself to be particularly susceptible," said Vanessa. "But how is dear Mr. Pemberton?"

"Very well indeed, actually," said Mrs. Dabney, sipping her tea.

Vanessa raised her brows in surprise. "How odd! I was told that he was laid down on his couch."

"I do not minimize my nephew's convalescence. Quite the contrary. However, considering the circumstances, he is doing extremely well," said Mrs. Dabney. She regarded Vanessa for a moment, before saying, "In the event that you called, my nephew requested that you visit with him personally. Would you be willing to do that, Miss Lester?"

"But of course!" said Vanessa. "I count Mr. Pemberton to be one of my dearest of friends."

Mrs. Dabney smiled and rose gracefully to her feet. "Very well, Miss Lester. Pray follow me. Howard insisted that he was well enough to rise and he is sitting up in the sitting room.

It is quite against the physician's orders, but gentlemen can be such stubborn patients."

"Yes, indeed. I well recall my father's impatience with his own convalescence. It tried him sorely. No doubt someone like Mr. Pemberton, who is naturally energetic, is even more restless," said Vanessa as she followed her hostess out of the drawing room and down the hall.

Mrs. Dabney laughed as she opened a door. "That is putting things mildly, I fear." She stood aside for Vanessa to enter. "Howard, here is dear Miss Lester come to visit with you."

"Miss Lester!" Mr. Pemberton tossed aside the newspaper that he had been perusing and stood up quickly. He swayed and had to grasp the back of a chair to steady himself.

Vanessa approached him swiftly. "Mr. Pemberton! Pray sit down again. You have not been at all well." As she neared him, she became shocked by his pallor. She scarcely heard the door close behind her.

Mr. Pemberton laughed and came forward to meet her. He took her hand and stood looking down into her anxious face. "Miss Lester, forgive me. I did not intend to alarm you. I simply got up too quickly and it made my head spin. But I am quite all right now."

"Are you certain? I should not wish you to faint, for I suspect that I could not catch you," said Vanessa, smiling as she made her little joke.

For an instant he stared down at her. There was a strange expression on his face. Then with a muttered oath he swept his arms around her, tilted up her startled face, and kissed her.

When he released her, Vanessa slapped him. Her eyes flashing, she exclaimed, "How dare you, sir!"

"I dared because I love you," said Mr. Pemberton quietly.

"Oh no, no!" exclaimed Vanessa, appalled. She stepped back. "You must not say so, Mr. Pemberton."

Her thoughts tumbled in distress. It was the worst thing that could possibly have transpired. She realized instantly that she had been wrong to befriend the gentleman. Poor dear Mr. Pemberton had fallen for what he had in his simple mind mistaken for her encouragement.

He took her hand and folded it against his chest. Vanessa

could feel his strong heartbeat and she tugged at her hand to be free. "Pray, pray do not," she choked.

Very quietly, Mr. Pemberton said, "My dear girl, look at me. Listen to my voice, and recall a certain moonlit night in the ruins of the abbey."

Vanessa abandoned her efforts to gain her liberty and stared up at Mr. Pemberton. Her color suddenly fluctuated. She whispered, "It cannot be. You cannot possibly be—no, I do not believe it!"

"Perhaps you should sit down, Miss Lester," said Mr. Pemberton sympathetically.

Vanessa allowed him to lead her over to the settee. She sank down on it in shock. Mr. Pemberton ranged himself on the settee beside her. She searched his face, and took note that he gingerly favored his left shoulder. Still not quite believing it, she asked, "Then you are my smuggler?"

"Yes, I suppose that I am," said Mr. Pemberton, amusement threading his voice.

That hint of laughter fully persuaded her. Vanessa stared at him for a moment more, her lips curving in a smile. Her reflections led to an inevitable conclusion. "But then you were not at all dull or stupid," she said.

"Not at all," agreed Mr. Pemberton, content to watch the expressions flit across her face.

Vanessa thought back over the last few months, seeing everything in an entirely new light. She remembered with perfect clarity every time she had gotten impatient with him, but forced it back because she had pitied him. She recalled each occasion when she had been angered at some unkind remark made about him or to him and how she had leaped to his defense. It had all been completely unnecessary.

"You were pretending all along," she said, beginning to realize how foolish she must have appeared in his eyes.

"Well, yes, I was," said Mr. Pemberton apologetically.

Vanessa looked at him, sparks in her eyes. "You have played me for a fool. When I recall how I defended you and took up for you and deflected Mark Nashe's cruelties!"

Hastily, he offered placation. "I could not reveal myself to you, sweetheart. I was under oath to certain parties that represented the Crown. You would most certainly have given me away by some inadvertent slip, for there is no guile in you." A smile lurked about his mobile mouth. "Besides, I rather enjoyed watching you take up the cudgels on my behalf."

Vanessa's annoyance vanished. "Yes, no doubt it was vastly amusing." She was distracted by the endearment that had fallen so naturally from his lips. More important than any question about his masquerade was the one that consumed her. What could he mean by speaking to her in such an outrageous fashion? He had said that he loved her. Could it be true? Did she want it to be true?

She was shortly left in little doubt.

Howard Pemberton folded her again into his arms. This time Vanessa willingly lifted her face. He kissed her thoroughly. Then he slowly set her aside, obviously reluctant to end their embrace.

Vanessa touched her lips with the tips of her fingers. Yes, that was precisely the same kiss that she recalled so vividly.

Pemberton was still smiling, but there was a peculiar light in his eyes that made her heart tumble. "I want you to wife, Miss Lester," he said quietly. "Dare I hope that you return a measure of my own warm regard?"

"Oh, yes," she said.

Vanessa was surprised by the breathless quality of her voice. She made an effort to get hold of herself. More matter-of-factly, she asked, "But why now, Howard? You've told me of this dangerous work that you are engaged upon and that you feared that I would somehow betray you for what you really are. Why have you revealed yourself to me now? Are you not still afraid, even more so, that I shall betray you?"

"It is a calculated risk, certainly," said Pemberton. "However, I sensed that you were already questioning my identity. I wanted to head you off from voicing your suspicions to anyone else. The disguise that I have chosen would not have withstood assault. It is only effective as long as others are willing to accept it, and if you had begun to plant seeds of suspicion, then it would have been only a matter of time before others began questioning it as well."

"Yes, that is true. And you were quite right that I was begin-

ning to harbor suspicions," said Vanessa. She flashed a smile.
"I could not quite believe, you see, that the boy I remembered
so vividly could have metamorphosed into the slow-witted
gentleman that you were portraying."

Pemberton nodded. "Yes, I wondered whether I could fool
you. I was fairly confident otherwise, for my parents and I had
left the county when I was still a boy. Few of the older generation knew me well enough to question my imposture, with the
exception of the squire. I took him into my confidence some
time ago. There were then only a few childhood friends who
had known anything about me."

"And you knew that Cressy and Eleanor had wed and gone
away," said Vanessa at a venture.

"Yes, and that Benjamin was safely away in the army," said
Pemberton with a smile.

"It must have come as an unpleasant surprise when Cressy
came back," said Vanessa.

"That is an understatement," said Pemberton dryly. "However, there was nothing to be done but to brazen it out and hope
for the best. As it turned out, Lady Akers accepted my distress-
ing change without question. That was a boon, particularly in
light of the danger I courted if I should have been challenged
even by some innocently put question."

"But what of Mark Nashe? Surely he might have been expected to realize that something was not right," said Vanessa.

"Mark Nashe I discounted, for we had never been particularly close. Quite the contrary, in fact. I was closer to Benjamin, both in age and in temperament. There was no reason
for Mark Nashe to perceive a radical difference in his brother's
old childhood friend. And with Lady Akers's acceptance of
me as I portrayed myself, I felt to be on even firmer ground,"
said Pemberton. He reached out to smooth a curl behind her
ear. "That left only you, Vanessa, who had known me well
from the past. However, I had been told of Sir Charles's death
and I knew that you would be in black gloves. I hoped to be
finished with my work here before you had emerged from
your seclusion."

"And then my mother took a hand in the game," said
Vanessa, a gleam of humor in her eyes.

Pemberton laughed. "Yes! You may imagine my dismay when Lady Cecily came to call and announced to my aunt that you were going to begin entertaining again at Halverton. I knew that it would only be a matter of time before you started to accept invitations as well. Then I was certain to meet up with you at some gathering or other."

"And that threw you into a positive quake of fear," suggested Vanessa with a quizzical expression.

"Not precisely that, but the possibility that you might see through my assumed stupidity greatly enhanced the risks that I was operating under. I could not afford to be unmasked just then," said Pemberton somberly, but with a slight grin.

"You could have avoided me," said Vanessa.

"That was my original intention. The task did not seem to form an insurmountable challenge," said Pemberton. With a lazy smile, he added, "Then you decided to befriend me and knocked my best intentions right out from under me. I found that I was firmly caught. I could not stay away. I was like a moth enticed by a flame. I knew the danger that proximity to you must mean, but I knew also that I wished above all else to court you."

He reached out and clasped her fingers. Very quietly, he said, "Then you appeared out of nowhere to save my life and I snatched the sweetest kiss of my career. I knew in that instant that I wanted to make you mine."

Vanessa felt the burning in her cheeks that his words had caused. "You were foolish, indeed. More than once I seemed to sense something more about you than what you showed to others. I could have said something damaging at any time."

He gently squeezed her fingers. "Yes, that is true. But I could not help myself. Do you understand that? Can you understand that?"

Vanessa felt slightly breathless. She nodded. "It was the same for me. At least, it was after that night at the abbey. I—I did not know who you were, of course. But I wanted to see you again. I tried to discover who you were. I thought you might be one of the guests staying with Lord and Lady Nashe or with the squire or that you made up one of the shooting parties that were coming and going in the county."

"Good Lord! I was running a greater risk than I knew," said Pemberton humorously.

Vanessa laughed. "Perhaps not, after all, for I never considered that dear dull Howard Pemberton was the smuggler."

"Did you ever confide in anyone that you were looking for the wounded smuggler?" asked Pemberton.

"Oh, no. I thought of asking one of my servants whom I know has ties to the smugglers, but that would have placed him in an untenable position. I could not do that to him, so I tried to discover some gentleman who was nursing a wounded shoulder," said Vanessa. She smiled ever so slightly. "It is fortunate that you had taken that tumble a few days before you were shot. It offered the perfect excuse for your stiffness at the Nashe dress ball."

"That was a hellish night. I was lightheaded from blood loss and shock and I wondered more than once whether I could last long enough through the evening to establish my alibi," said Pemberton grimly. "Fortunately, after I had trod on your gown, the squire suspected that I was in deep straits and bore me off with him. It was he who came up with the brilliant notion of the influenza. The last few days when I have been supposedly down with a bout of illness I have actually been enjoying a recovery period for this shoulder."

"I wish I had known. I would have been over here much sooner," said Vanessa. "But then, what would have seemed to be oversolicitation on my part would have brought about just the sort of questions that you would have liked least. Nor would I have liked it much." She shook her head, laughing at herself. "I would have looked all sorts of fool to have been forced to confess that I had formed a hopeless passion for a desperate outlaw, would I not?"

Chapter Nineteen

Pemberton pulled her close once more. His large hand stroked her hair. A frisson of laughter in his voice, he said, "My poor darling. I have been a sad trial to you. As you were to me! You seduced me with your kind smile into riding with you each morning. I thought that I could play the fool well enough for that short hour to escape detection. But you were also turning up at every function, when I had been so confident that you would be safely secluded at Halverston."

Vanessa caught his lapel between her fingers. She felt so safe and comfortable in his embrace. It was a marvel to her. "It was horridly inconsiderate of me. I see that now."

"As it turns out, I am glad." Pemberton eased her away from him again, catching hold of both her hands. His expression sobering, he said, "I am still engaged in dangerous work, Vanessa. I must trust you not to reveal me by word or look. It is vital that I retain that element of surprise on my side, for I am still unsure of the identity of the liaison to the French."

"But you suspect someone?" asked Vanessa.

Pemberton hesitated. "I can tell you this much. I know that he is in this neighborhood now. My freebooting friends have alerted me of that fact, for the word is that a Frenchman will be crossing the Channel soon. I want to be in position to capture both, the traitor and the spy, when they meet."

"You may rely on me," said Vanessa. "But what of the others who know what you are? Can you completely trust the smugglers?"

Pemberton laughed. "As far as I am able, yes. The freebooters know me exactly for what I am."

"But then—" started Vanessa, alarmed.

"My sweet life, the Pembertons have had connections with the gentleman's trade for generations. As far as my shadowy friends are concerned, I am merely following in a family tradition," said Pemberton. "If I choose to play the fool for the benefit of my neighbors and the excisemen, that is my business. Pray do not be anxious. They will keep silence about me."

Vanessa took a moment to readjust her thinking. "Then your father—"

"And my grandfather and his father before him," said Pemberton, smiling. "They all promoted the trade. Does that shock you?"

"Not as much as perhaps it should," said Vanessa. "My own father knew more than he actually told to me. I have that from Howard Tremaine. I suppose that I knew less than anyone. After all, you knew about the abbey before I ever told you that was where I was taking you."

"Yes. Halverton, too, has its traditions," said Pemberton with a grin.

"Howard, how many others besides myself and the squire and the smugglers know about you?" asked Vanessa.

"Have I not told you that you need not be anxious for me?" he asked.

"Yes, but I would still like to know," said Vanessa. "If ever I should need to send a message to you, for instance, whom could I trust?"

"There are only a handful here who are completely privy to my secret," said Pemberton. "My valet, the butler, and my housekeeper. I could not have done what I have nor escaped detection when I was wounded if it had not been for them."

"There must be others who suspect something," said Vanessa.

Pemberton rose and took a short turn around the room. His expression was reflective. He came back to sit down beside Vanessa. "Of course there are. But the rest of the household have been encouraged to think my comings and goings to be strictly related to the free trade. I am the brawn while others provide the brain."

"You are an exceedingly deceptive fellow," said Vanessa. She knew that he had decided to reveal no more to her than he had already. It did not particularly wound her, for she realized that he was protecting her as well as himself. Obviously the less she knew, the less she could inadvertently reveal.

"Do you think so?" asked Pemberton quietly. He gazed down into her face with a penetrating expression. "You must believe me when I say that I am not deceiving you, Vanessa. My declaration to you is honest and sincere."

"Yes, I know it," said Vanessa, reaching up to lay her hand gently against the side of his face.

Pemberton caught her hand and brought her palm to his lips, where he pressed a kiss. Still holding her hand clasped in his, he said, "We must bring this interlude to an end or even my good aunt will wonder at her wisdom in allowing us to be alone for so long. Tug on the bell rope, sweetheart. She will come when she hears it."

"What nonsense. But I suppose that the conventions must be preserved, even for a gentleman recovering from influenza," said Vanessa, rising. She turned away to carry out his suggestion and pulled the rope. "By the by, does Mrs. Dabney know about your escapades?"

"Indeed she does and highly disapproving she has professed herself. The greatest affront to her dignity is my assumption of stupidity. It so annoys her that she has little difficulty in treating me with all the impatience that my imbecilities deserve," said Pemberton. "But Aunt Cassie is a patriot to her backbone and so she supports me and my wretched disguise. However, she has informed me that my intention to court you is the only sensible thing that I have done since returning to the county."

Vanessa felt a blush warming her face. "She is a most admirable woman."

Pemberton settled himself more comfortably on the sofa and threw a rug over his long legs. He waved a negligent hand over himself. "Behold the patient on the road to recovery. I am a poor creature, am I not?"

"You shall come about," said Vanessa dryly.

"I confided in my aunt that I meant to offer for you. Do not be surprised if she asks for a private word with you," said Pemberton.

The door opened. Instantly Pemberton's face assumed the

wide, slow expression that had become so familiar. Vanessa turned as Mrs. Dabney and a footman entered. She remembered that not everyone in the household was in Howard Pemberton's confidences and she played the role that had been assigned to her. "Oh, Mrs. Dabney. I am glad that you came. I fear that I have overtaxed Mr. Pemberton with my conversation."

Aware that Pemberton's last remark had put color into her cheeks, Vanessa was not surprised by Mrs. Dabney's sharp glance. The elderly woman gave a quick, approving nod.

"Thank you, Miss Lester, but there is no need to concern yourself. My nephew is becoming stronger each day," said Mrs. Dabney. She narrowed her gaze on her nephew's guileless expression. "If he does just as the physician has ordered, he will no doubt recover his full strength very quickly."

On a spurt of mischief, Vanessa said, "Mr. Pemberton was just saying that he felt in need of a sustaining cordial." She was rewarded by a quick choked off exclamation behind her, but she did not dare to turn around to meet her betrothed's outraged expression.

Mrs. Dabney's eyes gleamed in appreciation. But she gave no other outward acknowledgment of her amusement. She marched across the room to the sofa and laid her hand on her nephew's brow. "I am not surprised. He is quite warm. I shall send Tobias down to ask Mrs. Dorrance to make up a cordial for you, nephew."

"That won't be necessary, Aunt," said Pemberton hastily. "I am perfectly well. In fact, I should like to go riding. Miss Lester needs an escort home."

"You shall do no such thing. You great silly creature, you haven't the least notion what is best for you," said Mrs. Dabney in a scolding tone. She tucked the rug more securely over Mr. Pemberton's limbs.

"But Miss Lester—" objected Pemberton.

"Miss Lester brought her groom with her. She will be perfectly safe," said Mrs. Dabney. She turned and held out her hand to Vanessa. "I shall not keep you, Miss Lester. I know that there is not the least cause for me or for Mr. Pemberton to feel anxious on your behalf."

Pemberton rolled his eyes in Vanessa's direction. She pretended not to see the appeal. "No, indeed, ma'am," said Vanessa with a quivering lip. "I shall take my leave of you, then. I trust that you shall soon be completely recovered, Mr. Pemberton."

"I am already well, but Aunt Cassie will not let me be," he said fretfully.

Vanessa turned away hastily, choking back a low chuckle. When she met the footman's wooden expression, she changed it to a slight clearing of her throat. Until that moment she had not realized how easily she could betray the man she had pledged herself to wed. Any inclination to laugh vanished.

The footman held open the door for Vanessa's exit. Upon Mrs. Dabney's reminder to order up a cordial, he followed Vanessa out and closed the door. "I'll be seeing you out, miss," he said courteously as he offered her cloak to her.

"Thank you," said Vanessa, wrapping the cloak around her. She gathered up her whip and gloves. She did not linger, but left Pemberton Place with almost unseemly haste.

On the return to Halverton, Vanessa addressed her groom suddenly. "John, if there is ever anything more rumored about the smugglers in these parts, I wish to be informed immediately."

"Yes, miss," said the groom.

Vanessa felt that there was some explanation due. "I must protect Halverton interests," she said. It was perfectly true in a sense. The future of Halverton very much depended upon the continued safety of a large and seemingly slow-witted gentleman.

"O' course, miss," said the groom.

Vanessa said nothing more, but set heel to her mare's side.

During the following week, Vanessa went about her usual duties and attended several social functions. She was unsurprised when Mr. Pemberton shortly reappeared in society, pronouncing himself ready to plunge back into circulation. She made an effort to treat him as did others, greeting his return with a mild interest and then accepting him into the fabric of her life much as before.

Vanessa tried hard not to smile at Mr. Pemberton with any

extra warmth or to seek out his company more than she would ordinarily have done. It was difficult, however, to keep away from him when her steps unconsciously wanted to carry her to his side or her gaze automatically sought him out. Vanessa constantly had to remind herself that Mr. Pemberton was supposed to be a dull-witted gentleman whose company no lady in her right mind would prefer over another gentleman, unless it was for the waltz.

Vanessa wanted to know what was happening in her betrothed's clandestine maneuvers, but she knew that she could not inquire. She felt anxiety for Mr. Pemberton's safety. No amount of reassurance to herself could rid her of it.

The uneasiness residing inside Vanessa became a perpetual companion. She was only relieved of its presence when she was in the same room with Mr. Pemberton. Vanessa almost wished that he had not declared himself to her. Ignorance of his true identity had spared her this tension. But no, she was glad she knew him now for what he was. She would not know otherwise what it was to love and be loved.

Lady Cecily announced that she was planning a grand ball, and one that would eclipse all that had gone before. Vanessa greeted the intelligence almost with relief. Halverton would be thrown into a flurry of preparations, in which she would necessarily be involved. Hopefully she would be able to turn her thoughts away from constant reflection about Mr. Pemberton and what he was trying to do.

Lady Cecily was astounded when her daughter encouraged her purpose. "Why, Vanessa, I did not realize that you were so ambitious," she said. "Surely this is a new come-out for you?"

"I have always wished Halverton hospitality to be of the best," said Vanessa.

"Indeed," replied Lady Cecily thoughtfully. Her ladyship did not understand what had come over her daughter. She was beginning to suspect that Vanessa had her own plans in the making and that did not sit easily with one of her managing character. However, Lady Cecily was not one to cavil at being granted her own way. She said nothing further to her daughter, merely filing away a mental note to herself to pay closer attention to Vanessa's movements.

It seemed to Lady Cecily that Vanessa was beginning to look a little worn. Perhaps her daughter was simply spending too much of her energy on the estate. It would not do to have Vanessa come down with some ailment, thought Lady Cecily ruminatively. It would not do at all.

Lady Cecily made an unparalleled decision. "I shall speak to Tremaine. He must see to it that Vanessa does not overtax herself," she said aloud, and at once sent for the elderly secretary.

The few minutes that Lady Cecily was closeted with Tremaine resulted in a short interview for the secretary with Vanessa. Vanessa denied that she was overburdened or wearied of her duties. She was astonished by her mother's surprising and unprecedented expression of concern.

"I, too, have noticed an unusual air of anxiety attached to you, miss," said Tremaine. "Her ladyship's queries merely confirmed my own conclusions. Is there anything that you wish to confide in me, miss? I assure you that I am quite prepared to shoulder any burden."

Vanessa realized again the validity of Mr. Pemberton's former wisdom in keeping her in the dark about his true identity and intentions. If Lady Cecily, who was completely self-centered, had deduced that she was concerned for some reason, then how much more observant must be those who were her closest friends. Now she must learn the art of dissembling and with all speed. She smiled at her secretary's concerned expression. "I am truly sorry if I have excited concern, Howard. It is but this round of entertaining and the consequences. I will confide this much to you, my old friend. I have rejected offers from both Reverend Haversaw and Mr. Nashe."

Tremaine's expression at once altered. "I understand completely, Miss Vanessa."

"Pray do not overly blame Lady Cecily for my disquiet, Howard," said Vanessa quietly. "It would be unfair."

Tremaine's expression was noncommittal. "No doubt." He bowed and left her, leaving Vanessa to somber reflection.

Vanessa resolved to be more on her guard. She could not allow herself to exhibit the least anxiety, for then she ran the risk of raising further questions. And that was precisely what she most wished to avoid. She therefore plunged herself full tilt into the arrangements for the Halverton ball, greeting every preparation with high enthusiasm.

Lady Cecily's ball was as elegant as her ladyship could have wished. Though the company was not as glittering as her ladyship might have liked, nevertheless everything else had the unmistakable air of London attached to it.

Lady Cecily had left nothing undone. Nor had her ladyship spared any expense. She had ordered everything from the refreshments to the decorations from the finest shops in London. The ball acquired a sophisticated cachet that no others in the district could ever hope to aspire. Lady Cecily was the object of envy of every other hostess in the county and she reveled in it.

The evening went marvelously well. There was nothing but a constant flow of compliments to Lady Cecily and Vanessa. Vanessa received the accolades with proper modesty and gave the honor to her mother for the success of the evening's entertainment.

Vanessa was in a fair way to relaxing completely. She had had the opportunity of a few whispered words with Mr. Pemberton, words accompanied by a passionate salute that had put roses in her cheeks and a sparkle in her eyes. She had heard wonderful compliments for Halverton's hospitality, which was a source of pride to her. Even Lady Cecily contributed to her sense of well-being by proffering an uncharacteristic compliment for her daughter's vibrant appearance.

"One might suspect that you had set up an ardent flirtation, Vanessa," finished Lady Cecily.

Vanessa laughed. Her eyes positively danced with secret amusement. "Might one? It is an enticing notion, indeed." She fairly glided off, leaving Lady Cecily standing with raised brows and staring after her.

Vanessa circulated among the guests, making conversation and accepting many invitations to dance. Mr. Nashe was favored with her lively company, as were several other gentlemen. Shortly before two in the morning, Mr. Pemberton came up to her. With his genial grin, he said, "There is a waltz striking up, Miss Lester. May I have the honor?"

Vanessa at once concurred, graciously excusing herself to those with whom she had been conversing. As she went into Mr. Pemberton's arms, she said with a smile, "I had hoped that you would ask me again, sir."

"I shall waltz with you anytime that you wish, Miss Lester," declared Mr. Pemberton.

Vanessa smiled up into his face. "I shall remember that," she murmured.

"Do not look at me like that. I might lose my head and shock these good people with a show of passion," said Mr. Pemberton softly.

"That would not do at all, of course," said Vanessa. She rearranged her features into a prim expression. "Is this better?"

"Much better," said Mr. Pemberton. He whirled her into a dizzying progress across the ballroom floor. For several minutes they enjoyed the fluid dance. Mr. Pemberton said suddenly, "I have hopes of shortly seeing an end to my masquerade."

Surprised, Vanessa glanced up into his face. He was faintly smiling and she responded with a quick smile of her own. "Oh, I am glad!"

"The moment that I am done, I intend to come for you," said Mr. Pemberton quietly.

Vanessa felt warmth steal into her face. "I shall be waiting," she said.

The set ended and Mr. Pemberton brought them reluctantly to a halt. He proffered his arm and Vanessa accepted it. He very correctly led her back toward her chair. There was a temporary lull in the activity around them so that he was able to speak a few private words. "I must leave the ball early, for there is something that I must do. But be assured that I shall wait on you in the morning."

"Of course." Vanessa put out her hand to catch his sleeve, a hint of her previous anxiety returning. "You will take care?"

Mr. Pemberton smiled. It was not the wide, genial smile that was characteristic of the part he played, but one of infinite tenderness. "You need not fear for me," he said softly. He lifted her hand to his lips and then was gone.

Vanessa watched his departure with a faint smile on her

face. She held the promise that he had given to her very close to her heart. All would soon be resolved and he would come for her. She felt as though she was dancing on air.

Vanessa's bubble of happiness was burst suddenly and quite brutally.

A few minutes after Mr. Pemberton's departure, she accepted an offer of refreshment from Lt. Copperidge. It had grown quite warm in the ballroom due to the multitude of burning candelabrum overhead and the press of people participating in the lively dancing, so that Vanessa was grateful for the suggestion.

As the excise officer handed the lemon ice to Vanessa, he suddenly thanked her again for her earlier help in providing vital information to him.

"You have already expressed your gratitude, Lieutenant. Nothing else need be said," said Vanessa with a smile. She had no desire to discuss that incident. It had been a harrowing experience, even though it had thrust her into the discovery of her life's love.

"I trust that we shall continue to enjoy one another's confidence," said Lt. Copperidge, his gray gaze penetrating.

"Of course, Lieutenant," said Vanessa, smiling. She knew that she spoke a lie, for she had no intention of providing the excise officer with any sort of information that might again put Mr. Pemberton into harm's way.

Lt. Copperidge nodded, apparently satisfied. After a few desultory statements, he got up to leave. He paused, then said, "I feel it only right that I should tell you that my investigation is coming along nicely. In fact, I have planned a raid shortly." He glanced toward the large clock in the corner, then returned his gaze to her face. "One I am certain that, if successful, will close the books on these elusive criminals."

Vanessa smiled again, though her lips suddenly felt stiff. "Indeed, I hope that all works out just as it ought," she said.

"I appreciate your sentiments, Miss Lester," said Lt. Copperidge, bowing once more before he left her.

Vanessa sat quite still, her eyes gazing blindly over the noisy company. The lieutenant's words, and his significant glance toward the clock, had struck a chord of fear in her.

Again she heard Mr. Pemberton's statement that he had something to attend to that night.

Vanessa expelled her breath slowly. Her pulse was pounding. Obviously there was to be a rendezvous of some sort within a very short time. And the excise troops knew all about it.

Chapter Twenty

Vanessa sat quite still for what seemed to her to be an eternity, though by the clock only a few seconds had elapsed. Her mind sped over conjectures and alternatives. One thing stood out from all the rest. She had to send a message to warn Mr. Pemberton. Her eyes sought out her butler. Perhaps Sims could help her.

Vanessa rose to her feet and threaded her way as quickly as she could across the ballroom. She was deterred several times by various friends and acquaintances, all of whom wanted to exchange a few words. Vanessa turned down an offer to dance, smilingly explaining that she wanted a word with her butler.

At last she was able to come up to the butler. "Sims!"

He looked around quickly. "Miss?"

"I should like a private word, please," said Vanessa, gesturing toward the anteroom off of the main ballroom.

The butler followed her and Vanessa, after making certain that the room was empty, closed the door behind them. She turned to the now-anxious butler. "Sims, I must get a message to the smugglers. I believe that you can help me."

The butler looked appalled. "Miss!"

"Sims, Lieutenant Copperidge has just hinted to me that he is leading a raid against them in a very short time," said Vanessa urgently. "They must be warned not to meet tonight."

"But—but I have heard nothing of a meeting," stammered Sims, shaken. "I would have had some word—" He suddenly realized what he was saying and broke off abruptly. "I am sorry, miss. I don't know what I was saying."

"No, nor I," agreed Vanessa impatiently. "Come, Sims! You must see that you can trust me."

"Aye, I know that I can, miss," said Sims quietly. He nodded suddenly. "Very well, miss. I shall tell you what I know."

A few minutes later, armed with the vital information that she needed, Vanessa slipped out of the anteroom. She did not return to the ballroom, but picked up her skirts and raced quickly upstairs.

In her bedroom, Vanessa changed her silk slippers for sturdy boots. She felt that there was not time to change into her habit. A warm cloak thrown over her ball gown would have to serve.

When Vanessa emerged from her bedroom, she did not approach the main staircase but took the backstairs instead. She prayed that she would not be intercepted by anyone before she was able to slip out of the manor house. The butler had been given orders to let it be known that she had the headache, but that excuse would scarcely do if she were discovered sneaking out of the back door.

Vanessa was successful in reaching the stables without detection. Her groom was surprised by her appearance, especially when he caught sight of her strange garb. At once he leaped to a shrewd conclusion.

"Miss, let me go for ye," he urged, as he reluctantly but swiftly followed her orders to saddle the mare.

Vanessa shook her head. She stepped into his laced hands and settled herself in the saddle. "No, I must go myself. It is for a very special reason, John." She could not betray Mr. Pemberton even to one as loyal as her own groom. Vanessa gathered the reins and turned the mare.

The groom hurried after her. "Ye'll never be going alone. Let me go with you," he begged.

"I am sorry, John. Truly I am," said Vanessa. She kicked her mare into motion.

It was a foggy cold night. Of necessity Vanessa was forced to keep her mount's pace in check, despite her anxious impatience. She could not afford to spur her mare to speed when she could not see more than a few yards in front of her. The danger of the mare stepping into an unseen pothole and breaking a leg was too real. She couldn't risk it.

Vanessa was certain that she had managed to tear her gown

in mounting. In addition the long skirt had twisted up to expose her legs to the cutting air. Her long cloak covered her, but it did not fully protect her from the icy drafts of wind. But she dismissed such small considerations. Her life's love was in mortal danger and she had to warn him.

Vanessa rode directly to the abbey. Her butler had thought that if there was indeed a rendezvous set for that night, the old ruins would be the most likely spot. She did not take precautions against being followed, trusting that her own familiarity with a scarcely-used winding track through the woods would give her an edge in time. The heavy damp mist was proving an advantage to her, as well, for even as it masked the way and slowed her, it must certainly prove nearly an insurmountable obstacle to the excise troops.

Suddenly, out of the mist ahead, she heard low voices. She called out as she emerged from the last of the trees, giving warning of her arrival. She did not want to catch the smugglers so unawares that they were startled into shooting at her.

The conversation ceased abruptly. One of the men in the clearing exclaimed as both whirled to face her.

Vanessa walked her mare forward. "Please! You must leave this place instantly. The excisemen know of this meeting."

As she spoke, she glanced over the two men, then around the remainder of the clearing. She saw in one sweeping glance that Pemberton was not one of the two, nor was he in immediate evidence. She assumed that the others must be hidden nearby among the trees and broken archways, however, and that Pemberton would soon come striding out.

The bridle of her horse was caught by the shorter of the two men. "So! Miss Lester, this is an unexpected surprise, indeed."

The familiar drawling voice astonished her. Vanessa peered down into the man's face in amazement. "Mark Nashe? Whatever are you doing here? I had no notion that you were involved."

"Did you not? But how felicitous, since I preferred it not to be known. Will you dismount, Miss Lester?"

She could see that he was smiling and that he was holding up his hands to her. Vanessa cast a glance again around the clearing, wondering where Pemberton was. But perhaps he was a little ways off and she would have to walk into the woods to meet him. She kicked free of her stirrup, swung her leg over the horn, and slipped down into Mark Nashe's waiting arms.

Vanessa was still surprised by his involvement. It seemed that the most astonishing people were involved in the smuggling. When she was on the ground, she thanked him and shook out her cloak and skirt. Looking around, she said, "But where are the others?"

"Others?"

"Why, yes. The rest of the smugglers," said Vanessa impatiently. She wanted to see Pemberton, but she did not want to use his name unless Mark Nashe mentioned it first. She had no way of knowing who was actually in Pemberton's confidence.

Nashe and the other man, who had not yet spoken, exchanged quick glances. "Ah, yes," said Nashe. "The others have already gone ahead. We tarried for a moment to discuss a certain matter of import. Now what was it you were saying about the excise troops?"

He was still holding one of her arms. Vanessa disliked the possessiveness of his grip, but doubted that he was aware he was offending her. Undoubtedly Nashe was feeling a sense of urgency over her hastily given warning and did not realize that he was clutching her so tightly.

"At the ball Lieutenant Copperidge hinted to me that he knew something was set for tonight. He has given orders for his troops to move in on the rendezvous point," said Vanessa.

The other man exclaimed under his breath. Mr. Nashe threw a warning glance toward him. "Did Lieutenant Copperidge mention the abbey specifically?" he asked.

Vanessa shook her head. "No. I wasn't certain that the abbey was being used tonight, but it seemed possible. I had to try to bring a warning."

"I do appreciate it, dear Vanessa. But why should you go to so much trouble for a group of smugglers?" asked Mr. Nashe.

Vanessa sensed suspicion in his quiet question. There was a tenseness about Mr. Nashe that she had never before encountered. "Naturally I would do so. Many of my own household are tied to the smugglers in one way or another. Nearly every household seems to be. But you know that, of course," she said.

"Of course." Mr. Nashe's voice was reflective. "I should have guessed that the feelings ran deeper than I had supposed."

Vanessa was impatient and bewildered by Mr. Nashe's attitude. Surely he had grasped by now the gravity of his circumstances. If they remained too long here, they ran the terrible risk of discovery by the excisemen.

"Mark, do you not understand? The excisemen may be upon us at any moment. You and your friend must be gone beforehand," she said urgently.

"Yes, yes, of course. But you see, my dear Vanessa, you pose a problem that I must solve first," said Mr. Nashe.

Vanessa felt a measure of relief. She at last understood his hesitation and could supply a remedy. "There is no cause for concern on my behalf, Mark. I assure you that I will be quite safe. There is a little-known track through the wood leading in the direction of Halverton that will avoid the excisemen altogether. I shall simply return home that way. It will not be the first time."

"Will it not? How very enterprising of you, Vanessa. At any other time I might be fascinated by the tale. However, I think now—" Mr. Nashe spoke swiftly in French to his companion. "Etienne, what think you?"

With shock, Vanessa absorbed the significance of the switch into French. She glanced swiftly at the other man, really taking note of him for the first time. She recalled with perfect, horrifying clarity that her betrothed had told her that a French spy was expected to appear in the vicinity. Her mind reeled with the implications of Mr. Nashe's apparent friendliness with the Frenchman.

"*Voyons!* You ask me? You have heard what she has said. We are shortly to be overtaken and you stand about dallying! Slit her throat and be done!"

"*Non, non.* That is too crude, *mon ami,*" said Mr. Nashe softly. He had felt the sharp recoil she made at the Frenchman's hissing words. He smiled up at Vanessa's appalled face. In the faint light, his eyes were slightly hooded. "We shall take her with us, Etienne. I do not wish to lose mademoiselle so soon, for she is to be my wife."

"You are mad!" exclaimed the Frenchman.

Vanessa silently agreed with the man's sentiments. Mr. Nashe's declaration was insane. She would never accept him. She had made that perfectly clear when she had thought him to be merely a particularly persistent suitor. Now that she knew him for a traitor, how much truer it was!

Mr. Nashe appeared able to read something of her thoughts, for his response echoed them. "But no, *mon ami*. Miss Lester is quite an heiress. When I wed her, I shall be a rich man. A very rich man, indeed. And it will be quite safe, for a wife cannot testify against her husband," he said softly.

Vanessa's aversion toward him rose up to an unbearable degree. She tried to pull away from him. "You *are* mad if you think that I shall ever consent to such an arrangement!"

Mr. Nashe continued to smile. Almost lazily, he lifted his gloved hand and flicked it against her cheek. The slight blow stung her face. Vanessa flinched, gasping in shock. "You will consent after tonight, Miss Lester. I promise you."

"Very well! Very well! Wed the wench and be damned. But we must be away from this place at once," exclaimed the Frenchman. His agitation had grown and he cast his glance from side to side as though he scented danger.

"Quite right, Etienne." Mr. Nashe's voice suddenly hardened. "Give me your handkerchief. I must secure Miss Lester."

Muttering, the Frenchman thrust the fine linen square into Nashe's hands. "There! Be quick. I thought that I heard something in the fog."

"Hold your pistol to her head, Etienne. If she moves or cries out, shoot her," instructed Mr. Nashe.

The Frenchman grunted. "That is the only sensible thing that you have said these past five minutes."

The cold touch of the pistol pressed firmly against Vanessa's temple. She held herself very still even though every fiber of her being urged her to pull free before Mr. Nashe could complete his quick ministrations.

"But give me the excuse, mademoiselle," breathed the Frenchman. "It will be so much more convenient."

Vanessa had no intention of offering such opportunity. She stood stoically while Mr. Nashe finished tying her wrists together in front of her. She lowered her tightly bound wrists, assuming that was the end of it. But then Mr. Nashe whipped his own handkerchief over her mouth, tying it securely.

He surveyed his handiwork with a satisfied smile. "Now we shall go. And you will lead us, dear Vanessa. Down your cleverly concealed path back to Halverton." As he spoke, he drew forth a small dagger and cut the long leading rein off of Vanessa's mare. Forming a noose, he put it around Vanessa's neck. When he mounted his own horse, he retained hold of the other end of the noose. "Etienne, you will lead Miss Lester's mare, if you please."

The Frenchman was already mounted and he had waited impatiently. Now he grumbled under his breath and caught hold of the mare's remaining rein. He did not like the circumstances that had been thrust upon him. It was not part of his character to overly trust anyone with whom he worked, but he had no choice now except to submit to Nashe's leading. He was too unfamiliar with the dangers of this country to strike off on his own. Until he had reached the beach and could make his rendezvous with the boat that was to carry him safely to France, he would have to comply with whatever decisions that Nashe might make.

A far-off crashing sounded somewhere in the wood. The noises were carried and accentuated by the heavy mist. The Frenchman cursed. "What if we must ride fast? What of the woman then?" he hissed challengingly, throwing a deadly glance in the direction of the female who walked ahead of them.

"Then I shall take her up before me," said Mr. Nashe indifferently. He jerked on the lead when Vanessa stepped onto a branch that cracked beneath her boot. She was pulled up painfully. "Careful, my dear. I do not wish to strangle you, but I shall do so quite cheerfully if you try to signal our friends yonder."

Vanessa cast a single glance backward, her face expression-

less. Then she returned her gaze forward, attempting to see far
enough ahead so that she could avoid the worst of the branches
that overlapped the track and dragged at her skirts. She used
her bound arms to push aside undergrowth that on horseback
would not have impeded her passage.

It was difficult walking and not just because of the obstacles
on the ground and around her. The leather strap around her
throat was an ever-present menace. She breathed shallowly
around the gag.

A small log loomed in front of her. Vanessa clutched up the
front of her cloak and gown as best she could with her bound
hands and clambered clumsily over it. She stumbled and the
leather strap jerked painfully around her throat. Her former ad-
mirer was reminding her that her present fate rested in his
hands.

She dared not try again to make any seemingly innocuous
noise. The swiftness of Mr. Nashe's discernment stunned her.
More and more the horror of Mark Nashe's character was becoming clear to her. He was a traitor to Britain, consorting
with the French for material gain. She had heard the rumors of
his addiction to gaming, but she had not paid close attention.
Apparently his obligations were steeper than anyone had
known.

He would have no compunction in killing her, Vanessa
thought distantly. He had already alluded to his willingness to
do so. Her safety thus far lay solely in his determination to use
her to gain possession of Halverton.

It occurred to Vanessa to wonder what her fate might be if
he was successful in coercing her into wedlock. Halverton
would be safely under his domination. Would he continue to
rely upon her silence or would he take steps to permanently in-
sure it? Vanessa shuddered.

At the moment she could see no hope of escape. Vanessa
was confident that, if given half the chance, her familiarity
with the surrounding woods would enable her to escape even
though she was afoot. But trussed up as she was, she could not
simply dart away into the woods. There was the Frenchman's
gun to be considered, as well. Even if she did manage to some-

how get the lead that was around her neck out of Nashe's grip, the Frenchman would no doubt be quick to shoot at her.

Vanessa had no choice but to lead the traitor and the spy off through the wood. Their path bore them away from the abbey and the danger presented by the excisemen, as testified by the sounds of men and horses falling gradually behind them.

Vanessa would have given anything at that moment to see an excise trooper with his rifle. Even better would be the sight of Howard Pemberton's dear face.

She wondered where Pemberton could be. Obviously she had gone far wrong in assuming that he and the smugglers would be at the abbey. Instead, she had stumbled upon Nashe and the spy and put herself into the gravest danger.

A lightning thought caused her to stumble. Vanessa scarcely noticed the resulting warning tug on the lead around her neck. The appalling thing that had come into her mind momentarily crowded out all other concerns.

Nashe had said that the smugglers had gone ahead, which meant that Howard Pemberton had done so, too. If Nashe was in collaboration with the smugglers and the French spy, that meant that Pemberton was also.

The suspicion that Howard Pemberton could himself be in league with Nashe and the French spy shook Vanessa to the depths of her being.

She did not want to believe it. It did not bear thinking of, and yet she could not quite dismiss the possibility. Unless Nashe had lied altogether about the smugglers, and there was no reason that he should since it was obvious that he had to have access to them to be able to get the Frenchman out of the country, then Howard Pemberton could well be up to his neck in treason. Howard Pemberton, her gentleman smuggler and her betrothed, a traitor to England. If it was true, then she had given her heart to a cad of the worst sort.

What did it matter now? she thought fearfully. She was going to die or else be forced by some hideous means to wed that monster, Mark Nashe. For Vanessa had no doubts that that gentleman had dreamed of a creative way to force her compliance with his diabolical wishes.

Something rose up inside of her, dispelling the spirit of fear and despair that threatened to overwhelm her. She was not alone. Never alone, for the God that she believed in assured her of that. "For I shall never leave you, nor forsake you." She had read that verse that very morning and now it came to life for her. Vanessa clung to that promise with every ounce of faith in her. She would survive. More, she would escape. She just needed to put her wits to work for her, instead of allowing her mind to work against her.

Vanessa thought about what lay ahead on the track. There was still some distance to be covered before Halverton was reached. She did not believe that Nashe intended to actually go up to the manor. He must plan to turn aside before actually emerging from the wood and coming into sight of Halverton's windows.

Therefore, if he did indeed want to take her with them, he would want her to be mounted. He had said something to the effect that he would put her up in front of him.

Vanessa gave careful consideration to that for several moments. She became convinced that that moment, when she was to be taken up on horseback, would be her best, and perhaps only, opportunity to escape.

Her desperate plan hinged on a very vital detail. There was the chance that Nashe would drop the neck lead in order to be able to reach down and boost her up onto his horse. That would be her moment.

Outwardly docile, Vanessa continued to lead the horsemen behind her toward Halverton. Inside she was filled with mingled anxiety and hope. Her nerves were stretched taut.

Chapter Twenty-one

Just as Vanessa began wondering whether she had thought out Nashe's intentions correctly after all, Nashe pulled up his horse. The Frenchman also stopped, his attitude one of alert suspicion.

"What is it?" asked the Frenchman sharply.

"Calm yourself, my friend," drawled Mr. Nashe. "As I judge, we are close to Halverton. Isn't that so, dear Vanessa?"

Vanessa nodded warily.

"Ah, yes, I can even see the end of the woods. You have done very well in guiding us. Now it is time to take a new direction. Come here, my dear bride. You must be quite worn out with your exertions. You will ride with me," said Mr. Nashe. "Etienne, let go of Miss Lester's mare. It will find its way home, riderless. A considerable alarm will be raised, which will be all to the good, I think."

"I do not follow your thoughts, Nashe, but it is nothing to me," said the Frenchman, letting go of the mare's rein. The mare shook her head, as though testing her freedom.

"It is simple, *mon ami.* Consternation shall arise over Miss Lester's disappearance and possible hurt. Tomorrow, after a suitable length of time, I shall produce Miss Lester with a credible tale of accident and rescue. I shall be the hero and Miss Lester will bestow her hand upon me, at last rewarding my ardent courtship," said Mr. Nashe.

The Frenchman snorted in disgust. "A pretty fairy tale!"

Nashe laughed. Then he tugged on the leather lead. "Why do you not obey me, my sweet? Have I not said that you do not need to walk one step further? Come, Vanessa! Surely you must see that you have no other option, so do be sensible and make things easy on yourself."

Vanessa slowly approached Nashe's horse. She stood looking up at him in a helpless manner, her bound hands slightly raised.

Realizing at last that without the use of her hands, she was unable to help him in lifting her onto the horse, Nashe gave an impatient exclamation. He let go of the lead and leaned far over to the side, his hand reaching for her waist.

Quick as a whip, Vanessa lashed out at Nashe's horse. The gelding threw up its head, startled. Leaning over the saddle as he was, Nashe was nearly unseated. He cursed, fighting to right himself even as he sawed on the reins of the sidestepping horse.

Vanessa plunged past the gelding's shoulder and darted into the woods.

The Frenchman wasted no time. He pulled out his pistol and fired. The shot whistled frighteningly close to Vanessa's head. Instinctively she ducked and went to the ground.

"You fool! You'll draw them down on us!" exclaimed Nashe furiously, turning his mount.

An answering shot sounded, very close.

"*Voyons!* They have found us!"

The Frenchman kicked heels to his mount and plunged clear of the woods. Another shot exploded. The Frenchman threw up his hands. He slid from the saddle to land heavily on the dark ground. His horse continued to run wildly away, empty stirrups flapping.

Nashe cursed awfully. He had gotten control of his own horse, cruelly cutting it with his whip. He cast swiftly around for any sign of his former captive. The heavy fog had separated and the faint moonlight showed an ugly expression on his face.

Urgent excited shouts came closer and closer. More shots were fired. Nashe lifted his head, listening. Then he pulled around his horse. Breaking from the trees, he set off thundering across the green toward Halverton.

Horsemen broke from the woods in close pursuit. More

shots were fired. Mark Nashe swayed suddenly in the saddle, but he did not fall. His gelding was stretched out in full gallop.

The troopers urged their own mounts to greater speed. "Don't let him get away, lads!" The pursuit swung out of sight.

Vanessa slowly raised up from where she had been crouched. She worked the gag free with her bound hands and then gasped at the sheer pleasure of drawing air through her mouth. The tight lead was next and when she had worked it loose, she threw it to the ground with revulsion.

Her mare had taken flight with the first pistol shot. Vanessa was afoot, but Halverton was within sight. She left the wood and started swiftly across the grassy lawns toward her home.

Suddenly she stopped.

A large figure was crouched over the downed French spy. When he rose, she knew him for Howard Pemberton. He caught sight of her then and stood very still.

"Are you friend or foe?" Vanessa asked, a quiver in her voice.

"I hope that I am still more than a friend," said Pemberton, approaching her. He was leading a tall stallion. From his free hand dangled a large deadly-looking pistol. The butt of a second firearm was thrust into his waistband.

Vanessa looked at the pistol in his hand. "If that is for me, pray recall that we are standing in sight of Halverton. All of the noise must have awakened my household. There will be witnesses."

"Vanessa! How could you think that of me?" exclaimed Pemberton. He had reached her by then. "Don't you realize that I was the one who fired on Nashe and the other?"

"Did you?" Vanessa reached up her bound wrists to brush the start of tears from her eyes. "Why weren't you at the abbey or somewhere on the track? Oh, Howard! Why didn't you save me?"

"Sweetheart, I—your hands!" Pemberton thrust the pistol into his waist with the other and then swiftly unknotted the handkerchief. Then he took her arm and led her around to the side of his horse. "Come along! We must get inside. Lieutenant Copperidge and his troops will return soon. Their temper will depend upon whether they capture Mark Nashe. I wish to avoid as many questions as possible and being caught flat-footed out here will not advance my desire."

"But what of the Frenchman?" asked Vanessa.

"He will not be going anywhere again," said Pemberton somewhat grimly.

Vanessa shuddered and allowed herself to be tossed up into the saddle. Pemberton mounted behind her and then set the stallion cantering swiftly across the green to Halverton's stables.

Vanessa was not surprised when her groom emerged. He did not ask any questions as the stallion was relinquished into his care. "John, is Ladyfly home?" she asked.

"Aye, miss. She came in not two minutes past," said the groom.

"Thank you, John." Without another word spoken by anyone, the groom turned away with the stallion and Pemberton took Vanessa's elbow to escort her to the manor.

The side door was standing open and the butler ushered them inside. There was a branch of candles burning on the occasional table against the hall wall, throwing odd dancing shadows across the dark paneling. "Come in, miss. You and Mr. Pemberton may be private in the drawing room. Her ladyship has gone up to bed. All of the guests have also retired or left long ago," said Sims.

"Thank you, Sims. I think Miss Lester needs to go upstairs and refresh herself first," said Pemberton, smiling down at her. He pulled a twig out of her tumbled hair.

Vanessa cast a downward glance at herself. Even in the dim candlelight it was obvious that her gown and cloak had suffered ruin. Streaks of dirt and leaves clung to the cloak and the hem of her gown showed a ragged tear. "Yes," agreed Vanessa. She glanced swiftly up at his face. "But you shall remain at Halverton until I return?"

Pemberton gave a slow grin. "Rest assured that I shall certainly do so. And I give you my word that I shall answer all of your questions in due time. Now go upstairs."

As Vanessa started to turn away, she saw her betrothed give an unmistakable signal to her butler, who gave a bare nod. She realized at once that her butler knew very well that Mr. Pemberton was not what he had seemed these past months.

"Sims, I presume that there is a fire in the drawing room. I believe that I can make my way there well enough. Do go up and light Miss Lester's way," said Mr. Pemberton.

"Very good, sir. I shall return to inquire your needs as soon as possible."

Even as Sims picked up the branch of candles and preceded her, Vanessa decided that she really didn't want to know what business her betrothed and her butler might have with one another. It was obvious that Sims knew very well that Howard Pemberton was not a dull-witted fool. Therefore whatever they were to talk about had to do with the smuggling. She had had enough exposure to the freebooters to last her a lifetime.

Vanessa went upstairs to her bedroom. She forestalled all of her dresser's exclamations and remonstrations by saying, "Pray help me, Mattie. A gentleman is waiting downstairs and he wishes to discuss something of importance with me."

The dresser at once assumed that her mistress was expecting to receive an offer. She saw her duty clear. Without another word over the state of Vanessa's cloak and gown, she helped her mistress wash and change into a long-sleeved gown of flattering cut. The dresser insisted upon redoing Vanessa's hair. Her nimble fingers created a simple topknot with a fall of curls. "There, miss. You go on now. You'll do," she said, gathering up the discarded, ruined garments.

Vanessa glanced at herself in the mirror as she arranged a woolen shawl over her shoulders. Her appearance was vastly improved. "Thank you, Mattie," she said in simple gratitude.

Vanessa at once made her way downstairs to the drawing room. She was half afraid that Pemberton had not kept his word and had gone away again. However, the butler was waiting for her and he opened the drawing room door with no sign of discomposure. When Vanessa had entered, he closed it again.

Vanessa stood looking across at the large gentleman standing before the blazing fire. As she had entered, he had been pensively toeing a log into place with one boot and he now turned to survey her. They regarded each other with equally grave expressions.

Pemberton came over to her. He took her hands and raised each in turn to his lips. "You are beautiful," he said quietly.

Vanessa felt herself blush. How strange it was that the same words when uttered by Mark Nashe had left her completely unmoved. "Thank you, sir. I am glad that I find favor in your eyes."

Pemberton drew her hand through his arm and escorted her over to the sofa. Seating her, he inquired, "I have had Sims bring up some sherry. Would you care for a glass?"

Vanessa glanced fleetingly around to discover a large tray set with a decanter and glasses on the occasional table behind the sofa. "Yes, please. After this night I am in need of a restorative."

"You have nerves of steel, my dear," said Pemberton. He walked around the sofa to decant the wine and pour two glasses. Lifting them, he came around again and seated himself beside her. He gave one of the wineglasses to her. "It has been an evening of shocks for you, I know. You were very foolish to go off on your own, my darling. You might have come to grave harm. I could not have borne that."

Vanessa sipped the sherry, eying him over the rim of the glass. "Perhaps I was highhanded in my method, but I was afraid for you. Lieutenant Copperidge gave me to understand that he knew of the smugglers' meeting place tonight. I felt that I had to warn you."

"I know, which makes it all the worse, for I had not gone to meet with the smugglers at all. I had followed Nashe, having already suspected him of duplicity of some sort," said Pemberton.

"Then you were present when I came upon Nashe and that Frenchman?" asked Vanessa quickly.

Pemberton nodded his head. "I had satisfied myself that Nashe was indeed the traitor. I was on the point of challenging him and the Frenchman when your mare crashed into the clearing. For an instant, I thought Lieutenant Copperidge had by some stroke of luck stumbled upon their rendezvous. By the time that I realized that it was you, Nashe had already taken you hostage. I knew that I could not risk challenging them then when you were in their hands. They would have had no compunction in killing you in cold blood or in using you for a shield. Your only safety at that point laid in Nashe's plan to take you with him. It was almost providential."

"That is not quite the way that I would have described it," murmured Vanessa with a slight shudder.

Pemberton chuckled. He touched her cheek with a gentle hand. "My poor lady. I did not know what to do at that point. However, I recalled the track that you told Nashe about. It was the same that you had followed when you aided my escape from the excise. I knew that if I could reach the end of the track before you, I could set myself in ambush. There would still have been a chance that you could be wounded if there proved to be shooting, but I hoped that I could wing one or the other before they knew that I was upon them. You would then have had a fairly good chance of escaping unscathed."

"I wish I had known that you were so near," said Vanessa, raising her eyes to his face. "I would not have been quite so afraid."

Pemberton took her wineglass out of her hands. He set both glasses aside on the occasional table. Then he gathered her into his arms. Against her hair, he said, "I thank God that you did not panic and that you came off safe."

"Yes, and so do I," said Vanessa earnestly. "I could not think straight at first, but then it was as though my mind cleared and I knew exactly what I had to do."

Pemberton chuckled again and his warm breath ruffled her hair. "You took even me by surprise. I was set to let loose my pistol at Nashe when you slapped his horse and bolted away. I knew then that I had them."

"And then Lieutenant Copperidge and his troops came flying onto the scene. I have wondered how they arrived so quickly," said Vanessa.

"The lieutenant followed you, of course," said Pemberton. "When he told you that he knew about a rendezvous, he was merely setting bait for you. He suspected that you knew more than you were telling."

"Are you saying that the smugglers were not out at all

tonight?" asked Vanessa, leaning back slightly to look up into his face.

Pemberton nodded, a smile curving his mouth.

Vanessa was stunned with the enormity of the implications. "Then when I stumbled on Nashe and the French spy, it was purely by coincidence," she said slowly.

"Quite," said Pemberton.

"I shall never go out on anyone's behalf again," she declared feelingly. "If you must continue your dealings with these smugglers, Howard, I trust that you shall take greater care, for I shall not rush to your rescue again!"

Pemberton laughed. He gently urged her head back to his shoulder. "You will have no need to do so, my darling. I suspect that I am nearly done with my nocturnal wanderings."

Vanessa felt cherished and warm. Her head rested upon his shoulder and she was held close against his broad chest. She had never felt such a sense of contentment. "Then it is all done."

"Not quite. Nashe may have eluded the excise troops long enough to destroy the papers that he was given by the spy. Those, together with the leather pouch of coins that was put into his hands, are the only things that will conclusively prove his treason," said Pemberton grimly.

"I see," said Vanessa slowly. "What will you do if he does succeed in eluding the troops and ridding himself of the evidence?"

"I shall remain in my role as the good-natured but slow-witted Howard Pemberton and wait for another day and another time, to catch Nashe out," said Pemberton. "At least, I shall do so if I was not unlucky enough to have been seen by anyone. If any of those excisemen chanced to catch a glimpse of me, then there will be uncomfortable questions to answer and that must inevitably lead to my unmasking."

Vanessa liked none of what she had heard. "But surely . . . Nashe was wounded. And I can testify about what he and the Frenchman said. Surely that will prove something."

"All it will prove is that Nashe was taking a moonlit ride and chanced to be caught in a crossfire between a French spy and the man's assailant," said Pemberton. "Believe me, Nashe is clever enough to stick to such a tale and his position is enough to protect him from close questioning. It would be your word against Nashe's. Your testimony would only be hearsay. And though you are well-respected, there will be many who will not believe you. Many will resist the thought that one of their own class has turned traitor."

"Yes. Yes, I do see that," said Vanessa, a parade of personages going swiftly through her mind. "Probably only Squire Leeds and Reverend Haversaw will give wholehearted credence to my story. But they do not care for Mark Nashe in any event."

"It will be better that you keep silent entirely. Lieutenant Copperidge already suspects you of being up to your lovely neck with the smuggling ring. If you come forward with this story, in his mind his suspicions will be confirmed. I do not think that you would find the resulting questions to be comfortable," said Pemberton.

"No, indeed," said Vanessa feelingly. "Then what am I to do? I cannot simply forget what Nashe has done and dance with him at the assembly next week!"

"No, I do not expect that," said Pemberton with a trace of laughter in his voice. "However, it is vital that if Lieutenant Copperidge should come here to question you and Lady Cecily, you should say nothing at all about being out tonight. You never left the house this evening, Vanessa. I do not wish you to be caught up in this thing any more than you already have been."

"That is all very well, my dear," said Vanessa dryly. "But you have forgotten one small detail. Assuming that Mark Nashe does win free of the excise, he will also be free to wonder just what sort of threat I shall prove to him. I know what I know. I will not forget. Nor will Nashe forget that I was a witness."

"Yes, that is quite true. Contrary to your supposition, I have given this matter consideration, which brings me to an important point," said Pemberton. He eased her away from him and he took both of her hands in his. "You must be protected and—"

The door to the drawing room was thrust open. Vanessa and

her companion both turned their heads. Lady Cecily stood on the threshold, regarding the startled couple seated on the sofa. There was a strange expression on her face. "My word! This is an enlightening spectacle indeed! When I went to your bedroom, Vanessa, and was informed by your dresser that you were entertaining the overtures of a gentleman downstairs, I could scarce believe it. But I see that it is all too true!"

Vanessa started to rise. "Mother, I can explain—"

Lady Cecily flung up her hand. "Not a word, miss! I shall deal with this as I know best." She turned to shut the door and was displeased to discover the butler hovering behind her. She frowned. "Attend to your duties, Sims. I shall ring for you when I need you."

"Yes, my lady," said the butler unhappily.

Lady Cecily closed the door. She turned back to her daughter and the gentleman. Pemberton had risen and was standing beside Vanessa, his hand on her shoulder. Lady Cecily regarded this detail grimly. "Sir, you have compromised my daughter. You shall wed her at once. Is that perfectly understood?"

"Mother!" Vanessa took a hasty step forward. Color flooded her face. "You shall not speak so!"

Pemberton slipped his arm about her shoulders. "Hush, sweetheart. Lady Cecily is acting perfectly within her rights. My lady, I shall be happy to oblige you. We shall have the banns posted tomorrow."

"But, Howard, you cannot wish to be forced into wedlock in this way," said Vanessa heatedly. "It is *abominable*!"

"Nonsense! Mr. Pemberton is showing uncommonly good sense. You will do just as your betrothed wishes, Vanessa, and count yourself fortunate that I have no objection to your choice," said Lady Cecily hastily.

Vanessa looked up at her betrothed helplessly. She met a gaze full of warmth and mirth. Suddenly her heart soared. "Very well, ma'am. Let it be just as Howard wishes," she said.

Lady Cecily was taken off guard, for she had set herself for a battle of wills. But she quickly recovered and surged forward. "Vanessa, my dear!" She reached up to place a swift kiss on her daughter's cheek.

She stepped back and smiled at them both. "I am very happy for you, very happy indeed. We must celebrate. I shall have Sims bring up one of those bottles of French wine to which Lieutenant Copperidge took such exception."

As she spoke, she crossed to the bell rope and gave it a vigorous tug.

Chapter Twenty-two

There was an imperative banging in the distance. Lady Cecily turned to frown at the drawing room door. "Why, that sounds as though someone is demanding entrance at the front door. What an ill-bred noise! Who might that be at this time of night?"

"Unless I am quite mistaken, that will be Lieutenant Copperidge," murmured Pemberton.

For the first time, Vanessa recalled the pistols that he had had earlier. She clutched his arm and whispered urgently, "Howard, your firearms!"

"They have been dealt with," said Pemberton softly.

Lady Cecily threw a sharp glance in his direction. She started to say something. Before she could do so, the door was thrown open and several people rushed into the drawing room.

"What is the meaning of this intrusion, Sims?" asked Lady Cecily coldly, drawing herself up to an imperious posture.

"My lady!" gasped the butler over his shoulder. He had literally been pushed into the room. He was valiantly still attempting to stem the tide of excise troops. "Pray forgive me! I could not stop them!"

Lady Cecily's cold gaze alighted on the officer in charge. "Pray, what have you to say that will excuse this outrageous behavior, Lieutenant Copperidge? Order your man to unhand my butler at once!"

Lt. Copperidge signaled and the trooper dropped his firm grip from the butler's shoulders. "My apologies, my lady. I am here in the dispatch of an unpleasant duty. I have come to arrest Mr. Howard Pemberton upon suspicion of consortment with illegal trade and in treason," he announced in a ringing tone. "I have also a few home questions for Miss Lester."

Pemberton's eyes widened in his guileless look. A particularly blank expression of confusion came across his face. "Why, what is it about? I don't understand."

"My sentiments exactly, my dear Mr. Pemberton," said Lady Cecily. She turned on the excise officer. "What basis have you for all this trumpeting, sirruh? It is enough, indeed, that you utterly destroyed my dinner party, but now you feel compelled to cut up my peace entirely! I will not have it, and so I warn you!"

Lt. Copperidge breathed audibly through his nose. "My lady, you must realize that I do not make rash allegations. This night we overtook Mr. Mark Nashe in possession of such incriminating material that there is no question that he is a traitor to the Crown. Nashe has been in league with a French spy ring operating through the smugglers in these parts. Once he was subdued, he made full confession. I will spare you the tawdry details."

"There is a bloodied handkerchief wrapped around your shoulder, Lieutenant Copperidge," said Pemberton in an interested voice.

Lt. Copperidge spared him a suspicious glance. "Nashe attacked me with a dagger when I ran him to ground in the front hall of his home. I believe that I owe Lord Akers my life, for it was his lordship who pulled Mr. Nashe off of me."

Vanessa was appalled. "Are you saying that this brawl took place before the eyes of the family, Lieutenant?"

Lt. Copperidge gave an abrupt nod. "Lord and Lady Nashe were preparing to retire. They were coming out of the drawing room, accompanied by Lord and Lady Akers, as Nashe and I came to grips. The ladies were naturally much upset."

"Oh, the poor Nashes! And Cressy! I must go to see them first thing in the morning," exclaimed Vanessa, distressed for them.

"I cannot believe that Lord Nashe docilely entertained your accusations against his heir, Lieutenant Copperidge," said Lady Cecily.

"No, my lady, he did not. However, the evidence found on

Mr. Nashe's person, as well as Mr. Nashe's confession, silenced all opposition," said Lt. Copperidge in a cold voice.

"He has disgraced and shamed his family," said Vanessa in distress. "They shall all be so very grieved and disheartened."

"Indeed. It is a tragedy. I myself am quite overcome at the thought of Mark Nashe . . ." faltered Lady Cecily, visibly shaken.

Lt. Copperidge gave a thin smile. "Now you will understand the importance of my errand to Halverton, my lady. I wish to make a complete end to this nefarious business at once."

Lady Cecily stared at the excise officer. She drew herself up. "If you are speaking of Mr. Pemberton and my daughter, sir, I assure you—"

"My lady, we found the body of the French spy just outside the wood below Halverton proper. Mr. Nashe testifies that someone besides himself shot the Frenchman and—"

"And on this you base such terrible charges! You have taken the word of a confirmed traitor," said Lady Cecily contemptuously.

Underneath her arrogance, she was alarmed. Her daughter's betrothed was in jeopardy. She could not allow this attack against Mr. Pemberton to stand, for if he was taken away there was every possibility that he would not wed her daughter. After all of her scheming and hard work, she would not stand by and allow this upstart puppy to destroy the fulfillment of her dream. "Lieutenant Copperidge, that is utterly ridiculous!"

Lt. Copperidge's lips thinned. His chiseled features grew harder. "Whatever else Mr. Nashe is, my lady, he is still a gentleman born. He swears that he caught a glimpse of a very large man in the wood."

He turned to face Pemberton. "That description fits yourself, Mr. Pemberton. In addition, your horse and Miss Lester's have been discovered in the stables to be still warm from a run. It is obvious that you, sir, and Miss Lester, I regret to say, have been involved up to your necks in this night's dastardly work. I must take you into immediate custody, Mr. Pemberton. As for you, Miss Lester, I shall wait upon you in the morning so that I may ask you a few questions."

"Nonsense. What have you proven except that a traitor saw

a large man and that two horses have been returned to our stables after being ridden by persons unknown?" inquired Lady Cecily. "It will not do, Lieutenant, it will not do!"

A breath of sound came to Vanessa's ear. "Bravo."

She cast a quick glance up at her betrothed's face. He wore an expression of amiable confusion, but she knew that he was tautly alert.

"My lady, are you contending that someone besides Mr. Pemberton and Miss Lester rode those horses?" asked Lt. Copperidge.

"Certainly I am! Are we to be condemned because some ruffians choose to borrow our livestock without our knowledge? Come, Lieutenant! Surely it is not unheard of for smugglers to take whatever mounts they needed without the owners' consent."

Lady Cecily regarded the excise officer's dropped jaw with grim satisfaction. She had scored and she hammered home her defense. "Mr. Pemberton and my daughter have been at Halverton all evening. Mr. Pemberton has done me the honor of requesting Miss Lester's hand in marriage. You may offer your felicitations, Lieutenant Copperidge!"

Lt. Copperidge stood as though turned to stone. Then he visibly shook himself. "Of course, my lady. I wish the couple most happy, naturally," he said, bowing stiffly.

Pemberton stepped forward to shake the excise officer's hand with enthusiasm. "You shall come to the wedding, sir. It is to be a grand affair. We shall have all of the county, of course."

Gazing up at the wide-eyed affable face, Lt. Copperidge wondered how anyone so thick-headed could ever be trusted by the sort of devious men that delved into treason and smuggling. Pemberton had scarcely seemed to understand that he was in grave danger of being hauled off to jail. Certainly the gentleman's present friendliness belied any anxiety or guilt on his part. But then, there must be more to Pemberton than what was readily apparent. The man had somehow managed to secure the hand of one of the most sought-after ladies in the county. "Thank you, sir. I shall certainly attend if my duties permit."

"Mr. Pemberton, let go of the lieutenant's hand. He does not wish his arm shaken off at the shoulder," said Lady Cecily acidly.

Pemberton's face at once registered consternation and remorse. He dropped the exciseman's hand as though it had burned him. "So sorry, dear fellow. I didn't realize. Just so happy, you know."

Lt. Copperidge's gaze shifted to the two women. Miss Lester was studiously staring down at the carpet as though ashamed to lift her eyes. He could readily understand her embarrassment over her mother's highhanded manner. As for Lady Cecily, her ladyship was frowning over at Mr. Pemberton with a peculiarly tight-lipped expression.

It occurred to Lt. Copperidge that Howard Pemberton was shortly going to find himself under Lady Cecily's domination. He felt a stir of pity for the large unsuspecting gentleman. All in all, Pemberton did not seem at all the sort to have been involved in anything nefarious. He made up his mind suddenly. "It is quite all right, sir."

He turned again to Lady Cecily. "Perhaps I was too hasty in my judgment, my lady. Certainly you have presented powerful arguments. I shall not bother any of you again with this matter. I am satisfied that with Nashe's apprehension and the death of the spy that we have broken the back of treasonous activity in these parts. That is the most important thing to consider. As for the smuggling . . ."

He shrugged and smiled a little, briefly meeting Miss Lester's eyes as she looked up. "As someone once observed to me, generations of tradition are very difficult to break."

"Quite true, Lieutenant," said Lady Cecily, inclining her head with a show of graciousness. She had taken the field and could afford to unbend slightly. "I know that you must still have many details pertaining to this business to see to. Pray do not let us delay you, sir. Sims, please show Lieutenant Copperidge and his men out."

"Gladly, my lady," said the butler. He went to the door. "This way, gentlemen."

When the last of the excisemen had exited and Sims had quietly closed the door behind him, Lady Cecily looked over once more at her future son-in-law. "You are a deceiving rogue, sir. I know very well that you have hoodwinked us all for months. You are no more slow-witted than I am!"

"Forgive me, Lady Cecily. It was a necessary subterfuge," said Pemberton, putting his arm around Vanessa.

Lady Cecily eyed his familiar embrace, but she did not comment upon it. "No doubt you are correct. And no doubt I shall one day require an explanation," she said coolly. "However, at present I urge you and Vanessa to wed as soon as possible. You may go on an extended honeymoon, well away from Halverton, until all of this smuggling and spy nonsense has been forgotten."

"A wise suggestion, my lady, and one that I heartily endorse," said Pemberton. He looked down at his lady. "Well, my dear? Shall we submit to her ladyship's wishes in this matter?"

Lady Cecily narrowed her eyes. "Vanessa, you will do precisely—"

"Mother, please! I have told you several times that I am perfectly capable of arranging my own business best," said Vanessa. She was smiling up at her betrothed and did not glance at her mother. "I shall be most happy to oblige you, sir."

Pemberton caught her up into his arms and roundly kissed her. Her fingers curled in his lapel and she returned his regard with full measure.

Lady Cecily regarded them dispassionately. "I shall pay Mrs. Dabney an official visit in the morning. We shall write out the banns together." As she moved toward the door, she said, "Pray do not keep my daughter up too late, Mr. Pemberton."

It was doubtful whether her ladyship's stricture was heard by either Vanessa or Mr. Pemberton. Or if they did, they chose to ignore her.

Not at all offended, Lady Cecily opened the door and exited. Her step was light.